a Promise to Remember

Kathryn CUSHMAN

a Promise to Remember

BETHANYHOUSE
MINNEAPOLIS, MINNESOTA

Published by Bethany House Publishers
11400 Hampshire Avenue South
Bloomington, Minnesota 55438

Bethany House Publishers is a division of
Baker Publishing Group, Grand Rapids, Michigan.

Printed in the United States of America

Library of Congress Cataloging-in-Publication Data

Cushman, Kathryn.
    A promise to remember / Kathryn Cushman.
        p.   cm.
    ISBN-13: 978-0-7642-0380-0 (pbk.)
    ISBN-10: 0-7642-0380-0 (pbk.)
    1. Middle-aged women—Fiction. 2. Children—Death—Fiction. 3. Loss (Psy-
chology)—Fiction. I. Title.

PS3603.U825P76 2007
813'.6—dc22   2007023749

to **Ora Parrish**—*mother, editor, best friend*

chapter one

Andie Phelps could not put the brush to the canvas. The blue paint seemed wrong now on the sable bristles. Brightness could not cover the dark, the darkness was too strong. Just like her sorrow and pain. Brightness and light were nothing more than lies.

Still, Chad had asked this of her. This one thing. By accomplishing this task, she would honor her son's memory.

The chill of January came through the windows, opened because of the fumes. Andie inhaled deeply, filling her lungs with the smell of turpentine and oil paint. She'd need her Ionic Breeze because her husband, even more than most people, hated this smell. Not Andie. To her, it meant release and relief. Usually.

But not today.

Carefully, she touched the brush to canvas. Nothing but perfection would do, and she knew she didn't possess the talent. Still, she had to try. "This is for you, Chad."

Her hand shook and dropped away from the canvas. She slid her chair back.

Focus, Andie. You have to get through this. Once again she looked at the yellow paper beside her easel. At the top of the page, handwritten in blue ink, were the words *Chad—notes from last year's chairman.* Then followed typewritten instructions, numbered one through twenty, detailing the proper procedures for conducting Climesdale Academy's Wash Your Car, Wax Your Board Scholarship Fundraiser. Number five—*Scan school logo onto posters and T-shirts for students*—had been crossed out. Beside it, in Chad's handwriting, *Boring. Mom can paint something cool.*

Two weeks ago, when she'd sketched the outline of grinning old-time convertibles and wagons loaded with surfboards, he had laughed. "How could anyone resist?" Chad, more than anyone she'd ever known, loved with complete abandon. Now she had failed him, and he was gone forever.

She looked at the dates written on the paper. The fundraiser was approaching fast. Time to get started. *Chad, I don't think I can do this.* She stared at the crown molding around the ceiling. *God, help me. Help me.*

Perhaps starting with a different color would help. And some surf tunes to change the mood. She crossed the room and pushed a button on her CD player. As Dick Dale and his surf guitar broke like a wave through the room, she selected another brush and dipped it into the sienna on her palette.

The old Woody at the front of the line began to take form, her wrist and fingers finding their own rhythm now. She had been away from it so long it surprised her how wonderful it felt. She realized again how much she missed painting.

The song switched. "Surfin' USA." Andie tapped her foot with the beat, until the Beach Boys sang the praises of Rincon Point. Chad's favorite surf spot.

Her eyes began to burn. She rubbed the left one with her shoulder and went to work on the convertible. She worked the red into the canvas. The brush slipped from her fingers and left a gash of red on the PT Cruiser's door.

An image of Chad floated before her. His pale face spattered with blood, his eyelids fluttering, his white lips whispering final words. "I love you, Mom. You're the greatest person I've ever known." A raspy breath, "Dad . . . I was on my way to get it back." Following quickly came another memory—his vacant eyes and lifeless form against stark white sheets in a room that smelled of antiseptic and pain.

Andie blinked and tried to turn her attention back to her work. That sight, those smells, would not go away. A drop of liquid splashed onto her thumb. She looked down at the fallen tear. Strange, she hadn't even felt them start this time. She wiped her cheeks with both hands, and as she did, the paintbrush rubbed against her left knuckles, leaving another wound of blood red in its path.

She screamed out in anguish, an agony she'd tried so hard to keep hidden these last days. "I'm sorry, Chad. I'm so sorry." She couldn't stand the sight of the red paint a moment longer. She threw the brush across the room, where it struck the picture window and splattered to the mahogany floor.

She swiped at her painting, the bright colors blending and cutting mournful gray across the canvas in four long streaks. Those eager, smiling vehicles could not pretend to be all right anymore. The cars were frauds and liars anyway. They weren't happy. Nothing could ever be happy again. Andie used both hands, wiping and mixing until the entire scene vanished into unrecognizable, unknowable darkness. A dark reflection of how she felt.

"What do you think you're doing?" Blair's voice was followed by the music clicking off. Andie had been so engrossed in her pain, she hadn't heard him enter the house. She didn't turn.

His footsteps paced toward her but did not stop, his shoulder brushing hers as he strode to the window, squatted, and picked up the brush, careful to hold it away from his gray suit. He turned. "Andie, if this dries, it'll ruin the sealant we just put down."

He dropped the brush into a cup of turpentine with a splash and snatched a rag. After scrubbing for some time, he stood and wiped his hands on the cloth. "I got it off the floor, but it smeared on the window. You'll need a razor to get it all."

Andie looked at her husband's handsome face. The salt and pepper of his hair only added to the lightness in his blue eyes. Eyes whose spark now dulled when he looked at her.

He hung the rag over the edge of the utility sink. "What is this all about?"

She wiped her eyes and choked on the words. "The painting for the fundraiser."

He brought her a towel for her hands and leaned over for a closer inspection. "No wonder you're in such a state. What are you thinking? No one expects you to do this now."

"Chad wanted me to do it. It was important to him."

Blair knelt before her, his eyes suddenly soft. "Andie, Chad is gone." He stopped, swallowed hard. "Torturing yourself over projects at his school—a school we no longer have a child attending—is not going to change that. This isn't healthy. You've got to stop."

"Chad was chairman of the committee. His dream was to double last year's fundraising. The least I can do is try to help."

She wouldn't say the rest, but Chad's words still bounced through her memory. *I'm going to show them all—just like Mom does with her cancer fundraiser every year.*

"Oh, sweetie." Blair wrapped his arms around her and pulled her close.

Andie sank into his arms. Sobs spilled forth, like a tube of paint bursting, splattering everything in its path.

Blair's arms trembled and she realized that he, too, was crying. Sometime later, they pulled away from each other, tears spent. Blair's face was set in decision. "How much money did the scholarship fund raise last year?"

"Twenty thousand dollars."

Blair lifted her chin with his fingers so that she was forced to meet his eyes. "Okay, here's what we're going to do. Tomorrow, I'll go to the school office and tell them that our family is donating forty-five thousand dollars to the scholarship fund. We'll do it in Chad's memory. How would that be?"

She looked back at the smeared scene on the canvas. "What about the painting?"

"That goes away. Things like this will only pull you down. We need to be strong and keep going. For Chad's sake."

Andie nodded. Chad would want her to keep going. "Okay. For Chad's sake." *I'm sorry I let you down again, Chad.*

———

Melanie Johnston placed the stack of mail on the frayed bedspread, then settled herself on the lumpy mattress. She sliced through the first envelope. The cream-colored card inside was embossed with a shining cross on a hillside and glossy doves flying in the sky above. She flipped it open, not bothering to read the poem of five or six verses. Why should she care what some poet thought about grief? She knew grief, lived it, and there was nothing poetic about it. She skipped instead to the handwritten message below, scrawled in blue ink.

> *Jeff's absence has left a hole in all our hearts. My greatest comfort is knowing I will see him again in heaven, someday. Please feel free to call or visit if you ever need to talk.*
> *In Him,*
> *Jake Sterling*

"Well, Mr. Sterling, it might give you comfort to think of seeing Jeff in heaven someday, but I want him here." She wanted to shred the note and mail it back to the man, but she knew his words mirrored Jeff's own beliefs. Besides, if she destroyed all the cards that said something similar, what would become of Jeff's memorial?

She looked at the length of twine she'd strung across his room. The middle sagged from the weight of so many cards.

Jeff would be so happy to see this. To see how his life affected so many others. He never understood how much everyone loved him. "Can you see this, Jeff?"

The yellowed ceiling paint responded with silence.

Her gaze turned to the walls. Posters of sailboats with colorful sails puffed out like crescent moons, expansion bridges lit with thousands of white bulbs, and Harley Davidson motorcycles rolling past the ocean filled every spare inch. Jeff had always been drawn to physics and mechanics. Now his dreams were gone like the puffs of wind pushing the sailboats.

Melanie sank back into her seat, intent on finishing her task before Sarah returned home from her sleepover with the youth group girls. Melanie had to admit, for a bunch of fifteen- and sixteen-year-olds, they had circled their wagons around Sarah, keeping her busy and supported. She was glad Sarah found a source of relief there, although she knew Sarah's wounds went deeper than her daughter would ever show.

Melanie strung up a second line, parallel with the first, and sat back down to her stack of envelopes. She didn't recognize the name on the return address.

Dear Mrs. Johnston,

Are your funeral bills piling up? Do you need help fighting the legal establishment? We at Fraker, Fritz, and Krutenatoffer full legal service to victims likeyou. Let us help you get the cash you deserve!

Don't delay, call today!

At the bottom was blue computer printing, designed to look like a handwritten signature. What kind of jerk sent a card like this?

This time, she didn't restrain herself and tore the letter to bits. She threw the shreds in the trash and went on to the next.

Fifteen cards later, she picked up a taupe-colored envelope that felt heavy, almost like linen. There was no return address.

> *Dear Mrs. Johnston,*
> *I am sorry for your loss.*
> *Les Stewart*
> *555-9553*

Les Stewart. The name sounded vaguely familiar. Then she remembered the recent news story. He was some big shot attorney from Los Angeles who had recently moved to Santa Barbara to retire. Why would he send her his phone number? His clients were movie stars and business magnates.

Melanie started to hang the note on the line, but it didn't honor Jeff in any way. She placed it back in its envelope and tossed it in the trash.

After she'd finished the complete stack, she walked into the kitchen, poured a strong cup of coffee, grabbed scissors, and sat down with the paper. Six days had passed since the crash. The articles were less frequent and less obvious now. She turned the pages over slowly, not wanting to miss anything.

There. A tiny article about Jeff's work tutoring underprivileged kids while attending college in San Luis Obispo. She lifted her scissors and began to cut, taking pains to be precise. She didn't want to miss one letter of a story about her son.

When she finished, she grabbed the scrapbook, which always sat in Jeff's empty chair at the table, and anchored the article inside, another page in his memory. She read it through once more, choking back a spasm of sobs when she read the quote of a boy Jeff had helped—"*He was the only one who cared*"—before closing the book and returning it to its place.

Only then did she continue through the rest of the paper for anything else of interest. The story waited for her on the back page. A half-page article, complete with photo, of the boy who had taken Jeff's life.

The muscles in her neck tightened so that breathing became difficult. She looked at the large headline beneath the photo. *Phelps family donates $45,000 to scholarship fund in son's honor.*

The coffee burned inside Melanie's stomach. How dare they? That family had no right to glorify their son. He killed Jeff. Jeff was the one who should be honored with a scholarship named for him. He was the one who was paying his own way through school, working part-time and taking out loans. The Phelps kid probably never did a hard day's work in his life.

The article praised the Phelps family's generosity. Generosity. Generous enough to give their son a brand new BMW, while Jeff had worked to pay for his old clunker. Generous enough to make certain their son's car came equipped with all the best safety equipment. Maybe if Jeff'd had the benefit of such generosity, he wouldn't have been crushed beyond recognition.

Melanie flung the paper against the wall. Things like this shouldn't be allowed to happen. People couldn't just act this way. Somebody should do something.

She would do something.

She walked back into Jeff's room. She dropped to her knees and fished through the trash until she found the taupe envelope. Her fingers trembled as she picked up the phone. She had a call to make.

chapter two

Andie unloaded the last of the bags onto the granite countertop, then sank onto a barstool. Everything these days felt complicated and overwhelming. The drain of grief made even a simple trip to the grocery exhausting. She dropped her head onto her folded arms and closed her eyes.

As soon as she put these things away, she could spend the rest of the afternoon in bed—or maybe working on graphics for the Cancer Center's upcoming fundraisers. Her charity work was the only thing left that mattered anymore.

Tires squealed in the driveway. That sound could mean only one thing.

Christi.

Act brave or she'll feel compelled to stay. Andie forced herself from the chair and looked out the kitchen window.

Christi Baur's fire-engine-red Mercedes Roadster skidded to a stop near the back door. She flounced out, wearing perfectly pressed navy pants and a white silk blouse. As usual, she breezed into the house without bothering to knock. "Andie?" Her voice floated from the family room entrance.

"I'm in the kitchen." Andie picked up some lettuce and went to put it in her refrigerator. Christi would see her up and busy, and be satisfied that things were going well.

"Really should lock your door, you know." Christi's voice drew closer with each word.

"Why? The driveway's gated. You're the only person who ever uses that door."

Christi entered the kitchen, a too-bright smile crowding her face. "Exactly. Don't want people like me just walking in, do you?" The laugh that followed sounded forced.

Andie closed the refrigerator door and turned toward her friend. A head-to-toe assessment was under way, and judging from Christi's scowl, Andie's faded jeans and USC T-shirt did not measure up. She chose to ignore it. "I need to put these things away. Have a seat."

Christi's perky smile dropped just a fraction. "Been to the grocery? Today?" The last syllable came out with a squeak.

"Yeah. Everyone's been bringing in casseroles, but you have to get some milk and fresh veggies every now and then. Know what I mean?" Andie reached inside the nearest white plastic bag and pulled out a large bag of Oreos—her new best friend in the battle against grief.

She headed for the walk-in pantry, trying to hide the cookies from view. When she emerged, Christi had crossed the room and was holding a sack in her hands. She thumped her hand against her chest in exaggerated relief.

Andie stopped walking. "What?"

"Safeway bags! What a relief! Scott sent me over to tell you to stay away from Alfords for a while."

Andie's eyes began to sting. She picked up a bag of carrots and hurried to the refrigerator. "Really? Why would he say that?" Her voice came out too high, but Christi wouldn't acknowledge it. Christi hated dealing with heavy issues, and that suited Andie just fine. She wanted time alone with her pain.

"*She* works there. You know. The Johnston kid's mom. Scott's afraid she might look for some quick money."

Andie thought about the woman in question—saw her face. Attractive in an earthy way, no makeup, brown curly hair that just reached her shoulders. Her easy answers and quick smile, the cheerful way she stopped what she was doing to help customers find the sugar aisle. "I don't think she's the type." Melanie Johnston's eyes were the only thing that made her doubt her words. They sometimes narrowed with the grim determination of a woman used to a fight. A woman who would not back down if she thought she was right.

"Never know. Scott says don't go anywhere near her until this whole thing blows over."

Andie put her hand across her stomach. "Blows over?" She turned away from her friend, then began to forcefully unload another bag into the refrigerator. "How long does it take for the death of your child to 'blow over'?"

"Oh, Andie. Didn't mean it that way. You know I didn't. But you have to understand. Say the wrong word to the wrong person, and you find yourself in court."

"Yeah. Thanks for the advice." She knew her tone belied the polite words. Good. Maybe Christi would get the message. Not that she ever did.

Christi picked up a loaf of bread. "I'll help." She walked into the pantry. Seconds later, she emerged, shaking her head, bread still in hand. She tossed the loaf on the counter and rummaged through the cabinet under the sink, where she emerged with a bottle of 409 and a sponge.

Andie took a few silent steps to watch her.

Christi emptied three full shelves. There were scattered crumbs and a round sticky spot where Andie knew syrup had hardened into a sugary mess. This Christi targeted first, then scrubbed the shelves before putting things back. Though not necessarily in their original location. When she turned around and saw Andie watching, her eyes opened a bit wider. "Didn't know you were back there."

"So I gathered."

Christi extended her upturned hand as though she were a *Price is Right* model, demonstrating a new appliance. "Isn't it amazing how much having a clean, organized kitchen can brighten your mood?" She raked her hand across the top shelf. "See, all the cereals together, the bread products, the cooking supplies. Better, hmm?"

Andie looked at the shelves. They did look better. But why did it matter? "Yes, of course." She turned and walked out of the pantry.

Christi followed. The silence grew awkward, and Christi kept looking out the window toward her car. She jingled the keys in her purse. "Want to go for a ride? I promise I'll drive like a grandmother so I won't scare you."

Andie shook her head, ready to be alone. "No thanks, but you go ahead. You shouldn't be cooped up inside on a beautiful day like this."

Although Christi's face remained fixed, a brief spark in her eyes gave away her relief. "Sure you're okay? Anything I can do for you?"

Leave me and my dirty shelves in peace. "No, I'm fine."

Christi nodded. "Okay, then. Expect to see you back at tennis next week."

"Maybe."

Andie walked Christi to the back door. Just outside, Christi turned. "Remember, stay away from Alfords for a while." She removed keys from her Prada bag. "Shame our world has come to this."

Andie's eyes puddled in spite of defensive blinking. *Hold it in so she can leave.*

Christi looked at her car, then back again. "Need to be going." She beat a hasty retreat to her convertible, where she revved her engine and threw up a parting hand as she escaped down the driveway.

———

The Lexus glided to a stop in front of Melanie's house. The driver emerged, surveyed the neighborhood—one- and two-story homes, tidy yards, cars spilling out of the driveways. Probably not what he was used to, but nice by most standards. He smoothed the slacks of his expensive-looking suit. When he reached inside his car, Melanie moved away from the window and opened the door.

She already knew what he looked like from television and news reports. In person, he was shorter than she'd expected, his hair a tad more gray. He started toward her, and his swagger revealed every bit of the cockiness she despised.

What was she thinking in bringing him here?

"Les Stewart." He smiled at her and extended his hand, a hand that looked as if it had been manicured recently. The handshake was, as she had supposed, firm, but his skin was so soft she decided the man had never done a decent day's work in his entire life. He, too, seemed to feel this difference for a moment, looked at their hands, then pulled his own away as if ashamed.

She would force herself to be polite to the overstuffed turkey. For Jeff's sake. "Please come in, Mr. Stewart. Would you like some coffee or tea?"

His eyes opened just a little wider. "Tea sounds wonderful."

She pointed toward the worn blue-and-orange-plaid sofa. "Make yourself comfortable. I'll just be a minute." She went into the kitchen and smirked as she poured tea into two glasses. No doubt he was expecting Earl Grey, or Tazo, or one of those fancy teas she saw in the coffee shop windows.

When she walked back into the living room, he had assembled an impressive array of official-looking papers on the scarred coffee table. She set a cork coaster on the table and watched his face when he saw the tumbler of iced tea she set before him.

The corners of his eyes crinkled, but otherwise he suppressed any hint of surprise. He lifted the glass in a mock toast and took his sip. Then his eyes opened wide. "This is delicious."

"I've yet to meet a highfalutin hot-tea drinker who didn't prefer my iced tea to any of that fancy stuff. It's the homegrown mint that makes a difference."

He looked into the glass where the green leaf floated on the surface. "Hear, hear." He looked at her this time with genuine appreciation. No doubt he expected a woman of her social and financial status to be totally cowed in his presence, but Melanie had never been one to like pretension. Or chitchat.

"What, exactly, do you think you can do for me, Mr. Stewart?"

"Mrs. Johnston—"

"It's Melanie. I prefer to leave Mr. and Mrs. to old people—and the younger ones who think they're too important to have a first name. If you ask me, those are the kinds of people whose names I'd just as soon not know."

He smiled and offered a single nod. "Have you read the newspaper accounts of the accident?"

"Read 'em all. Saved the ones about Jeff in a scrapbook in the kitchen."

"Good. Then you are aware that Chad Phelps was driving with a suspended license."

"Yeah, I read that."

"In a California court, his parents are liable for his behavior. They should have made certain he didn't have access to a car, whether or not they were home."

"What's a kid that age doing with keys to a BMW, anyway?"

"As I understand it, Mrs. Johns—Melanie, it was a birthday present for his sixteenth birthday."

She already knew this, but it never failed to anger her. "What kind of parents give their kid a car like that as a birthday present?" She twirled her glass around, then set it on the coaster. "Jeff bought his car with his own money. Still has two years of payments on the thing." She laced her fingers together and pulled against her right knee. "I suppose that fancy car is what helped that other kid live long enough to say good-bye to his parents. All that high-tech safety equipment." She sniffed and looked away. "Maybe those parents had the right idea after all."

He took a deep breath, no doubt preparing the high-pressure "take me because I'm high-powered" spiel. She would force herself to listen, but knew that she could not go through with this.

"Melanie, I would be honored to help you fight this battle. Your son's life was snuffed out, not by simply an accident, but by careless behavior. If you take action now, and we make certain that everyone knows what has happened here, then we show the world that this kind of lax behavior will not be tolerated."

At least he didn't have the gall to tell her how much money he could get her, and how it would change Sarah's life and her own. Their life had been just fine. Before.

"You just might save the life of another kid like Jeff. I think your son would like to leave that as his legacy, don't you?"

Legacy.

The word snagged somewhere inside of her, and she knew she flinched a little. Les Stewart certainly saw, but Melanie didn't care. A spark of determination kindled deep inside. Every story about that other family showed how, with nothing but dollars, they were buying a legacy for their son. But she couldn't do that. She had no other choice. Two strings of cards wouldn't last. A scrapbook wouldn't last. How else could she make certain that something of Jeff lasted when he couldn't? This would be for him. This would be about Jeff.

The front door swung open. Sarah's blue duffel bag came flying through and landed in a heap, *Santa Barbara Volleyball League* in bright gold letters across its side. She exchanged a few shouted good-byes back toward the driveway, then came inside, stopping almost immediately. Her eyes locked on Les.

He rose to his feet and extended his hand. "Hello there, young lady. I'm Les Stewart."

Sarah lifted her hand but did not take his. Instead, she moved it past him and up to her twisted ponytail. She narrowed her eyes, looked him over, then crossed her arms and looked at Melanie. "Who's this?"

"Honey, he just *tried* to introduce himself." Melanie looked from Sarah's gray BMX T-shirt, volleyball shorts, and kneepads around her ankles, to the fancy-suited man beside her. At six feet, she was almost as tall, and not one bit intimidated. *Good girl.*

Still, manners did matter. "Mr. Stewart, please accept my apologies on Sarah's behalf. I'm sure she'll offer some herself when she realizes how *rude* she just sounded."

Sarah glared at her. "What's he doing here?"

Les took a step forward. "Sarah—is it?"

Sarah did turn to look at him, although her expression told him he was not worthy of the attention.

"Your mother invited me here to talk about your brother's legacy." His voice was smooth, ingratiating.

"My brother's legacy, huh?" Sarah leane[...] could see out the front door. "That's a pretty fa[...] It yours?"

He hesitated. "Yes."

"Thought so." She studied his tie, looked down at h[...] "You're a lawyer, aren't you?" She looked him straight [...] face, daring him to prove her wrong.

"Yes, I am. I can help your mother make certain that Jeff'[...] death was not in vain. That something good comes out of it."

"Something good like you getting a newer model Lexus? You're not doing this to help my mother, or to make sure my brother has a legacy." She shook her head. "I'll bet you want to build a bigger house in Montecito. That's where you live, isn't it?" She folded her arms. "You must figure you can win a lot of money if it's worth your time to drive all the way over here to the slums of Goleta."

"Sarah, stop that this instant. Mr. Stewart is a guest in our home, and I'll not have you talking to him that way."

Sarah flashed a look at her mother, and in it Melanie saw not the teenage sullenness she'd expected but something fragile and wounded. For a second she thought her daughter might even cry, but Sarah shifted her hips and set her jaw, and the anger returned to her eyes.

Les dropped his chin a half inch. "Sarah, it's important that we send a message to parents that they are responsible for their children."

Sarah pulled at a loose strand of hair, stared at the lawyer with a withering glance for three painfully silent seconds before snatching her duffel out of the entryway and fleeing down the hall.

"I'm sure she misses her brother very much," Les said after Sarah's door slammed.

...age girl who can use up the
...en she gets something in her
... Stewart."

...I won't. And please, call me
...r of your categories for the
...is facial muscles relax into
...der what I've talked to you

...e's not much to consider. I don't
...uppity lawyers—"

"But what about—"

"I wasn't finished." She looked at him, waiting. He needed to learn the ground rules, right now. He was no "Mr. Big Shot" around her house.

"Sorry."

She stared at him through another second of silence. "As I was saying—I don't care for uppity lawyers, but that other family is naming scholarships after their son, making him out to be some kind of hero. My Jeff is going unnoticed and forgotten. My son talked all the time about making a difference in the world. But he didn't get the chance. And if taking this to court could save another kid's life...if one other kid could be saved because of this, Jeff would want that—and so that's what I'll do. How do we get started?"

chapter three

Melanie took care to place the flowers in exactly the middle of Jeff's grave. Everything needed to be perfect for him. "There, that's better, huh?"

Tiny shoots of grass were already filling in the outline of the newly laid sod. Soon, no one who walked by would have any idea of the fresh grief buried beneath it.

Melanie would. And thanks to this lawsuit, everyone else would remember, too.

She put a blanket on the ground beside the headstone, sat down, and pulled the journal from her bag. "So, Jeff, this lawyer that's helping me, he says I need to keep a journal of my thoughts and emotions during this time. And memories of you, too. He says it's 'loss of companionship' and will help drive the lawsuit. I say it's a lot more than that.

"Remembering you is easy, bud. What would you like for me to tell the world about you?"

She looked at the blank pages and wondered where to start. This first memory seemed the most important somehow. But how could she choose? His whole life needed to be in these pages. Every moment. Not just bits and pieces. She'd lose him that way. The last thought fell like a hammer, and she swallowed hard, forcing herself to concentrate. She would not cry in front of Jeff. She needed to be strong.

"Let's…" She decided to just write down the first thing that came to mind. "Let's write about the time you 'fixed' Sarah's bike. Remember that?"

Jeff's eight-year-old face formed in her mind, smeared with dirt and wearing a knowing smile. "Don't worry, Sarah, I'll fix it for ya." He raked his hand across his nose and turned his ball cap backward. "I'm a mechanic. This is not a problem."

The wind blew Sarah's blond hair; a few strands stuck to her wet cheeks. "But I wrecked it." She pointed at the broken chain and dangling kickstand. "See? It's ruined." Her chin began to quiver.

He put his hand on her shoulder and shook it. "You're riding a big kid bike now, and big kids don't cry. You straighten up and go get me a screwdriver and oil can."

A doe-eyed five-year-old, she stared at him with open adoration. "Really?" Her shoulders drew back.

"Really. Now get." He gave her a gentle shove toward the garage, then looked at Melanie and shook his head. "Kids. The first crash is always the hardest."

Melanie blinked frantically, refusing to cry.

"Remember that, Jeff? You took that whole bike apart, right down to the seat. It took two days to get it back together again. As I recall there were a couple of parts left over, and it always made a funny clicking sound after that." She choked out a laugh. "Remember? Sarah asked you about it, and you told her it was 'bike music.'"

The granite stone sat cold and unmoving, seemingly untouched by the memories. She finished writing, then looked at the ground.

"This is good for us, Jeff. To remember these good times. We need to focus on what we did have. It'll help us stay strong."

She touched the sod with her fingers. "You were so special." Again, the choking threatened to close her throat, and the last thing she wanted was to lose it in front of Jeff.

"I start back to work tomorrow, so I won't see you until late afternoon."

Silence. A deep emptiness.

Jeff had never liked the quiet; she couldn't leave him this way. "Work's going to be a little odd now. That other boy's mother shops at my store."

Again, the empty silence.

"She's a lot like you'd expect. Thin. Beautiful. Long, wavy black hair. She doesn't know about the lawsuit yet, but I still don't want to see her.

"You know, she was always friendly in a shy kind of way." She bent down and gathered her blanket. "I just wish she'd have been a better mother."

––––––

The next morning, Melanie pulled into the parking lot, prepared for her first day back at work. She dreaded the day ahead, the inevitable offers of sympathy, the whispers when no one thought she could hear. Her journal lay in the passenger seat, ready for an afternoon visit with Jeff. She would make it through this day for him.

She climbed from the car and looked toward Alfords. The building, though now a year old, still amazed her. The thing looked more like a concert hall than the upscale grocery that it was—a concession to the planning commission. If you're going to put a grocery store on the outskirts of Hope Ranch, then it needs to be appropriate in architecture and style.

Just down the road stood stone pillars, the words *Hope Ranch* in a wrought-iron arch above. Beyond that, the enclave of Hope Ranch nestled on cliffs overlooking the Pacific Ocean.

Beautiful homes, hidden behind gates and imported trees, shared the landscape with Thoroughbreds and Arabians that slept in heated stalls.

The Phelps family's world. A world where they showered their son with presents—like BMWs—then turned him loose without any supervision. Did the Phelps family have a heated barn?

Would Mrs. Phelps come into the store today? Melanie would be expected to treat a customer with respect, but how could she? Best to avoid the confrontation if possible. She'd keep a close watch on the door. Maybe have someone up front keep up an alert.

Once inside, she stowed her purse in the employee lockers at the back of the store and practiced a plastered smile and the words she'd decided on in the shower that morning. "I'm doing okay. We're going to carry on. Jeff would want it that way." Maybe after repeating them a few hundred times, it wouldn't sting every time she said his name.

"Hey, Melanie." Joe Server, head butcher, put his thick, scarred palm on her shoulder. He squeezed once, lightly, then dropped his hand and continued on his way. Joe was never one to say much. Melanie appreciated that more than ever right now. The unspoken words in the shoulder squeeze, and keeping the subject out of conversation, were just what she needed.

She walked to the customer service booth and scanned the names of the employees who would be with her today. "Morning, Melanie." Peggy from the floral department climbed into the booth and threw her arms around Melanie's shoulders. "How you doing, hon?"

Tears stung Melanie's eyes, but she blinked them back and remembered her line. "I'm doing okay. Jeff would want us to carry on." She knew the words must sound as hollow and memorized as they felt.

Peggy pulled away, wiping a tear from the corner of her own eyes. "You are so brave. Jeff would be so proud of you." She scurried on her way as if trying to escape the grief.

Would Jeff be proud of her? Melanie hoped so. She picked up her stack of price-alert signs and walked onto the floor to begin her day.

———

Friday afternoon, Blair Phelps reached for the next set of papers on his desk requiring his attention. The stack remaining still loomed tall—and for that he was truly grateful.

The work of owning a company, which so often had been a burden, now provided just what he needed. Much better to spend the time at work, busy, than to be at his too-quiet home—reminded of what he'd lost—trying to console an in-consolable wife. Yes, work was good. They said the pain eased with time. Garbage. Two weeks had passed without an infini-tesimal measure of ease. Work at least masked the anguish, if not alleviating it.

Especially now, with the impending buyout by Vitasoft. The deal would be a shining moment in this field of all black. He just needed to keep things running top-drawer until the offer was solidified.

The intercom beeped. "Blair, there's someone here to see you."

"Yeah, who is it?"

"Something or other Smith. Said it's important."

Probably a salesman, but Blair could deal with them easily enough. "Okay, send him up."

The hulking man appeared in the doorway. The wrinkles in his cheap suit and his unkempt hair made it appear he might have been sleeping in the alleyway only moments before. "Blair Phelps?"

Blair stood, his muscles tense. "Yes, I'm Blair Phelps. Who are you?"

"Name's Smith." The man's eyes were dark, hard.

"What can I do for you, Mr. Smith?" He looked at his phone, a hand's reach away, then toward the giant of a man pacing toward him.

Smith smiled, revealing yellowed teeth. "I've got a delivery for you." He reached into the breast pocket of his suit, removed an envelope, then dropped it on Blair's desk. "You, Mr. Phelps, may consider yourself officially served."

The man doffed an imaginary hat, then ambled out of the office, whistling.

Blair looked at the envelope. A summons? Not uncommon in his business, but still, there hadn't been so much as a complaint from a client in the last few months. Something like this would look bad to the power players at Vitasoft, and he didn't need that kind of distraction right now. Who would do something idiotic like this, without even talking to him about it?

He sliced the flap open, unfolded the paper, and began scanning the jargon. Words like *negligent entrustment* stood out from the jumble of letters on the page. Then he saw the words that took the air from his chest. He dropped into his seat and stared, wishing he could delete the offending legal verbiage. It remained unchanged.

Wrongful death.

chapter **four**

Andie clung to Blair's arm as they walked into the church. The United Church of Montecito had been their church home for almost two decades. Why should it be so difficult to come here today? She had worshiped beside most of these people her entire adult life. After the accident, they had deluged her in casseroles, sent cards, hugged her in sympathy. So many caring, kind people. So many prayers. So why did she feel like she had to put on her happy face and pretend that everything was fine when she came here?

At least no one knew about the lawsuit yet. It wouldn't hit the paper until Monday or Tuesday, if their lawyers were right. Something to be thankful for.

"Andieeeee . . . Andie darling . . ." The unmistakable singsong of Mattilda Plendor's voice rose above the subdued murmur in the foyer. Andie turned and could see a single hand raised above the crowd. Immaculate fingernails, painted bright orange, crowned fingers heavy with emeralds and diamonds, platinum and white gold. Occasional glimpses of fiery red hair appeared as the hand's owner pushed through the crowd.

Andie moved toward her, hoping to save someone from losing a rib to Mattilda Plendor's sharp elbow.

"Oh, Andie darling." Mattilda emerged from the circle of people, her expression startled. She wrapped one arm around Andie's back. "I am so, so, sorry, my dear. I wish I could have been here for you. I got back into town last night and only then heard the terrible news." She began to pet Andie's back like she would one of her award-winning poodles.

"Thank you for your kindness, Lady Plendor. There really was nothing you could have done, though."

"Please, dear, call me Mattie."

Mattie? No one under the age of seventy dared to call Mattilda Plendor by her first name, especially since her husband acquired the family title a decade ago. Andie had never known her to suggest a breach in etiquette until this very second.

Mattie—it sounded strange just to think the name—brought her head to within inches of Andie's, squinted, and began a methodical study of her face. She started with the right cheek, moved across the forehead and down the left cheek, over the nose and down to the chin. Then she stepped back and scanned Andie from head to toe, as though inspecting a car or large appliance. "My, my, the grief is just written all over you. And of course it would be, you poor thing. I must do something to cheer you up. Something from my shop, perhaps?"

Lady Plendor owned a posh boutique in Montecito, the Santa Barbara region's most exclusive city. In spite of the fact that she was pushing seventy, she wore a wool dress in a wild leopard print, three-inch heels, and ample jewelry and accessories. Her appearance left no one to doubt that she came from very old and very substantial wealth.

Her eyebrows remained lifted in shock, even though it had been several minutes since she first approached. What had her so perplexed? The answer slowly revealed itself as Andie studied Mattie's face. She wasn't surprised—she'd had another facelift.

"We'll get together for tea and share our stories of grief. When my Milton died, I thought I'd never survive it."

"I know that was very hard for you."

The woman nodded, and although her facial expression remained locked in place, her eyes clouded. Just last year she had lost her husband of the past five decades in a skydiving accident. It had been a terrible shock.

Organ music floated out into the vestibule. It had started none too soon for Andie.

"I've got to get to my seat now, dear, but we'll talk more about a little something from my shop, okay?"

Andie nodded and watched Mattie walk down the aisle to her seat. Several women in the surrounding area stood and performed their usual air-kisses ritual with Mattie. The woman's apparent contradictions never failed to amaze Andie.

Only because she was on the Mission Board did Andie know why Mattie had just returned to town. She'd been in Africa for the last few weeks, painting, cleaning, and helping with the children at the new orphanage she'd helped pay for. A donation no one knew about except Andie and the other members of the Mission Board—and they'd been sworn to secrecy. Few would look past the couture and elective surgery, but there was more to Mattilda Plendor than most people would ever understand.

Blair put his arm under Andie's elbow as they started up the aisle. His shoulder brushed against her, and he leaned closer. His breath was warm on her ear when he whispered, "Doth my ear deceive me, or did her ladyship actually tell you to call her Mattie?"

Andie looked at him and stifled a giggle. The first since Chad's death. What kind of mother could ever think of laughing when her son was gone forever? She took a shaky breath. *I'm sorry, Chad. It won't happen again.*

———

On Wednesday morning, Andie stood outside the mahogany doors of Baur, Campbell, and Associates and cast a nervous look over her shoulder. No one seemed to notice her. Good. After the story in this morning's paper, anyone who recognized her would misconstrue her presence here. Santa Barbara wasn't that big a city, and it didn't take much more than a whisper for rumors to flourish. She was at least thankful it had taken the lawsuit five days to go public. It gave them time to come to terms with it in private. As much as possible, anyway.

She pulled open the door and entered through a warm exhalation of air, taking care to plaster a smile on her face. Everyone would be watching her. Some would watch in concern, some in pained fascination—like watching a train wreck—and some, the most perceptive, would recognize her failures as a mother and think smugly how she was getting what she deserved.

Maybe it was what she deserved, but what about Chad? He didn't deserve to die for her mistakes, did he?

"Good morning, Mrs. Phelps." Diana, the front-desk secretary, smiled sweetly up at Andie.

Andie forced the muscles in her cheek to hold up her farce of a smile. "Good morning, Diana."

Diana's perky voice and bright eyes seemed a bit reserved today. Andie wondered if she was hiding pity or contempt. "Mrs. Baur is waiting in the conference room."

Andie nodded and started down the hall. She knew where to go.

The Charity League's executive committee had been meeting in this conference room every week for the last six years. Since Christi's first term as president.

Every year now, Christi was reelected without a hitch. No one had the organization, determination, and energy to even attempt to outdo her. She kept things moving. She also saw to it that the conference room at her husband's law firm was reserved every Wednesday morning at eleven o'clock.

Andie walked down the hallway, pretending fascination with the portraits of brilliant lawyers that lined the wall. Normally, she would voice greetings to several acquaintances who worked here. Not today. She darted through the door into the conference room, thankful to have avoided contact.

"Got to stick together and fight this. That's the only way this kind of thing will ever stop—" Christi stopped midsentence and jumped to her feet. "There you are." She walked over to give Andie a hug but didn't meet her eye. In fact, both she and Carol looked as though they'd been caught cheating on a test. "Glad you're here. We were just talking about you."

Andie grimaced. She had a pretty good idea what they had been talking about. "Really?"

"Yes. Andie, you are doing such a great job organizing the silent-auction baskets for the Rescue Mission benefit. Last year, it was such a disaster." Christi looked toward Carol, who must've gotten the hint.

"Yes. We think that should be your job from here on."

"Well, I—"

Christi grabbed Andie's arm and pulled her forward. "Forgive me for being so rude. You walk in the door and I start loading you with more assignments. Here, put your bag down and get some coffee and a scone. Susie and Janice will be late, as usual."

Andie walked to the sidebar for coffee, feeling the women's stares burning through her back. She knew they were dying to see her reaction to the news. Well, she planned to pretend nothing had happened. She had a job to do and she was here to do it. The people in the cancer treatment wards and detox facilities didn't have time to worry about Andie or the lawsuit aimed at her. They needed her creating for them, planning for them, and it felt nice to think of something outside of her pain, if only for a moment.

Susie and Janice burst into the room, arms loaded with shopping bags. "Sorry we're late, ladies. We stopped by Nordstrom and one thing led to another." The words spouted from Susie's mouth in one breath. She paused to inhale, dropped her bags, and looked around the room. Her wandering gaze stopped at Andie. She covered her gaunt cheek with her right hand and held out her emaciated left arm for a hug.

"Oh, Andie honey, I saw the paper this morning. I can't believe what that woman is doing to your family. How can we help you?" Susie had never been one for tact, or keeping quiet about things best kept quiet.

She threw her arms around Andie's shoulders and squeezed so tight Andie fought to breathe. *Her heart's in the right place. Be polite. Count to three, then you can pull away. Make it through this meeting and you can go home.*

"I'm just fine, Susie. Thanks for asking." Andie looked toward Christi with all the dignity she could still muster. "I believe everyone is here now. Shall we get the meeting started?"

Christi nodded. "To your places, ladies."

As Andie went to her seat at the table, she saw Christi exchange a look with Carol. Whatever they had been talking about, it would be continued later. Andie's presence would stop it for now, but they would talk plenty after she left.

The business of helping others filled the next forty-five minutes. *Not long now.*

"One last thing for you, Andie." Christi tapped a finger at something in her notebook. She looked apologetic. "Carolyn Patterson, from the Cancer Center…she wondered if the board should appoint another director for the Fair this year."

This jolted her back into full attention. "Of course not. Why would she ask that?"

Of all the myriads of Andie's charity projects, the Old Time Fair for the Cure was the one closest to her soul. She had invented the concept three years ago and had watched the attendance grow and mushroom until they were expecting this April's crowds to perhaps triple previous records.

Christi cocked her head. "Probably just concerned you need a little time to yourself." She looked hard at Andie. "Do you?"

Andie thought about Chad's notes on his own fundraiser. *"I'm going to show them all—just like Mom does with her cancer fundraiser every year."* Chad and his friends had always talked about how much they loved the Fair. This year's Fair would be in honor of Chad. It would be her best yet. "Absolutely not. The Fair is my baby, and I can handle it."

"Okay, then." Christi looked around the table. "If there's nothing else, ladies, this meeting is adjourned."

———

Christi Baur reclined on the back deck, checking her fingernail polish. She held the portable phone between her ear and her shoulder, waiting. Finally, on the third ring, she heard the telltale click on the other end. She gripped the receiver with her right hand and sat upright. "Kaitlyn, hi. You saw the paper?"

While murmuring agreement with Kaitlyn's words of outrage, she noticed a dandelion sprouting in her lawn. She stood and walked toward it. "I've talked to some of the others. We're going to boycott Alfords." She pulled the offending weed up by the roots and carried it to the trash can.

"Boycott Alfords?" Kaitlyn's shriek blasted through the line with enough decibels that Christi almost dropped the phone. "But it's the best grocery store in town. Their meat is better; the produce is fresher. I was planning to get the hotdogs and hamburgers for the kids' car wash from them."

"Make new plans. I'd already ordered salmon and ribs for Scott's firm's barbeque. Called this morning—canceled the order. Told the manager he'd seen his last business from me as long as he employed a heartless money grabber. Told him that a lot of others would feel the same way." She paused, long enough to let her words sink in. "Told him we would all stick together."

"Well . . . yes . . . I suppose you're right. I want to do what I can to help Andie. I suppose we can drive across town to Gelson's."

Christi made a fist and pumped her arm. Victory. This had been easier than she'd expected. "Yes, we can. Honestly, it's just shameless what the woman is doing."

"Yeah. I guess so."

Christi heard the lack of conviction in Kaitlyn's voice and decided to squash it for good. "Remember Benjamin's fender bender last month? Could just as easily have been your family. Teenagers get into accidents. We need to send out a message that those accidents are not a get-rich-quick ticket."

A sniffle sounded through the line. "Of course you're right."

"Yes, I am."

"Sure. Okay, count me in. Umm, I've got an appointment. I need to go."

"See you at the Charity League meeting tomorrow night. Oh, by the way, I haven't told Andie about the boycott yet, so don't mention it." Christi smiled and hung up the phone.

She knew what Kaitlyn's "appointment" was. It was her standing Wednesday afternoon massage at the club. Knowing she would be the most difficult to convince, Christi had specifically picked this time to call because the less time Kaitlyn had to think and argue, the better. Christi smiled. If Kaitlyn, who prided herself on her cooking and insisted on doing her own shopping, could be convinced that easily, the rest—many of whom hired chefs or paid assistants to stock their pantries—would be as simple as procuring sponsors for a high-profile charity event.

She picked up the phone to make the next call. By the time this day ended, she would have an entire armada of Hope Ranch residents driving their grocery business across town. Their exodus would work like a vacuum, sucking the life's air from Alfords. It could not go unnoticed or unanswered for long.

chapter five

Andie jerked her hands back from the sink full of scalding water. "Ouch! That's hot!"

Mrs. Greenfield, the cook for the soup kitchen, scowled. "Did you see the crew that ate out there today? Honestly, they were dirtier than Silas on a bad day. I believe we need the extra sanitation of the higher temperature, so I cranked it up."

Since Mrs. Greenfield was not the one who would be sticking her hands in the almost boiling liquid, that was easy for her to say. Andie tried again.

On her third attempt she managed to keep her hands in the water long enough to remove the first bowl from the hot suds, scrub it, then rinse—in much cooler water. Fifty more dishes waited their turn.

"I would venture to guess that you will be more than delighted when we raise appropriate funds for a dishwasher. Yes?"

Andie jumped. "Silas, I didn't hear you sneak in here." *Or smell you,* she thought despite herself and turned to give him a hug.

Something about him looked different. The mannered speech was the same—always a strange contrast with the brown dreadlocks. But today his clothes were relatively clean, and his face less grimy than usual. Patches of white skin showed around the edge of his collar. Interesting. Must have found a girlfriend.

He bowed in his formal way. "I did not sneak, ma'am. I simply walked with care. It is delightful to see you back at your old post."

She nodded, not trusting her voice. They all knew where she'd been for the last weeks, and she didn't want to talk about it.

"I must go tend to the window cleaning now." He bowed once again and left the room.

Mrs. Greenfield waited until he was out of the kitchen. "Did you hear he finally used his shower?"

Andie stopped washing and turned. "The one in the back room? You're kidding."

"Nope. He used it before the funer—" Mrs. Greenfield's eyes grew wide, then she looked down at the tomatoes she was chopping. "I mean . . ."

Andie turned back to her dishes, the steam blurring her vision. "The funeral?"

"I'm so sorry. I promised myself I wouldn't bring that up."

"It's all right." Andie searched through her fog of funeral memories, and could not find Silas's face among them. "I don't remember seeing him there."

"You didn't."

"But I thought you said . . ."

"He got all ready, went over to the church, then lost his nerve. Said there were a bunch of fine people in fine cars, and he didn't want to embarrass anyone. Came back here and cried."

Silas crying. Alone. Over Chad.

So much pain. It seemed to touch everything and everyone. How could they keep moving?

She swallowed the lump in her throat. "He loved Chad, didn't he?"

"We all did. Especially Silas, though. Chad's the one who gave him his dignity back."

"I remember." Andie scrubbed harder, remembering the skeleton of a man who refused to take "charity," waiting for his buddies outside the door, starving while they ate.

"He needs to feel like he earned his food—that's all." Chad's voice still echoed so clear in her mind. "I'll take care of it."

He grabbed a bottle of glass cleaner and some paper towels and made for the door. "Hello, sir, I need some help washing these windows. How much would you charge?"

From that day forward, Silas cleaned the windows every day before he ate. Months later, Chad came up with the idea for the "caretaker" title and convinced Silas to move into the back room, complete with bathroom and shower—a shower he refused to use. Except once. To honor Chad.

"I thought you were in a hurry today." Mrs. Greenfield's voice chased the memories.

Andie looked at her watch. "You're right, I better get on it." She needed to get some paperwork done for the Fair. And she needed to get tonight's dinner together for Blair, who might or might not show up to eat it. As much as she wanted to curl up in a ball and die, the duties of her life were piling up around her. With the exception of the Fair, she just didn't want to deal with them.

———

Blair pulled onto the freeway and realized he was so slumped that he couldn't see out of his rearview mirror. He tried sitting up but felt too worn and eventually just adjusted the mirror. Next to him waited a mound of paperwork requiring his attention before the night was over. He patted the stack like an old friend.

His phone chirped and he pressed the button on his steering wheel while changing lanes. "Blair Phelps."

"Hello, Blair. Mike Daniels."

A green VW cut in front of Blair, forcing him to hit his brakes. *Idiot. Where do these people learn to drive?* The car swerved across the final two lanes and off the exit, followed by the angry blast of horns.

When the horns quieted, the following silence felt thick, suffocating. "Mike, you still there?"

"Yeah, I'm here."

The presence of grief seemed to block people's ability to carry on a normal conversation, even for lifelong friends. Even for Mike—the life of the party. He, too, fought the silence and lost. The hush, louder than any spoken words, screamed out the agony. Blair couldn't take another second. "So what's on your mind?" He exited the freeway toward home.

"The bank president paid me a visit today."

Blair turned onto Las Palmas Drive. "Really? Is there a promotion in the near future? I've been wondering when they were going to make you VP. Will you still have time to surf?"

A choked sound came through the phone. "Oh man, Blair. It's not me. It's about you. Your loan."

Blair turned onto his street. "What about it? The principal's not due for another few months."

"Let's just say he's . . . concerned."

"Concerned?"

"We've had a couple of major loans go bad lately. Then he gets a call from his brother-in-law up in Seattle—those two hate each other like you wouldn't believe—and he's telling him the Vitasoft geeks are shaking in their white socks about the buyout."

"I've seen no indication of that on my end." Blair's company had the product Vitasoft needed—it was as simple as that. Acquiring Phelps, Inc., would save them millions of dollars in the long run, and make millions for Blair in the short-term. It would pay off all loans, with plenty to spare.

"I'm just telling you, the talk up north is that the lawsuit has those guys nervous. Vitasoft's putting out noise that they might not pay up until they know for sure they won't have to pay out."

Blair stopped at the gate to his driveway. He didn't have the strength to push the remote to open it. If Vitasoft backed out of the deal . . .

"Blair, you do remember I tried to talk you out of that loan, right? A personal guarantee on an unsecured loan . . ."

Blair remembered the conversation. Mike had paced back and forth, ranting, while Blair signed the Continuing Guarantee. "Man, think before you do this. Something goes wrong, they can come after you. You could lose everything. Your house . . . everything. Don't do this."

"I won't default." Funny how the same words, a few months later, felt paper-thin.

Blair pushed the button for the gate. He started up the winding drive, looking around at his front lawn in a way he hadn't in a long time. The manicured grass, well-tended flower beds, giant oaks. It was *his*. No way would he allow anyone to take this from him.

"How is Andie holding up?"

"Like you'd expect, I guess. She's pretty wrecked." His phrasing was too mild to be precise, but it was true enough.

"Give her my best, okay?"

"Sure."

Blair hung up the phone as he reached the top of the drive. *This deal cannot fall through. I won't lose this house. It would kill what's left of Andie. And me.*

The house sat in darkness. Andie always turned on the porch light to welcome him home, unless something was wrong.

Usually, a dark porch meant she was angry with him. Since the accident, it could also mean she was having a hard day. He didn't really want to deal with either option at the moment.

He pulled the car into the garage and sat without moving. Maybe he should have stayed longer at the office. *I can't handle one of Andie's crying spells. Not tonight.*

The advent of cable and DSL negated the millions of dollars he'd invested in dial-up technologies just a few years ago; he had been forced to spend twice that to upgrade. Until their latest software unveiling, things tottered on the knife-edge of financial failure. Then Vitasoft stepped forward, waving big money and big promises.

Blair looked at the digital clock on the dashboard. Eight p.m. Of course. Andie probably made dinner and was mad because he hadn't called or shown up to eat it.

She hated to cook. Although he came home late and forgot to call at least once a week, it never failed to make her angry. You'd think that after twenty years she would have moved past that. *I'll get an earful of "taking her for granted" tonight.* He took a deep breath, gathered his papers, and entered the house.

The kitchen was dark, save for the one light over the sink. No dishes sat on the counter, no dinner waited at the table. "Andie?"

No one answered, but Blair saw a glow coming from the back room. Andie's studio. He followed the shaft of light and found her sitting in the chair, staring at the wall, stone-faced. A large bowl sat beside her chair, empty. Only the brown traces against the white of the china told him she'd been eating chocolate ice cream—again. A lot, apparently. Her hair looked as though it hadn't been brushed since morning, and there were three brown spots on her white T-shirt.

Since Chad's death, Andie had begun to medicate her pain with chocolate and other sweets, and greasy food. She'd been skipping the gym, too, and after only three weeks, there was a noticeable difference in her appearance.

He took a deep breath, too tired to even attempt compassion. "Andie, what are you doing?"

She looked at him. "Thinking." She swiveled in her chair so that her back faced him.

Tempted though he was to take the cue and walk out, he knew it would only make things more difficult in the end. He set down the stack of papers, urgently wanting—no, needing—to get them taken care of, yet forced to deal with Andie's grief as if his own didn't matter. Sometimes it was hard to be the man of the family.

"What are you thinking about?" He reached over and put his hand on top of hers.

She didn't pull away, but made no attempt to return the gesture. "Did you know that a group of women from Hope Ranch are refusing to shop at Alfords because of this lawsuit?"

"Scott Baur told me about that. He said Christi started making calls." He forced a lightness into his voice that he didn't feel. "You know how Christi is. Once she sets her mind to something, things are going to happen."

She swung around to face him. "You sound like you approve of what she's doing. Don't you think it's wrong?"

"No. Those women are trying to support you. Why would I condemn them for it?"

She shrugged.

Blair used his last ounce of energy to point out the obvious. "You know how excited they all were when the planning commission finally approved the proposal for a grocery store in this area. Now, not a year after it opens, your friends are driving across town again. They are inconveniencing themselves because they care about you. How could that be wrong?"

"Why do they want to punish that other boy's mother? She didn't do anything wrong."

The stress that had built up in Blair over the course of the day exploded from him before he could think to calm it. "Andie, she's trying to ruin what's left of our lives. What purpose does it serve her to sue us, other than to make herself rich? We lost our son, too, didn't we? She should be thankful for the child she still has, instead of trying to destroy what remains of our lives. How can you say she's done nothing wrong? She's selfish—that's what she is."

Andie gasped. She stared at her fingernails and picked at the chipped polish. "I'm sorry." Her words were a barely audible whisper.

Blair exhaled, thankful that she had seen the truth so easily. "That's all right. I know you just didn't see the whole picture."

She looked up, her eyes glistening and red. "I didn't mean for questioning the boycott. I mean, I'm sorry that you don't have any other children at home. I know you wanted more. I'm sorry you got stuck with a defective wife."

Oh no. Surely she's not going down this road. Blair didn't have the strength to deal with one more piece of sorrow or regret. "Andie, it's not your fault you couldn't have more children. You were a terrific mother to Chad. He was blessed to live his short life with you. I'm blessed, too." He gathered his papers to signal her that the conversation had ended.

"Listen, hon, I've got tons of paperwork. I'm going to go lock myself in the office and plow through it, okay? We'll talk about this more later."

She nodded and swiveled her back to him again. Blair left the room. When he walked through the kitchen, he grabbed two granola bars and a bottled water. So much for dinner.

———

The front door slammed with such force the entire house rattled.

Melanie jerked around, dropping the ladle she'd been using. It clattered across the white linoleum floor and splattered everything, including her bare feet, with scalding drops of tomato-beef broth. She yelped and reached for a dish towel.

Sarah stormed into the kitchen. "That lawyer of yours has ruined everything!"

Bone-weary grief and exhaustion blended with such force, Melanie didn't have the energy to rise to this fight. She wiped her foot with the towel and picked up the ladle. Inhaling a deep breath, she made a great effort to speak in her most interested-mother voice, hoping to disarm whatever it was that had Sarah so worked up. "What did he ruin, sweetheart?"

She dropped the ladle into the sink and reached into the cabinets below for the all-purpose cleaner. She sprayed the reddish-brown spots on the floor, counted to five, and then straightened up and looked at Sarah.

The beautiful oval face flushed with frustration. Framed by long blond hair that had been meticulously straightened before tonight's Groundhog Day pizza feast, bright blue eyes glared at her. Since Jeff died, those eyes always seemed to be bloodshot or puffy from tears or slitted in anger, and Melanie wanted nothing more than for the beauty to return to them, that the spark of hope and joy might glimmer in them again. It was too much to ask for her own to do the same—she knew that. Still, she had hopes for Sarah.

Sarah must have seen something of the concern on her mother's face and her own expression softened. She turned away and began to rummage through the refrigerator. "The mission trip. You know, the one our youth group is supposed to take this summer?"

"What does Les Stewart have to do with building houses in Mexico?"

"We have to raise our support, *remember*?"

The sarcasm spewing from Sarah's voice broke through Melanie's weariness. Exhausted as she was, she wasn't willing to listen to sixteen-year-old sass.

"Sarah, if you want to continue this conversation, you will change your tone of voice now."

Sarah looked over her shoulder, rolled her eyes, and turned back to the refrigerator.

Melanie counted to ten. Then twenty. She had worked so hard to not burden Sarah with her pain; she didn't want it to pour out of her now in a fit of anger. She tore a paper towel off the roll, then bent down. The stew, now diffused to a pale shade of pink in the cleaning solution, began to soak into the white cloth. After she'd wiped up the last of the mess, she turned toward her daughter.

Sarah had jumped onto the kitchen counter and sat cross-legged, peeling an orange. She did not look up.

Sufficiently calm to be sure of her voice, Melanie said, "Okay. Tell me what Les Stewart has to do with your raising support to go build houses in Mexico."

Sarah continued to study her orange. "We sent out our support letters as a group, from the church. I found out tonight that a bunch of people who'd pledged money decided not to give it after all. It's because you're suing that other family."

Melanie felt the heat rise in her face. What kind of church people were these? "Honey, it's only been two days since the lawsuit hit the paper. People are just in an uproar right now. Besides, why would it change anything?" How dare these people even suggest this? Hadn't her family been through enough already?

Then again—perhaps it was a teenager's overactive imagination doing the talking. "Maybe those other people just realized they weren't financially able to give the support right now. Have you thought of that?"

Sarah glared over at her. "Jake Sterling told me!"

Melanie's hands began to shake, and she crossed her arms so that Sarah wouldn't see it. "In front of everyone, he told you it was because of the lawsuit?"

"No. He just announced we'd had some unexpected issues." She popped a slice of orange into her mouth. "Sally told me her mother said it was all my fault. I didn't believe her, so I talked to Jake. Privately. He didn't say anything to the group. Not that everyone won't figure it out soon enough." She wiped her eye with her sleeve. "Even if they don't, I promised Juanita I'd be back this summer. I promised to bring her a volleyball. I promised I'd help build her house this year. Now what am I supposed to say?"

Melanie thought about the dark-eyed young girl whose haunted eyes stared out from the photo on Sarah's bedroom wall. She thought about the half-dozen crayon drawings of hearts, volleyballs, and Sarah. She thought what this meant to her daughter. "We'll just see about this." She stomped down the hall to Jeff's room, where she searched through the three lines strung with cards. She lifted Jake Sterling's from the line and stalked out of the room. She'd have a little talk with Mr. Sterling.

chapter **six**

The next morning, Melanie looked again at the address she'd scrawled on the back of an old grocery list. She pulled it closer to the window to read it in full sunlight, then looked at the number on the building before her. This couldn't be right.

After driving several miles out of the city, she'd expected a small driveway, a cottage or rambler. What she found was a tiny parking lot outside a huge aluminum-sided warehouse, the large sliding door thrown open to let in the crisp February air. No signs adorned the building in any way—only smudged windows and a rusting tin roof.

She pulled her car into a marked space, turned off the ignition, and made her way cautiously toward the entrance. Perhaps the people inside could help her.

A loud roaring sound boomed out through the parking lot. Melanie covered her ears and moved closer.

The place smelled of exhaust and hot metal. The combination blended into an intoxicating aroma that reminded her of her old life, when she'd been young, carefree, and stupid. The sound ceased for the moment.

She peeked inside the door. A man lay on his back, an engine mounted on a block above him. She moved beside him and knelt down. "Excuse me?"

He jerked up, followed by a thud and a groan.

Melanie stood and took a step backward. "Sorry."

"No worries. Didn't hear anybody come in, that's all." He pulled himself from beneath the engine and sat up, rubbing his head.

He was young. Very young. Not much more than twenty, if that. His blue coveralls were covered with grease, as was his face and the LA Dodgers baseball cap on his head. He pushed himself off the ground and stood. "Can I help you with something?"

"Sorry to bother you, but I think I've written down a wrong address. I'm looking for Jake Sterling. Would you happen to know if he lives around here?"

The kid smiled, revealing a row of straight white teeth. "You wrote it down just fine. The address, I mean. This is Jake's shop."

Melanie felt her mouth open, but no words came. She looked around the massive garage, trying to take it in. This was wrong.

"I'm Tony, by the way." The boy extended his hand.

Melanie reached to take it, but Tony yanked it back and wiped it against his pants. "Sorry. Been working on that engine all morning. Forgot about the grease."

Melanie hadn't even noticed. Her shock was too great. This was Jake Sterling's garage? The place where Jeff and his cell group met once a week to study the Bible? She couldn't believe it.

Places like this she associated with fast bikes, fast times, and not much else. What kind of man was this Jake, and what would he be doing with a motorcycle shop?

"Jake's just in the back workshop. It's pretty dirty back there. You can go wait in the office if you want, and I'll tell him you're here. What did you say your name was?"

"Melanie. Melanie Johnston."

The kid's eyes grew wide. "Are you Jeff's mom?"

She nodded.

He threw out his arms and engulfed her. "Oh, man. That whole thing just ripped me up." He squeezed her tight and held on.

The shock of his emotion hit her in the gut. *Oh, Jeff. How can we bear this? How can we bear it?* She took a deep breath and held it until she was sure of her composure. Today needed focus. Today was about Sarah.

Tony pulled away, his eyes tinged pink. He looked at his greasy clothes, then back to her. "Oh, sorry about that. I lost myself there for a minute."

Melanie looked down at her red T-shirt. It was dotted with grease, but she didn't mind. "Don't worry. A hug like that is worth a thousand T-shirts as far as I'm concerned." It was true. It was people like Tony who helped her believe Jeff just might not be forgotten.

"Where'd you say Jake was? Back through there?"

"Yeah. You really should wait in the office. I'm not kidding—it's pretty grimy back there."

She smiled and looked at her shirt. "I don't mind." She started toward the back room, then looked over her shoulder. "Thanks."

"You kidding? My pleasure."

Melanie walked around a scattered group of chrome pieces, stepped over a set of handlebars, and did her best to avoid a pile of metal shavings. She managed to make it to the doorway without mishap.

The smell, the look of the place, sent a little shiver down her spine. It came from the kind of thrill she thought she'd left behind. This place could make her forget her obligations. How could Jeff have been coming here and she didn't know it?

She stuck her head over the threshold. "Hello?"

The clattering of metal against concrete drew her attention to the far right wall. A man with a gray ponytail bent over and picked up a wrench from the floor. As he straightened, Melanie noted he was taller than she would have guessed, and quite thin. Not your stereotypical Harley mechanic. When he was fully upright, he looked toward the sound of the interruption.

A full second after he first looked at her, his eyes flew open. "Oh!" He dropped the wrench on a nearby counter and hurried over to her. "Mrs. Johnston. Please, come in. I wish I'd known you were coming—I'd have been waiting for you."

Melanie noticed the way the gray in his hair seemed to darken the brown of his eyes. Tinge them with mystery and danger. Well, she didn't have a place in her life for any of that. "Mr. Sterling, I've come to talk with you about Sarah, and the upcoming trip."

His face clouded. His fingers touched her elbow while the other hand gestured back from where she'd come. "Please, let's go sit in my office."

He directed her toward a small door in the middle of the back wall. The contents of the office surprised her.

Though a cramped workspace, he'd kept it pristine. She'd expected to see a desk piled high with invoices and biker magazines, but the scarred metal surface was almost empty. There were a couple of posters of bands. Melanie recognized the names as Christian groups. She'd bought their CDs for Jeff at Christmas. Melanie shook her head the tiniest bit. She couldn't let herself disappear into memories. She scanned the rest of the room.

Several filing cabinets neatly lined the far wall, a wall filled with pictures of boys from the youth group involved in various activities. Jeff's smiling face could be seen in almost all of them.

She walked over and allowed her fingers to trace one of the frames. The boys were barely recognizable beneath a thick layer of smudge, the victors after the annual "mud war." Jeff stood grinning, his arm around the boy to his right, his left hand raised in victory.

Why him? Why did he have to be at precisely the wrong spot in that curve? Ten seconds difference, maybe even five, maybe three, is all it would have taken, and her son would be alive today. Why?

Why?

Jake joined her at the wall. "Things will never be the same without him." He cleared his throat. "You want to sit?"

She moved away from the wall and sat on a worn vinyl chair. Jake settled in its twin just a few feet away.

Melanie waved her hand around the office. "You know, in all the times Jeff told me the youth group met at Jake Sterling's garage, I pictured a garage to your house. I never knew you had an actual, you know, *garage*. No wonder Jeff always came home with grease on his hands and jeans."

What else had she missed in her son's life? Her throat tightened. "Funny, I always prided myself on knowing where my kids were and with whom. It's hard learning about your failings when you don't have a chance to change them."

She managed to clamp her mouth shut against further ramblings. Jake Sterling must think her a blabbering idiot. Still, somehow more words forced their way out. "Of course, there's still Sarah. I still have a chance with her."

"Mrs. Johnston—"

"Melanie."

He smiled. "Melanie, no mother knows exactly where her children are and what they are doing all the time. You knew he met with a group of guys to *study the Bible* in a garage. What does it matter if you didn't know what the garage looked like? You knew what he was doing, and that it was something most parents only dream about their children doing."

Melanie shrugged. In fact, his words did help.

Jake continued. "It was obvious in Jeff's life that you were a very strong presence. The boys always talked about eating your homemade ice cream. You were 'a cool mom' because you not only allowed them to watch motocross on TV but you actually watched with them. You shouldn't have any regrets."

A flash of a half-dozen boys, sprawled across her living room, eating pizza and watching dirt bikes on TV, filled her mind. The smell of pepperoni and popcorn, the dirty feet all over the furniture, the good-natured insults and raucous cackling. It all seemed so precious now.

She felt herself disappearing again into the memories, times when Jeff still laughed, and roused herself sufficiently to remember this visit was not about her. It wasn't even about Jeff. It was about Sarah. "Sarah tells me that the youth group is having some trouble getting the funds to go on the mission trip. She believes I have something to do with that. Do you have any idea what might have given her that impression?"

Jake Sterling studied his right hand, flexed his fingers, then clenched them. He repeated the process with this left hand, never making a sound. He finally looked up at her. "What made you come to me with this question? Why did you not go to Sue Jameson, the director of the girls' group?"

Melanie had expected this question and was prepared. "If I may be frank, Mr. Sterling—"

"Jake. And frank is good."

"Okay, Jake. I've met Sue Jameson on a few occasions. My gut impression is that she avoids conflict at all costs. I don't want to waste my time on someone who will only tell me what they think I want to hear."

Jake gave a single nod of begrudging agreement. Melanie pounced on the opportunity. "Also, the impression I got from your sympathy card was that you were available to help during this time in any way that you could. In fact, you specifically said to feel free to visit or call if I ever needed to talk. Well, I need to talk about this."

He tilted his head forward, peering at her in bafflement. "From all the cards you must have received, you have that clear a memory of mine?"

"I have a clear memory of all of them. I've tied strings across Jeff's room and hung every condolence, every prayer, every note Jeff received on them. I couldn't afford a big statue in the cemetery, so this is the memorial I could offer. I just don't want him to be forgotten."

Jake leaned forward, placing his elbows on his knees. His face had taken on a serious cast that Melanie found unnerving. "Melanie, Jeff will never be forgotten. He is with his Father in heaven right now. With the One who loves him more than even you. He will spend eternity loved, and with his name known and praised because of the life he lived."

Anger began to burn in the pit of Melanie's belly. "Perhaps that's the way you look at it. To me, a *father* who loved him that much would have let him live a full life before bringing him up to *heaven*." She spat out the words with more venom than she had intended but did not regret it. She spoke the truth.

He flinched, but his expression didn't change. "I understand this is a difficult time for you." He looked at her and waited.

This man had some nerve. Where did these religious people come off thinking all that mumbo jumbo was comforting? Now he was patronizing, which was worse. "I am not here to discuss Jeff or me. I'm here because Sarah's all upset about the trip. Can you help me with that, or not?"

"Do you want help understanding the problem, or do you want help fixing the problem?"

"Both."

He nodded. "Fair enough. Why don't we start with understanding?"

"I'm all ears."

"Our church is full of young people and working-class families. Most do not have a lot of extra income, so when they give money to send the youth on a mission trip, it might mean that they cut back on the grocery budget for a week or two."

"I've lived on a tight budget my whole life. You're not telling me anything I don't completely understand. What I want to know is, how does that have anything to do with Sarah or me?"

"Do you read the *News-Press*?"

"Yes."

"So do a lot of our church members. When that whole spate of articles came out this week about the lawsuit, your lawyer made it very plain that he expects to handily win this case, and that he expects to get you a whole pile of money in the process." He paused and looked at her, as if to see if she understood his words.

"And?"

"Would you shortchange your family to support a soon-to-be millionaire?"

Heat surged through every vein in her body. She jumped to her feet. "This is *not* about the money. This is about sending a message to parents that they are responsible for their children. If those other parents had done their job, Jeff would still be with us today."

"Whether or not it is *about* the money, the fact is, a large amount of money is involved."

"I can't believe what a bunch of hypocrites you Christians are. How dare you judge me when you've never lost a child?"

Jake's head jerked back as if she'd slapped him. Good. Point made. She started toward the door.

He jumped from his seat and blocked her. He extended his left arm and gestured at her chair. "Please. Sit. I didn't mean to sound judgmental, because I don't judge what you're doing at all."

He motioned with his head toward the red vinyl. "Please. You *did* say you wanted to understand what the problem was."

She couldn't argue that. Begrudgingly, she took a step backward, but made no move to sit.

He sat on his chair and folded his arms. "We do have a few other options."

Melanie finally perched on the end of the seat, her hands against her knees, prepared to jump up at a second's notice. "What other options?"

"The kids will have to do twice the fundraising as normal. Usually, with this type of thing, we do a couple of fundraisers and the church matches the amount we earn. In this particular case, we may just have to raise all the money ourselves."

Melanie relaxed against the back of her seat. "I don't get it." She stretched her legs out. "It's not like Sarah is going to Mexico on vacation. She's using part of her summer vacation to build houses for people who need the help. She won't be staying in some fancy hotel; she'll be living in a tent with six other girls."

"You don't have to explain that to me. I'll be sleeping in a similar tent with the boys." He rubbed his face.

The lines around his eyes suddenly seemed deeper, and his eyes faded into a dull weariness. His hands had left a smudge of grease on his forehead. "Just give this a little time, okay? Most likely, it will sort itself out. If not, the kids will have to work a little harder this year. There's no harm in a little hard work, now, is there?"

"No. I suppose not."

"I'll talk to Sue Jameson and make sure she puts a stop to the whispering in the girls' group. Sarah should never be faced with something like that."

Melanie nodded her head. "I'm sorry I lost my temper." She stood and offered him her hand.

He shook it with a warm and firm grip, then opened the door. "I understand why you were upset. How about if we meet again in the near future? I'll update you on anything I've learned. You can tell me how things are going with Sarah."

Melanie nodded. "Sure." Her feet didn't seem to want to move forward. In fact, her entire being screamed at her to stay put. It was as if Jake Sterling held the answers to questions she didn't even yet know how to ask. And what did he mean by "the near future"?

"Thank you." She forced her legs to carry her out of the garage. Since Jeff's death, her normally placid emotions often surprised her with an unexpected reaction, like not wanting to leave right now. Would her life ever regain an even keel? Jeff's life was snuffed out forever. So what if she felt a little out of whack?

Tony looked up from his spot on the floor and smiled. "Bye, Mrs. Johnston! Come back around so we can talk sometime, all right?"

"Good-bye, Tony. I'll make a point of it."

———

Melanie pushed open the swinging doors that led from the storage room to the front of the store. Her time back at work had passed in a blur of well-wishes, awkward moments, and mind-numbing pain. Today, the aisles were surprisingly empty of customers. She looked at her watch. Nine o'clock. Although Monday was not their biggest day, or morning their busiest time, the store felt empty.

By the time her lunch break rolled around, she had immersed herself in work, but an uneasiness played on her nerves. Most likely because she was still awaiting a confrontation about the lawsuit from Andie Phelps or one of her rich friends. She almost wished it would happen and get over with, so she could quit thinking about it.

She took her lunch bag and sat in the employee break room beside Joe. She pulled out her yogurt and peeled open its foil lid. "Where is everybody? I don't remember ever seeing a Monday this slow. How are things in your department?"

Joe choked on his sandwich and took a sip of Red Bull. "Uh, it's a little slow for us, too."

"The sun's shining. Maybe everyone loaded up and went to the beach today, huh?"

"Yeah, maybe." Joe took another bite of his sandwich and stared at the squares of bread as if he expected them to move. He looked around the empty table, then leaned forward. "Look, Melanie, there's something you probably need to know."

An opening like that could only mean bad news. "What?"

"Word is, the Hope Ranch women have banded together and are boycotting this place."

"Why?"

Joe didn't answer.

"Because of me?"

Joe shrugged and looked back toward his sandwich, now sitting on the table. "Not exactly you. But the lawsuit. You know?"

Those arrogant rich women. "How long has this been go-ing on?"

He looked up at her. "Things started to slow down the end of last week. Today is even slower."

"Does management know about this?"

"Yeah. They know. Mr. Mortensen says they'll just monitor the situation for a while. Expects it will fizzle out after a few weeks."

"Fizzle out?"

"Yeah. He says the Hope Ranch women will get tired of driving across town for groceries. They won't like losing the precious hours from their stables and tennis courts. He says they'll give it up soon enough." His words might have reassured, except for the expression on his face.

"What if they don't?"

He stared at the table, his face draining of color. "Potential layoffs if it stays this way."

Melanie gasped.

Joe shifted in his seat and looked away. He always avoided controversy. He wouldn't have said a word if things weren't really serious.

"How bad is it?"

"I've had several major orders canceled. I know some of our standing company events have been canceled, as well." He began to put away his mostly uneaten sandwich. "You won't have to worry, though. I'm sure your job is secure. The ACLU would be all over them if they laid you off because you filed a lawsuit."

She chose to ignore the last comment. Joe had stuck out his neck to tell her any of this; she wouldn't demean that. "Thanks for telling me."

"Well, I've probably said too much. But you're going to hear it anyway. Better to hear it all at once from a friend than in bits and pieces of gossip that float around the store." He hurried from the break room as if afraid he'd have to keep talking.

What more did those women think they could do to her? Did none of them have any shame, care about anything besides money?

She sat in her chair and seethed. What was she going to do about this? She needed to talk to someone. But who?

She fished through her purse for her cell phone. Next, she found her wallet and pulled out the piece of paper tucked there. She stared at the numbers for a moment and then pushed the necessary buttons.

Peggy strolled into the break room, lunch in hand. "Who ya calling?" She plopped at the table.

Melanie turned off the phone. "No one." The call would have to wait.

chapter seven

Andie set the McDonald's bag on the coffee table and kicked off the sandals she'd worn for the trip to the drive-through. Grasping the remote firmly in her right hand, she picked up her milkshake with the left and extended her feet onto the glass coffee table. Blair would have a fit if he saw her now, but she'd clean the smudges before he got home. He'd never know.

The screen before her blinked as she pushed the button past infomercials, talk shows, and *I Love Lucy* reruns. She finally stopped at a home-makeover show, though she didn't really watch it. To her, it was just noise. Something to fill the quietness of the house.

The phone rang.

Probably Christi, wanting to know why I didn't make it to the committee brunch. The machine could get it, but if I don't answer, she'll call every five minutes until I do.

Andie took a slug of milkshake and reached across the end table for the receiver. "Hello."

"Andie darling, it's Mattie. How are you doing today, you poor thing?"

Andie was glad that Mattie couldn't see her roll her eyes. Mattilda Plendor knew everyone's business in the entire church. No one would think to call her a gossip, because she didn't spread rumors, and even though busybody might be appropriate, her genuine love and concern precluded that label, as well. She was simply "involved"—whether you wanted her to be or not.

"I'm okay." Andie wanted to end this call and dig into the bag of fries on the coffee table. "Thanks for checking in."

"Well, I've got to tell you something. My driver—you've met Rodrigo, haven't you, dear? He'll be at your house in just a few minutes. Remember how we decided that you needed a new outfit to cheer you up?"

"Oh, Mattie, thanks for the offer, but I couldn't possibly buy anything right now."

"And I don't want you to buy anything now. At our last store meeting we discussed the possibility of using some living models."

Andie had no idea what she was talking about, but bit back the obvious sarcastic comment—*Have you been using dead ones?*

"We want to find three or four women who are involved around town to wear our creations. They will draw notice and bring more business. It costs less than running an ad in *Harper's Bazaar*, you know." Mattie paused.

Andie had the distinct impression she was expected to insert a squeal of joy at that point. She didn't want to hurt Mattie's feelings, so she worked up the energy for at least polite acknowledgment. "Oh, well, I'm honored, but—"

"No more arguments. You jump in the car with Rodrigo and do as you are told."

"But, Mattie, I haven't even showered yet." Andie felt her cheeks flush at the admission—after all, it was almost noon. Before the accident she would have been up, exercised, met with the committee, and been to her elbows in paperwork by noon. These days, she found excuses to skip all but the most vital charity commitments. Nothing social warranted the energy required to get out and put on a happy face. Or a fancy dress.

"That's fortunate, dear. I called Camille the Day Spa—you're going there first. You'll get a massage, soak in the hot tub, then get a facial and a hairstyle. I thought you might want a little boost to get you out and about."

The speaker from the gate buzzed.

"He's at your gate now. Hurry, or you'll be late for your appointment. Don't worry about what you're wearing, because as soon as you're done at Camille, Rodrigo is bringing you here."

Too exhausted to keep up the argument, Andie pushed the button to open the gate and went in search of a hairbrush. There was no stopping Mattilda when she was in one of these modes, and Andie knew it. The next problem that faced her was what to do about the clothes. She didn't like the clothes at Mattilda's boutique and wondered how she could get out of that part gracefully.

She didn't want to hurt Mattie. Or the women boycotting Alfords. Or any of the others trying to help her. But they weren't helping her. They were making things worse. Why couldn't they just leave her alone?

———

Melanie walked to a remote corner of the parking lot. She didn't want to take the chance of being overheard.

The call was answered on the first ring. "Les Stewart."

She poured out the story of the boycott, and the talk of layoffs, and all her pent-up anger and fear. She hated showing her weakness to him. He might be on her side, but he was, after all, one of *them.*

"This is just the kind of thing I'd expect." His voice was reassuring, but perhaps a touch eager, too. Did he enjoy this added conflict? "I want you to keep doing your job to the best of your abilities. If it comes down to layoffs, we need to make absolutely certain there are no reasonable grounds for your name to be on the list."

If it comes to layoffs? She had hoped he would tell her that could never happen. Somehow the fact that he acknowledged the possibility made it more real. "Okay." She hated the way her voice cracked.

"You go back to work today like nothing's changed. I'm sure your co-worker was right—things will get back to normal in the next few days."

Maybe contacting him had been an overreaction. "All right."

"Thanks for calling and telling me about this. If I don't know about a situation, there is no way I can help. Don't ever hesitate to call. Okay?"

"Yeah, sure."

"Don't worry. If they want to play hard ball, they are about to come up against the best in the business."

Melanie could almost hear the smile in his voice.

Andie looked in the mirror at her made-over self. Still in her jeans, she stood in the dressing room of Discerning—the shop Mattilda owned. She had to admit that the visit to the spa did help. It gave her a bit of a lift to feel fixed up again. But not enough to make her want to exert her own limited energy in keeping it up.

"This will look divine on you." Mattilda breezed into the room and held up a snake-print dress for Andie's inspection.

"I don't know, I don't usually wear anything so flashy."

Mattilda's eyebrows twitched. "It's not flashy—it's fabulous. It's from Roberto Cavalli's new line."

Andie had always favored traditional clothes, varying her wardrobe only to stay out of the "out of fashion" ranks. Although she appreciated couture on other people, it wasn't her line of interest. She preferred not to stand out.

Mattilda looked her up and down. "Hmmm, you have gained a little weight. Let me see what else we've got."

Andie looked down at her body. Was her lack of discipline that apparent? What did it matter, though? Blair didn't even look at her anymore; Chad was gone. Why should she care what she looked like? It required too much effort to maintain.

"This is it!" Mattilda came in, her face beaming, holding a dress that Marcia Brady might have worn on a bad day. "I can't wait to see you wearing this at church on Sunday."

At that very moment, Andie began to pray she would develop a case of the flu before Sunday services. This was going to be a nightmare.

Later that night, Andie scraped her barely touched salmon off the plate. Neither she nor Blair had finished much. They didn't speak, didn't eat, didn't look at each other. She didn't risk talking to him about it because she dreaded the sharp retort that would follow. No reason to go asking for more pain.

She reached up to tuck her hair behind her ear. The shorter length, from the morning's makeover at Camille, felt strange to her fingers. Blair hadn't even noticed. He'd barely bothered to look at her during the silent dinner. Instead, after five minutes he announced he had work to do and shut himself in his office.

She rinsed the plates silently and loaded the dishwasher. Tension knotted her stomach. When Blair was in one of these moods, she could do nothing right, and the thing that annoyed him most of all was her tendency toward messiness. She glanced around for anything that needed straightening.

The knots pulled tighter. Everything seemed messy tonight. Why did she never notice these things until Blair—or Christi—came barreling through the door?

These were the nights when she missed the easy company of Chad. His quiet hugs. His understanding smile. His "Gee, Dad, do we need to put our trays in the upright and locked position? Looks like you're flying through some bumpy weather" comments that always calmed Blair's temper. He'd have everyone sitting at the Monopoly board within minutes, forgetting there had ever been disquiet.

She rubbed her eyes and placed the last of the dishes in the dishwasher, started the cycle, and walked into the living room. She needed to get some of this picked up before Blair came out of the office and began a tirade.

On the couch, she saw her latest *Artist's World* magazine lying open. Better put it away, and quick. Blair considered art a waste of time. For the most part, she had abandoned her passion, but she still looked at the magazine once a month and dreamed of sitting on a secluded beach, easel before her, brush in hand, empty canvas waiting.

Chad had been the only source of encouragement in her painting. Now he was gone.

She opened the drawer to the end table, removed last month's edition, and placed the new one in its spot.

Okay, one less thing for Blair to get angry about. Though with sudden awareness she knew it wouldn't matter. One magazine in a drawer meant nothing. Their problems and Blair's frustrations lay deeper. She knew something at the office was not going well, but more than that she felt that deep down Blair blamed her. He blamed her for Chad's death. How could he not?

She threw herself on the couch and buried her face in the pillows. Why had she not intervened in Chad's problems sooner?

When she lifted her head, she noticed the smudges on the coffee table from her fast-food lunch. Couldn't she do one thing right?

Just then Blair's voice boomed from the back of the house. "Andie, is it too much to ask for you to put your shoes back in the closet? I just tripped over your sandals in the hallway and spilled my papers everywhere."

"Sorry." Yes. She had failed at everything.

chapter eight

Melanie's fingers tightened on the phone. "They filed a what?"

"A demurrer."

Something in Les's voice reminded her of a parent trying to explain the obvious to a toddler. *Control yourself. Getting irritated with your lawyer will not help you or Jeff.* "What does that mean, and how will it affect us?"

"To simplify the explanation, basically they are saying there is not a legally sufficient reason to proceed with this suit."

These people would stop at nothing. "Did they see the pictures? Did they see my son's car—so crushed the police couldn't identify the make? Did they see Jeff—so battered his own mother could barely identify him? What, have they been out of the country during all this?" Hysteria was setting in, but she didn't care. "How dare they say we don't have sufficient grounds! I'll show them some grounds."

"Melanie, you need to calm down. They know there are grounds. This is just standard practice. I've been expecting it."

"Expecting it? You would *expect* such garbage?" She looked from the faded paint on her walls to the cracked linoleum, then pictured the Phelps family laughing and drinking champagne in a fancy kitchen with imported tile and granite countertops. Money spoke louder than common sense, it seemed.

"Don't worry, it just takes patience to meander through the process. Next on the agenda is the hearing. I expect our complaint will be sustained."

"How long do we have to wait for all this?"

"It usually takes three to four weeks. After that, I file an amended complaint and we start again. All in all, we lose maybe a month of time, but we *will* keep moving forward, and we *will* win this thing."

"Seems to me they're fighting dirty."

"It's the way the game is played." He paused and cleared his throat. "Maybe you should keep that in mind."

She shook her head, felt her grip tighten. "Don't start in on me about going to a psychiatrist again. I told you, I'm not doing it. I'm keeping my journal of thoughts and memories like you asked, but even that seems silly to me. Any jury with half a heart would know that I'm grieving myself sick. I don't need a journal for that, and I do *not* need some shrink asking me 'how that makes me feel' because he's too stupid to see the obvious."

"An expert witness testifying on your behalf would strengthen the case."

"Well, I don't want to strengthen my case that way. I'm in the right, and I don't need a high-priced medical puppet to confirm it."

He laughed. "I have to admit, I like the strength of your convictions, even if they don't help our case."

———

"Here are your phone messages, and Shane Greyton from Vita-soft is on line one," Blair's secretary said and skittered from the room before he could respond. Rumors must be getting around the office.

He lifted the phone and pushed the button. "Blair Phelps."

"Hello, Blair. How are things in sunny California today?"

Blair looked out his window, low misty clouds shrouding everything. "I think we've got your weather. Things are pretty murky, I'm afraid."

"Yes." Shane cleared his throat. "That's what we keep hearing."

This discussion was no longer about the weather. Blair began to mindlessly flip through his phone messages. One drew his attention. *Mike Daniels at Parsons Bank and Trust wants you to call him.*

This deal could not fall through. The few things that Blair had left depended on it.

He reached for the Vitasoft file on his desk. "Only a fool would let a little fog keep him from doing what needs to be done. Myself, I stay focused on the big picture and walk right through it."

"Good man. Unfortunately . . . I'm not so certain that our major stockholders feel the same way. Some of our directors are asking tough questions—questions I'm having trouble answering."

Blair picked up a paper clip and began to straighten it. "You can tell your directors that there is no need for worry."

"A lawsuit worth several million dollars might be perceived as a rather large reason to worry. Know what I mean? Our legal counsel is telling us to cool our jets a little on the timing of the close."

"My personal problems have nothing to do with the well-being of this company. I'm continuing on with business as usual." He worked the clip into a circle.

"Good. I expect you to do everything in your power to provide the warmth and sunshine we'd all like to see in a California experience."

"I'm taking care of things on my end. You do the same on yours."

"Got it covered. I'll check in again soon."

Blair hung up the phone and fought the urge to bury his face in his hands. Too many people could walk by the office. Instead he stared at the paper clip he'd bent out of shape. It'd never go back, he thought. He could try, could maybe get it close, but it'd never be back to its original shape. Blair somehow felt that was true of his own life, too. One more twist, one more bend. He wondered if so much could happen that you'd forget where you started in the first place. And then what would he be left with? What kind of complicated knot would his life look like then?

———

The buzz from the front gate jerked Andie to her feet. It was nine o'clock on Friday night. Blair had once again barricaded himself in his study and she expected no visitors. The surprise of the buzzer rose a dread deep within. But really, what bad news could be left?

She walked to the intercom. "Yes?"

"Andie, it's Sam Campbell. I need to talk to you." Andie couldn't move. Sam was their lawyer—Scott Baur's law partner and a longtime acquaintance. This probably wasn't social. Not tonight—at this time.

"Andie?"

Mechanically, she opened the gate, flipped on the porch light, and waited. When she heard his car stop at the front of the house, she braced herself, turned the deadbolt, and opened the door. It took all her energy to force her voice out in a casual, friendly manner. "Good evening, Sam."

"Good evening, Andie. I'm sorry to bother you at home this late, but I've got something I think you need to know." His grim face told her she might *need* to know it, but she definitely did not *want* to know it.

"Please, come in." She held the door. *Close it. Leave him outside. Don't let him in.* "Would you like a cup of decaf?" She surprised herself with the control she managed to keep in her tone.

"No thanks. Is Blair home? I'd like to speak with him, as well."

"Yes, I'm home." Blair stood in the hallway, watching. The weary look on his face told Andie he, too, feared the cause of this visit.

Andie continued her illusion of calm. "Come into the living room." From the look on Sam Campbell's face, he needed to sit down while he delivered this news. She was certain she needed to sit to hear it. She pointed at the gray wingback chair. "Please, have a seat."

She walked on wobbly legs to the couch, where she sank into the cushions. Maybe she should just order him out of her house. Lock him and the bad news he brought out of her life.

It wouldn't help. The truth would find them.

Blair sat beside her. He rubbed his hands together and leaned his elbows on his knees. It was his "let's get down to business" position that Andie recognized so well. "What news do you have for us?"

"The toxicology reports have come back." He pulled a white sheet of paper out of his jacket pocket but didn't look at it. "Your son had a 0.03 alcohol level in his blood. Not enough to be legally drunk, but of course, any amount at his age is illegal."

Andie gasped. "There must be some mistake. Chad never touched alcohol. He spoke out against it."

She remembered his birthday party last year. Dozens of teen-agers splashing about in the softly lit pool, the smell of hot dogs carrying over from the grill, the girls' giggles at the boys' belly-busting competition.

Chad had walked over, dripping wet and smiling. "I think this is the best party yet. Don't you?" He put his arms around Andie's shoulders.

She laughed. "How come the only time you hug me in front of your friends is when you're soaking wet?"

"Oops. Sorry about that." He lifted his arm, then put it back on her shoulders. "Ah, you're already wet now. May as well enjoy it, huh?" He looked around. "I wonder where Dan and Kurt went."

"They've been in and out several times tonight. They must be up to something." Andie smiled. "They better not be TPing all the trees out front again. It took a week to clean that mess up last time they did it."

Chad sniggered. "Yeah, Dad was pretty mad about that, too. I better go see if they're out there."

Three minutes later, he returned, his face solemn. He went over to a group of boys and pointed toward the door. The boys looked at him, grinning, waiting for the joke that didn't seem to come. After a minute of heated conversation, three of them left. Only later did Andie ask him what had happened.

"They were going out to their cars and mixing rum in with their Coke. I told them they were disrespecting my family. I told them to get out and not come back."

Chad could not have died with alcohol in his system. It had to be a mistake.

"He was underage. Surely we can track down the person who sold something to him. They should be called to answer for it." Blair's voice came out gravelly, and his lips had gone so tight they hardly moved as he spoke.

Sam shifted in his seat and adjusted his tie, as if he needed to breathe. "Yes, that is true. First of all, I need to ask you, is there any way he could have gotten into the alcohol cabinet at home?"

Andie lifted her chin and looked at Sam. "Neither of us drink, and we do not keep alcohol in our home." Had someone sold that poison to her son? Whoever it was, he was responsible for the accident and needed to face up to it. She wanted to punish him, make him pay. Let him feel some of her pain. They would drag him into court so fast . . .

An uncomfortable sensation formed deep in her gut. No. *This* was different. This was . . . different.

Sam nodded. "That's good to hear. I asked because, upon searching through the wreckage, the police found a bottle beneath his backseat. They kept it quiet for as long as possible.

He tugged at his tie again. "The reason I thought it might have come from home is because of the bottle they found. I'm told, with kids, they usually find beer, or some form of cheap liquor. Chad had a bottle of Scotch."

Blair's face went white. "Laphroaig? Thirty-year-old Laphroaig?"

Sam pressed his lips into a thin line. "Yes, as a matter of fact."

"Oh, dear God, help me." Blair buried his face in his hands. He didn't cry, nor did he speak, but he rocked back and forth over and over again.

Andie watched her husband, and an entirely new dread crept through her. "Blair, what is going on?"

He looked up, his eyes haunted and hollow. "The day of the wreck, I got a package. It was from Rex Grimes, an old college friend I hadn't seen in years. He'd just gotten back from a tour of Scotland and sent a bottle to all the old gang."

"What kind of person sends a bottle of Scotch to a friend who's been clean and sober for over twenty years?"

"I haven't talked to him in almost that long. He had no way of knowing." Blair rubbed his hands against his knees. "Chad was with me when I opened it. I set it on the counter beside the sink, planning to pour it out. That's when I found out about the midterm grades, and everything else started to happen. I forgot about it."

Sam rose stiffly from the chair and walked over to touch Blair on the shoulder. "I'm sorry, Blair. I know this is devastating. But you've got to understand, this just made our case a whole lot harder."

chapter **nine**

Melanie scanned through the list of price changes as she waited for the weekly meeting to begin. One by one the others moved into the conference room and took their seats. When Joe Server entered she smiled at him. He offered a brief nod, then turned away. It was then she noticed that everyone in the room seemed to be conspicuously focused away from her.

Quit being paranoid.

Mr. Mortensen flipped the papers in front of him. "Randy, I've gotten several complaints about the new man in produce. What are you doing about the situation?" He scanned the table but avoided eye contact with Melanie.

What was going on?

The meeting was brief and to the point. When it ended, everyone scurried from the room except Joe. He shuffled through papers and rubbed at a spot on the table until Melanie stood to walk out. He followed her.

When they were away from everyone else, he tugged her arm. "Is it worth all this?"

Fighting for Jeff's memory was worth any price. "All what?"

"Your past, plastered before the whole world."

"What are you talking about? What about my past?"

Joe's eyes grew wide. "You didn't see the paper this morning? I thought you always read it first thing."

"Not today." Not since the stories had stopped being about Jeff and started being about the lawsuit. She waited until later in the day to read now, when she felt less vulnerable than she did first thing in the morning. Her tongue seemed thicker as she asked the next question. "What's in the paper, Joe?"

He shook his head. "I'll let you see it yourself." He spun around and hurried from the room, carrying his notepad under his arm.

Melanie went in search of a paper.

————

Andie had just settled on the couch when the phone chimed. She'd collapsed there this morning after making Blair's coffee and sending him out the door with a packed lunch. *See, no matter what they say, I am making an effort. And my effort for today is complete.*

There was nothing on today's calendar. She'd canceled a few meetings and planned to skip the ladies' luncheon. She wanted to sit in the quiet house and feel her pain. She was too tired to try to find something to keep her busy and pretend the agony wasn't there. Exhaustion killed pretense.

She lumbered over to the phone but decided to let the machine get it. Whoever it was could wait.

"Andie, this is Carolyn Patterson from the Cancer Foundation. I have a rather urgent need to talk to you regarding the Old Time Fair for the Cure. Please call me as soon as—"

"Hi, Carolyn. It's me. Sorry. It took a while to get to the phone. What's up?"

A sudden glimmer sneaked up on her. Perhaps Blair had put Carolyn up to this call. He knew the Fair was the one thing that might get her motivated.

He had been nagging about getting out of the house and back into life. For Andie, there was no life to get back into. Not without Chad.

Oh, she still attended church faithfully—no need to get all the women in an uproar about her backsliding. Still attended meetings that were absolutely necessary, but nothing else. No tennis. No coffee with the girls. And no gym. She suspected that was the one that troubled Blair the most.

"What's your question about the Fair?" *A fair that doesn't happen for another two months.*

"I just got a call from one of our major corporate sponsors. It seems their CEO has heard a rumor about your family."

The *News-Press* kept a running documentary on the accident, the lawsuit, and this week's toxicology results. What could possibly still be open to speculation?

"I'm so sick of all this. I'm sure he has heard a rumor, probably lots of them, but I would think he has better things to be doing with his time. Besides, how is my personal life any of his business? He runs a company; I run a charitable fundraiser."

"This is a little different."

"Because of gossip? A rumor like what?"

"Like your family is trying to bankrupt the mother of that other kid. The one from the wreck."

Andie gasped. "That is a lie! *She* is the one suing *us!*"

"I don't know where the information came from, but he is concerned and is considering withdrawing sponsorship. He says they cannot afford a publicity problem right now."

"What kind of publicity will he get for letting a lie stop him from supporting cancer patients and their families?"

Carolyn paused. "Andie, I certainly don't judge you, but what about Alfords?"

Andie's legs wobbled; she collapsed into a chair. "What about it?"

"Word is that you have called for a boycott by all Hope Ranch residents. A boycott that will not lift until the other woman is fired or transfers out of there."

Andie thought she might throw up. Why hadn't she stopped Christi when the boycott idea first started? "Some of my friends are staying away from the store, although I had nothing to do with their decision."

"Are you telling me that you're still shopping there, then?"

Smack. "No." She remembered Blair's outrage when she suggested the unfairness of the boycott. In this instant, some of that outrage flowed into her. "Anyway, why should they support someone who's trying to ruin my family? Haven't we been through enough?"

"It's not my call, Andie. I'm just telling you what I was told."

"What does that have to do with corporate sponsorship?"

"Supposedly, there is going to be an editorial in tomorrow's paper. It will describe the rich families in Hope Ranch banding together to destroy a struggling single mother who dares to challenge them. It sounds like things are about to get pretty ugly and pretty divided in this town."

How dare those people try to hurt her by keeping her from helping other people? She wasn't paid a penny for the countless hours she spent doing charity work. Didn't these people see they were only hurting the cancer victims by doing this?

"So what am I supposed to do?"

"Just lay low for now. We're going to make certain your name is not publicly attached to anything involved with the Fair. If things die down quickly, and I'm sure they will, we will continue with business as normal. By Fair time, we'll forget we ever had this conversation."

"And if things don't die down?"

"Well . . ."

"Well, what?"

"We may have to ask you to resign as director."

"No." They couldn't rip Andie's only measure of comfort from her grasp like this. "Please, no." She wiped a stray tear, her hands ice-cold against her cheek.

"We won't do anything in haste, Andie. I just wanted you to know what's happening. In case."

Andie found it almost impossible to speak, but somehow she finally swallowed and answered in a most civil voice. "Thank you for calling. Of course I want what's right for the Cancer Center, so I'll do what I have to do. Thank you for your support."

As soon as the click sounded at the other end, Andie hurled her phone across the room. Those horrible people! For the first time since Chad's accident, she was able to feel something besides overwhelming pain. Outrage. It bubbled into her blood and spread through her limbs, restoring the energy that grief had drained from them.

If they wanted a fight, she would fight. No one was going to take away the gains she had made in cancer fundraising just to win sympathy in a lawsuit.

Andie bolted toward her bedroom, pulling the sweatshirt over her head as she went. She hopped into a burning hot shower and scrubbed away the dirtiness that seemed to cling to her.

She emerged from the shower as a woman with a renewed sense of purpose. She would save the Fair, and make certain everyone who threatened to bring it down got what was coming to them.

———

Christi Baur watched Susie's face closely. So far, no signs of shock or outrage. Next to Andie, Susie was the biggest wimp of the group. Her reaction would most closely resemble Andie's.

Susie's forehead gathered in the wrinkles of deep thought. At one point, she gasped and covered her mouth with her hand. Christi pictured the rest of Santa Barbara doing the same as they read about Melanie Johnston's checkered past. All of the city was being enlightened today.

She wondered what the most outspoken supporters of the valiant and hard working single mother would say about this. By now, everyone would realize the woman they rallied behind had not been married when Jeff was born. By the time her second child came around, she had married the guy, but of course there were several drug arrests in the interim. Christi smiled. About time the truth came out.

Susie lowered the paper, took a deep breath, then carefully folded it before placing it on the round table. She didn't look at Christi, but instead seemed fascinated with the barista and the steamed milk she was spooning into a customer's latte.

Christi couldn't take it. "Well? Come on. What did you think?"

Susie looked at her. "It was a bit . . . rough. Don't you think? Bu—"

"A bit rough? Are you kidding me? That woman has been coming across like Mother Teresa all this time, when she's probably not even a fit mother at all. Who's to say she's kicked the drug habit?"

Susie leaned forward. "You interrupted me. I hate it when you do that." She quirked her eyebrows and sat back into her seat.

Christi recognized the look in Susie's eyes and knew the information would be slow in coming. Susie tweaked Christi's impatience anytime she got a chance, and now she had the perfect opportunity.

Christi assumed her most humble expression and tried to look bored, as though she had all the time in the world. "Sorry. What was it you were about to say?"

Susie took a sip of her double decaf latte. She set the cup onto the wooden table and ran the tip of her index finger around the plastic lid.

Oh, she's going to draw this out, all right.

"What I was about to say . . ." She paused for another sip of her coffee. "Is that it was a little rough. The woman did lose her son, after all. But—and this is the part where you interrupted me before—there are some things here that need to be taken into consideration. Up until this point, it seems to me that all the negative talk has been centered on Andie and Blair. It's nice to see her taking some heat for a change."

Christi felt a growing sense of satisfaction. She'd been certain there was some trash to be found, but Scott's partner feared public backlash too much to use it. Public backlash did not concern Christi at all. *Andie* was her concern. Softhearted wimp though she was, Christi did love her.

So she'd hired her own investigator, who uncovered this part of the story. She had then fed these juicy tidbits to her favorite *News-Press* reporter, and no one would ever know she was the source of this most helpful information. Her biggest fear was that this story would upset Andie into doing something stupid.

She had planned to drive to her house this morning and see how she was taking it. After seeing Susie's reaction, maybe she'd call on the cell phone and see if that was necessary after all.

"I've gotta run. See you tomorrow at nine?" Susie stood and smoothed her tennis skirt over legs Christi couldn't help but admire.

"Yep. Court three."

Christi carried the paper out of the shop and slung it in the backseat on top of her tennis racket. She fired up the engine and waited only until the first light to call up Andie's number on her cell phone.

Andie answered on the second ring. "Christi, did you have anything to do with that article today?"

Christi both loved and hated caller ID. How could you surprise anyone anymore? "Well…yes and no." The light turned green. She needed to ask the question she really didn't want to ask. It was the only way she would know whether to turn right or left at the next light. "What did you think?"

"It surprised me. I had built her up into some kind of sainted martyr. You know what? I think I'm ready to fight for what's mine. What else can you think of that I should be doing?"

chapter **ten**

Melanie put away the last of the dishes and looked at the clock. She still had time to clean the floor before Sarah got home from youth group. Good. She had some aggression to work out.

She filled the bucket with pine cleaner and water, dipped her brush, and began to scrub. Today, more than usual, she was glad for the old-fashioned way she cleaned her linoleum. As she scrubbed, she allowed all the pent-up anger to flow through her arms and out the brush. This floor would never again be so clean.

It had been two days since the article appeared in the *News-Press*, but the sting had not lessened. How dare those people dredge up her past like that? She knew why they did it, of course. The resulting feeding frenzy turned the public's attention to her, and off their son's toxicology report. Did they have no conscience at all? Was money so important to them that they would ruin another person to distract people from their own fault—all to hold on to their precious possessions?

Apparently so. Their lack of caring about anything had cost them a son. If only their selfishness hadn't cost Melanie hers, as well.

The important thing now was to make certain that Jeff's memory served a purpose, and to help Sarah make it through life as well as possible. A stab of pain in Melanie's chest reminded her that things had not been going so great with Sarah lately.

The kids at school had been only too happy to whisper through the halls about the "partysville" past of Sarah's mother. Sarah had been so mortified, she planned to stay home from youth group tonight. She couldn't bear to face her friends. But Beth fixed that.

Good old Beth.

She called this afternoon, told Sarah her parents had agreed to let her take the car, since it was Valentine's Day. "I can't waste this one-time offer on just myself. I'll pick you up at quarter till seven."

Sarah couldn't refuse.

Melanie knew the excuse was a ruse. Beth was the truest of friends. Most likely her parents had helped contrive a reason to make certain Sarah didn't retreat to her room and hide from the world. They were a nice family. Good people.

Melanie scrubbed the last section of floor, emptied the bucket, and was rinsing out her brush when the headlights pulled into the driveway. She pretended to stay busy at the sink, wanting to give Sarah space to make the first move.

Would she disappear into her room without a word? Vent her frustration on Melanie? Whatever it was she needed to do, Melanie would make certain she had the opportunity to do it. She promised herself no matter how angry she got, she would not allow it to spill over onto Sarah. She was her only child now. She couldn't afford to mess that up.

"You're not going to believe what happened tonight."

Melanie turned to find Sarah leaning against the doorjamb, red heart stickers all over her T-shirt. She saw no hint of anger in her daughter's face. In fact, her eyes danced with excitement.

"Let me guess—you got some Valentine stickers."

Sarah looked at her shirt and smiled. "Well, yeah, that, too. We played 'sticker tag.' Whoever got the most hearts lost." She held out her shirt. "I came in next to last, but Kevin beat me out by two stickers. But that's not what I'm talking about."

"Really? What, then?"

"Jake Sterling—you know who he is, right?"

A bolt of apprehension shot through Melanie. She wiped her hands on a dish towel. "Yeah, I know who he is." In fact, she had a meeting scheduled with him for tomorrow night—a meeting she planned to cancel. No need to talk more about the mission trip thing after that article. She figured that sealed her doom.

"Well, he marched all the youth into the auditorium where the adults were having their Wednesday night class, then got up and spoke to the entire church about me—and you—and our situation."

The towel dropped from Melanie's hand to the floor. She didn't bother to pick it up. "He did what? What did he say?"

"He told everyone that Jeff had been a devoted member of our church, and that I still was. He said no matter what, we were a hurting family and deserved the love and support of our church. He said he didn't want to hear a word whispered by a single member of our church about this week's article."

"Why would he say that? Isn't that what churches do, tell people like me we need to clean up our act?"

"He said he'd met you and you were one of the finest, most upstanding women he'd met in a long time. He said that his past was much worse than yours, and if people in the church could not accept our family, then they could not accept him, either."

Melanie couldn't believe it. Jake had taken the hit for Sarah—and for her.

Late that night, when she finally turned out the light, she lay in bed and thought about what he had done. *One of the finest, most upstanding women he had met in a long time.* That's what he'd said about her. Of course, he was probably building her up for the sake of his cause, but still. To have someone say those words, even with questionable sincerity, instilled vague warmth into a heart that expected nothing but cold ever again. Maybe she wouldn't rush to cancel tomorrow night's meeting after all.

———

Andie forced herself to transcribe the phone numbers, though anger burned with each stroke of the pencil. Bitterness finally burst from her in screams—screams no one would hear in her empty house.

"The Fair was my brain child! My baby!" she shouted to the air, stabbing at the paper and cutting rather than writing the numbers. The lead snapped. She flung the pencil across the room. "Those people have no right to try to take this away from me." She pushed her chair away from the desk and walked to the window, where she stared at the distant Pacific. Three pelicans flew low over the water.

Although she had not officially been removed from planning, it was agreed that Susie, Janice, and Christi would make all phone calls and keep Andie's name out of it. They asked her to go through her piles of supporters and contributors and make a phone list for the other women.

Until she had come up with the idea of a county-fair themed fundraiser-for-the-masses three years ago, the Cancer Center had lagged in their fundraising efforts. Bringing the event back to the people, and away from black ties and fancy dinners, they had basked in the added public support and increased donations. After all, cancer affected everyone.

"Those troublemakers want to ruin everything." Of all the charity work she did out of obligation or guilt, this was the one that came straight from the heart. A heart that had first been broken twenty-two years ago. The year she lost her mother to cancer.

She still dreamed about that tennis match—the first of the season. She could see her mom's face behind the chain-link fence, watching, cheering. Then she'd had one of those epic points, maybe twenty or twenty-five back-and-forth returns before she hit a winner. When she turned back, her mother wasn't watching and someone was shouting.

"Doctor! Someone call a doctor!"

Andie remembered looking down. Her mother lay on the ground, arms and legs spasming, eyes rolled back in her head.

The remaining memories from Andie's senior year were a blur of scenes, pieced together by fuzzy mental images and haunting words. Words like *cancer, chemotherapy, pain management, terminal illness.* The process lasted barely two months. Then Andie and her father were alone.

Andie picked up the pencil and thrust it into the sharpener, her anger still burning. "I'll bet all those troublemakers had a fabulous senior year—dates, proms, future plans."

She collapsed back into the chair and rubbed her face. *And the cancer didn't stop there, did it?*

She wiped her eyes and attempted to return to her task, trying in vain to block her mind from the rest of the story. It didn't work. The memories flooded of the next September, when she started USC still wrapped in the cocoon of grief that never seemed to loosen.

The second day on her new campus, Grandpa Jim called. "Andie . . ." His voice sounded funny, choked. "It's your father."

The heart that Andie thought would never feel anything again suddenly convulsed in her chest. "What about him?"

"Andie, he's gone."

Her own father had put a pistol inside his mouth and pulled the trigger. The memory still hit her like a physical blow. What was the reason for it? Simple, really.

Cancer.

If there had never been the cancer, her father would never have sunk to the depths of pain he couldn't rise above. *Okay, let's be honest, Andie. There are two reasons. If you'd been less self-absorbed in your own pain, been a better daughter, maybe you could have pulled him up out of his pit. Part of the reason you lost your father was your own failing.*

Her guilt helped tamp down the anger and pushed her forward in the task at hand. She looked at the list of names yet to be copied.

No other family should have to face that pain. No other eighteen-year-old girl left on her own to fend for herself. *That's why the Fair is so important. Can't they see that?* She forced herself to finish the work.

"I'm going to show them all—just like Mom does with her cancer fundraiser every year." Chad's words continued to echo. She *had* to do this. She had failed him by not doing the painting for the car wash. The Fair was her last chance to make him proud.

She shoved her chair back and paced around the house, looking at nothing. It was almost nine o'clock. Blair had always worked long hours, but these days he barely made it home to sleep.

She walked into her little studio and didn't even bother to turn on the light. She sat on a small stool and stared into the darkness, engulfed in pain.

A large white rectangle against the back wall drew her attention. The blank canvas looked almost gray in the darkness. She crossed the room and stood before it.

A familiar longing stirred within her. The itch to have her fingers wrapped around a paintbrush, to be creating something with texture and imagination and planning.

She crossed the room and flipped the light switch. Slowly, she walked over and picked up a brush. Blair wasn't around to make a big fuss about it. Not that it mattered. At this point, he didn't seem to care what she did with her time as long as he didn't have to deal with her.

She was alone. Shouldn't she be allowed to do something that offered her the slightest bit of joy? She removed her charcoal pencils from the drawer. A flash of realization told her she'd known for a long time what her next painting would be.

Several hours later, she had completed a sketch and begun to paint. She mixed the blues on her palette until they reached the perfect shade for the perfect sky. Just right. It was coming together in a way she never dreamed possible. At last, she found a reason to hope.

When she heard Blair's car coming up the driveway, she flipped off the lights in her studio and moved quickly down the hall. It was past midnight. She could rush upstairs and pretend to be asleep if she moved fast enough.

chapter eleven

When Melanie walked into Jake Sterling's garage this time, Tony jumped from his seat on the floor. He leapt over the pile of engine parts surrounding him and rushed over to greet her.

She nodded. "Hi, Tony."

He looked down at his shirt. Apparently satisfied with its cleanliness, he threw his arms around her and squeezed tight. "It's great to see you."

"It's great to see you, too."

"How're you making it? You doing okay?"

"Fine." Her answer came out wheezy and choked.

He released her and smiled sheepishly. "Sorry about that. Got a little carried away."

"Tony, the good you do my heart is worth the damage you do my ribs. I know those hugs are because of Jeff. That means a lot."

His face turned pink and he looked over his shoulder. "Jake's waiting for you in his office. He said to send you right in." He wiped his hands against his work pants. "Probably thought I'd keep you out here all night talking to you."

The door to the office was open. Jake sat with his back turned, filling out paperwork at his desk. He looked busy.

Melanie tapped on the open door. "Knock, knock."

Jake swiveled in his seat. "No need to knock around here. Open door policy, you know. How are you doing?" He smiled at her and his eyes glowed with a hint of something tantalizing.

Melanie wanted to know more about what went on behind those eyes. She dismissed the thought. "Thank you for what you did at your church last night. Sarah told me about it. It means a lot to her—and me."

He shrugged one shoulder. "Someone needed to stand up and say it."

Melanie nodded in full agreement. "Will it solve the problem about the mission trip? Sarah befriended this little girl last year. Just the thought of not going is eating her up with guilt."

Jake tilted his head thoughtfully to one side. "It won't *solve* the problem, but it certainly can't hurt. I've been thinking a lot about that. You know what might? If you were to come to church a time or two."

She should have known. It had to come around to religion sometime. Melanie felt the heat rising in her face and willed herself to maintain control. "What kind of hypocrite would that make me, if I came to your church just so they'd give my daughter money to go on a trip with the youth? A *mission* trip! My lawsuit is not about the money. If I won't go to court for the money, I certainly will not go to church for it."

He held up his hand to stop her. "I didn't mean it that way. I think it would help all the people there to see that you are just like them. Let them see that you are not the ... uh ... financially motivated person they might think you are."

Melanie felt her anger fade, and in its place shame took what remained of her will to fight. "I know you read the article."

He blinked an acknowledgment.

"It's all true, you know. Every detail about my past life that was spelled out for all of Santa Barbara to read is true. Why would it help my daughter if a woman with my past showed up at your church?"

"Melanie, your past is just that—past. No one is perfect. We've all sinned, all made mistakes."

"That may be true, but most people don't make mistakes as big as mine were."

"I did. Bigger. It's only through God's grace that I'm where I am today, and that I will one day stand before Him—forgiven."

"Jake, like I used to tell Jeff, 'If it works for you, that's fine with me, but it doesn't work for me.' Besides, you and I both know everyone in the church would be talking and whispering if I walked in."

"Not everyone. Some would—I can't deny that. But the ones who would talk and whisper will do it anyway. Do you want Sarah to endure their talk, or do you want to do it for her? Just show up once—give it a try, and see what happens."

Melanie stood. She couldn't think of anything else to do. "As I said before, I'm glad that stuff works for you. Thanks again for helping Sarah." She rushed out the door and out of the shop, thankful Tony was occupied elsewhere.

———

Blair Phelps forced himself to dress for church, although he did not want to go. He needed to go to the office and bury himself in paperwork. The Vitasoft people kept calling, asking questions, offering vague, unsettling comments. He needed to give them answers. Needed to focus.

But every time he closed his eyes he saw that bottle sitting on the counter. Why had he left it there?

Andie's groans brought him back to reality. One more reason he didn't want to go to church today—she looked ridiculous.

In some ways, he welcomed the changes this week had brought in her. Some issue with one of her charities had given her the drive to get up and going again. That fact alone improved life at home. Not perfect, but at least he wasn't coming in from the office to find her still in sweats, with candy wrappers and ice cream bowls sitting all around her.

But this deal with Mattilda Plendor overshadowed many of the changes for the better.

Andie had always dressed in classics, and he liked that. Even when some of her friends started moving toward high-end fashion, she resisted. She never looked gaudy or tacky, always elegant and ladylike. Until now.

Today she wore a dark green dress that looked as though a freshman failing remedial Home Ec had sewn it. The hemline was shredded, hanging in stringy long panels of every length and width. The material would have been less out of place marching in a military parade. Perhaps the designer of this particular number had taken out her frustration on some army-surplus fabric and decided to make a little money off the result. She was probably perched right now in a penthouse on Park Avenue, laughing at the fool who would pay for such a scrap as high fashion.

Andie spun around and took one last look in the mirror. She scrunched up the right side of her face. "I hate this dress."

Blair breathed a sigh of relief. She'd go change, and at least one of his problems would be solved. He stepped aside to clear the way to her closet. She didn't move.

He'd been married long enough to know that the wrong words in a situation like this could land him in husband detention for weeks to come. *Think. Choose your words with prudence. No need to create more problems than you have already.*

He made a point of looking at his watch. Taking care to speak in his most oblivious husband tone so she wouldn't see how he strained at the truth, he yawned. "Really? Well, we've got a few minutes. Just enough time to don a new outfit."

Andie turned and looked over her shoulder into the mirror. She patted her rear end with both hands. "Talk about unflattering."

He couldn't have agreed more. "You need to get moving if you're going to change. We need to leave soon."

Andie pivoted away from the mirror and grabbed her purse. "I can't." She rushed through the bedroom and out into the hallway.

Blair groaned. By the time he made it through the door, she was halfway down the stairs. He knew that to say any more would move dangerously close to explosive grounds, but the ugliness of the ensemble caused him to take the risk. "Why not?"

"Why not what?" By this time she had reached the bottom of the stairs and turned to look up at him.

"Why can't you change?"

She shrugged. "Mattie would be upset." She turned and started walking toward the garage.

Blair jumped over the last three stairs and rushed up beside her. "Mattie?"

She kept moving.

"What about you?"

When she didn't seem to hear him, he put a hand on her until she turned. "You've said you don't like the dress. You just said it's unflattering. Why would you let that woman bully you into wearing something that you will only feel self-conscious about?"

Andie's eyes cut toward him, a flash of anger showing. "The same reason I let everyone around here bully me into doing things I don't want to do—and *not* doing the things I do want to do." She flung open the door to the garage. "Funny how no one complains until someone else is doing the bullying." She shoved through the door and disappeared into the garage.

Blair did not follow. He would regret anything he said—better to let it go. He heard the car door slam. Her attitude was getting old.

He walked into the garage, determined not to say or do anything that would escalate the situation. He could see Andie in the passenger's seat with her arms folded across her chest and her head turned away from him.

Why should he take the brunt of her frustration? With everything else going on, to willfully dress in something you hated seemed ridiculous. He wasn't going to apologize for saying otherwise.

In fact, he didn't know what more he could apologize for. The bottle Chad had taken continued to haunt him; he'd be sorry about that forever. But he'd been a faithful husband and a good provider all these years. Where was her appreciation? Hey, he'd only been trying to encourage her to stand up for herself. If she wanted to wear that sack of rags, so be it.

They rode in silence. Andie kept her head turned toward her window the entire way, pouting. By the time they pulled into the parking lot, Blair had never been so happy to see the church.

Andie appeared to share his relief, because she yanked open the door and jumped from the car. She had no sooner put her foot on the parking lot than Mattilda Plendor rushed across the asphalt, a sheath of purple flowing around her. "There you are. I was beginning to think you weren't going to make it." She looked Andie over with obvious approval. "Doesn't she look fabulous, Blair?"

Blair couldn't bring himself to lie, so he didn't speak. Only because his parents had ingrained in him courtesy to women was he able to offer a polite nod. He hurried away before the words he really wanted to say found voice.

As he walked away, he heard Mattilda. "Come along, dear. We want everyone to see this glorious creation." He quickened his pace to avoid being caught in her trap. Why hadn't he feigned illness this morning? He looked at his watch. Only two more hours and he'd be on his way to the office. Just two hours. Surely he could make it.

———

Melanie drove through downtown Santa Barbara and into the part of town where old warehouses stood beside shacks and funky offices for trendy architects and artists. A homeless man lay napping between the roots of an ancient oak, his shopping cart parked beside him, a bottle perched between his laced fingers. She turned left into a narrow street that led between two rusted storage sheds, then emerged at a huge red warehouse. This must be the place.

She backed her car into a space at the very edge of the rapidly filling parking lot. Best to make a quick getaway when this was over. She took a deep breath and took a moment to simply observe.

A family walked toward the large warehouse together, talking and laughing. The woman wore an ankle-length wool skirt, the man plain jeans.

Melanie glanced down at her khakis, her nicest pair. They ought to blend in there somewhere. She left the comfort of her car and pushed forward.

Three sets of glass doors stood propped open. They reminded her of the mouth of a hungry whale, prepared to swallow a school of krill. Two people stood before each of these openings, wearing name tags and directing the tiny fish into the whale's mouth. Wasn't there a story in the Bible about a whale eating someone? It was one of the few she knew anything about. The couple offered greetings and handed some sort of folded paper to everyone brave enough to pass through. Their strategic placement made it impossible to enter unnoticed.

Melanie stopped walking. If she turned now, maybe she could make it back to the car without being seen. She disliked cowardice above almost anything else, though, and besides, this was for Sarah.

Several years ago, when one of her neighbors started taking Jeff and Sarah to church, it seemed like a good idea. She knew the dangers of a missing father figure and a mother who worked full-time and wanted them to learn good morals. But in the intervening years she'd met enough people who called themselves "Christians" to know they weren't a lick better than she was. These days, in fact, she was probably a morally better person than most everyone going inside. What did she need church for?

"Good morning. How are you today?" The woman who greeted her had perfect hair, a perfect sweater, and perfect makeup.

Her last chance for escape had passed. "Fine. Thanks." She took the offered paper and walked forward. Panic built with each step. She followed the crowd through another set of doors that led into a huge auditorium.

There were no somber pews, no stained-glass windows. The chairs were individual and a muted shade of plum. The carpet carried the same color, with contrasting circles of black and tan. Interesting. Not quite like the vague memory she had of churches from her past.

"Hi. I'm Trish." A woman with shoulder-length, frizzy blond curls stood beside Melanie, offering an extended hand and a bright smile.

"Melanie." Melanie shook her hand, annoyed at the woman's cheeriness. She knew with one word she could wipe the smile off the woman's face. Now would be just as good a time as any. "Johnston."

"I'm sorry, I didn't hear you. What did you say?"

"I said Johnston, my name is Melanie Johnston." She waited for the smile to fade, the sparkle to dim from the eyes.

Trish's face did change. It took on a quiet consideration, but Melanie did not sense the outright hostility she had braced for. "Melanie Johnston." Trish nodded her head thoughtfully. "I'm so glad you've come."

"Yeah. Well, thanks."

"You know, I have my things in a seat up toward the front. Will you join me?"

Something about the woman seemed real, not at all like the phoniness Melanie had expected. She considered the offer for a split second, but remembered her vow to get out of here quickly. "Thanks, but I was planning on sitting toward the back. I need to leave as soon as the service is over, and don't want to get caught in the crowd."

Trish nodded her head. "I know what you mean. Tell you what, I'll get my things and join you—how about that? I'll just be a minute." Before Melanie had a chance to respond, Trish rushed up the aisle toward the front.

Melanie found a seat on the outside aisle of a row near the back. Seconds later, Trish slipped in beside her. "I've always meant to try a new spot. You get in a rut of sitting in the same place week after week, and you never see any new faces. Know what I mean?" She adjusted her purse and looked toward the front. "Oh good, we're getting started."

Melanie watched a group of people, most dressed in baggy jeans and casual shirts, walk to the front. Some pulled guitars from stands, while others perched behind drums, keyboards, and microphones. Two large screens at the front of the auditorium displayed projected words, and the music began.

The musicians were as talented as they were young. Melanie decided they looked more like a rock band than a choir. They should call themselves the Dirty Dozen.

Somewhere during the course of the singing, Melanie began to relax a bit. She looked around the room. The mix of people surprised her. Some were fashionable, while others wore jeans. There were young children and elderly couples, and near the front she saw a row of teen boys. Melanie's son had come here. Week after week. Maybe even sat with that gang of guys. And yet she'd never been part of this. She couldn't even imagine him here listening to the music. Why had he come?

After a handful more songs, the man who had to be the pastor came forward. He looked to be in his fifties, with balding hair and a trim physique. He wore khakis and a dress shirt but no jacket, no tie. A microphone—the kind pop stars use in their televised concerts—looped across his ear and extended forward toward his mouth.

He smiled at the crowd and gestured with both hands opened toward the audience. "Forgiveness." He walked back and took a seat on a chair previously occupied by the guitar player. After several uneasy seconds, the crowd began to shift in their seats. He finally stood, walked forward, and put his hands on the wooden lectern at the front of the pulpit. "Forgiveness."

Part of Melanie just wanted the guy to get on with it, but somehow, during the silence, another part of her began to feel a growing uneasiness.

The pastor began to pace. "If you don't leave here with any other thought today, I want the word *forgiveness* to ring through you like a bell in a tower for the rest of the day. Maybe even the rest of your life. That's what we're all about, people. Forgiveness.

"Sure, you're thinking, 'Yeah, Pastor, Jesus told us to forgive seventy times seven—we know all that.' But what you're not remembering is that God watched His Son die a terrible death, able to stop it, but unwilling. Why did He do that? So that He could offer *forgiveness*—to you."

Melanie heard little else of what was said. She'd gone to church intermittently as a child, depending on the inclination of her current foster family. She knew a passing amount about the Bible and the major stories from it. But this seemed different from the fire-and-brimstone stuff she remembered hearing as a kid.

This preacher, in this warehouse called a church, had put something in a completely new light to her. God *allowed* His son to suffer and die. For her. It was almost too awful to bear. She would've gladly taken Jeff's place in that car, anything to keep him safe, and yet God *allowed* it....

There had to be more to it. Jeff and Sarah were too kind-hearted to believe in a God that cruel. There had to be more... but Melanie couldn't come back. Things were never as they appeared at first glance. As soon as these people figured out who she was, they wouldn't want to see her again, that much was certain.

The preacher finished, and the Dirty Dozen returned to the podium. As the music cranked, Melanie knew now was the perfect time to make her escape. She'd made her appearance. She wanted to get out before the service ended and she had to swim through the sea of krill again and out of the whale's mouth. Jonah. The name came back to her. She didn't move.

Somehow she knew there was more to it than making an appearance. The pastor's puzzling words. Trish's unexpected kindness.

Of course, Trish most likely had no idea who she was. This was a large church. She probably hadn't known Jeff, and didn't recognize Melanie from the paper. Maybe Trish didn't even read the paper. She would be the exception to the rule.

The service ended with a final prayer. People began to file down the aisle and out the back. Melanie pretended to fumble with her things to give people a chance to see her there. Word would get around. Maybe they would scowl at her and leave

Sarah in peace. Maybe they would at least send the youth group to build a house for Juanita.

A woman from the aisle grabbed Trish. "There you are." They started chatting and Melanie walked through the lobby, alone.

"Mom? What are you doing here?" Sarah pushed through the crowd at the door, her mouth hanging open.

"Mrs. Johnston, how are you?" Beth followed close behind and threw her arms around Melanie. Several other girls gathered round. "Mrs. Johnston, so good to see you."

A flood of something warm seeped through Melanie's cold and weary heart. The genuine welcome of these girls made her wish for something she couldn't quite understand, something just out of reach.

"Mom, why didn't you tell me you were coming?"

Melanie shrugged. "I wanted to surprise you." Truth was, she hadn't been certain she'd have the nerve to go through with it.

They moved toward the parking lot, the girls chattering full speed.

"Melanie. Hang on a sec." Trish's voice came from the doorway. Melanie turned and saw her frantically trying to catch up.

While Melanie stopped and waited, Sarah and her friends rambled on through the parking lot, all gangly limbs electric with teenage energy.

Melanie glanced at her car, parked at the ready for a quick exit. It would be a relief to escape. "Thanks for the warm welcome, Trish."

"I hope you come again. It was nice sitting somewhere new and with someone different. You're just the spark I've needed."

Melanie doubted Trish would say that if she knew who she was. She managed to mumble thanks, and something about maybe coming back next week if she didn't have to work.

Trish practically bounced up and down. "Oh, I do hope so."

What was it that drove this woman, anyway? Melanie mumbled a last good-bye and walked to the car. She opened the door and sat in the driver's seat.

" 'Bout time you stopped gabbing."

Melanie jumped. Her knee banged against the steering wheel, a shot of pain shooting up her leg. She reached down to rub it. "Sarah! You scared me halfway to the moon."

"More like three-quarters of the way with how high you jumped."

Melanie looked at her daughter, and something seemed to lodge in her throat. "You're…riding with me?"

Sarah reached across the console and hugged her. "Thanks for coming today, Mom." Another surge of warmth seeped in through the barrier. Sarah had avoided her almost completely for the last month. When Melanie turned the key, she began to think maybe coming here hadn't been such a bad idea after all.

chapter twelve

The other managers were already seated when Melanie walked into the conference room. The Monday meeting wasn't due to start for another five minutes, and she was usually the only one on time. Something was wrong.

She slid into one of the blue upholstered chairs and placed her notepad on the table. She made a conspicuous point of looking at her watch. "Am I late? My watch must have stopped." She shook her wrist and stuck the timepiece to her ear. "No. Still ticking."

The others shifted in their seats. Still, no one looked at her. This was starting to feel strangely familiar.

Mr. Mortensen rose from his seat at the end of the table. "No, Melanie, you're not late. I asked everyone else to come a few minutes early. To talk about some ongoing problems."

"Problems?" She glanced toward Joe. He stared at the table and didn't move.

Mr. Mortensen said, "Melanie, I'm going to lay it on the table. Our business has dropped more than fifty percent in the last three weeks. The boycott is hurting us more than we initially realized it would. If things don't pick up, we'll have to start layoffs soon."

"You can't do that! Several of our people are still struggling to make up for the financial ground they lost during the lockout two years ago."

Mr. Mortensen leaned across the table, his blue tie swinging over the stack of papers before him. "Well, that's not my fault, is it? I never told the union to strike."

Melanie wanted to argue the point but restrained herself. Two years ago, when the grocery workers' union decided to strike one major chain, the other chains banded together and locked out their union employees. It had been financially devastating for everyone involved. Melanie knew that arguing the fine points of that event would not help her now. She needed to take another approach.

As if sensing her hesitation, Mr. Mortensen continued. "We simply can't afford to pay employees to service customers who are not here." He ran his hand down the length of his tie and sank into his chair. "We're starting to get pressure from the home office. I don't like it any more than you do, but those are the facts."

Melanie shook her head and looked around the room. "Those may be the facts, but this is not right."

He sighed. "A lot of things in this situation are not right. Unfortunately, we can't change that." He looked down at his papers. "Now, let's get on with our other business."

The meeting continued for the next thirty minutes, but Melanie heard none of it. She sat in stunned silence, wondering how much worse things could get.

She thought of Tina. A struggling single mom at the bottom of the seniority totem pole. She would most likely be one of the first to go in a layoff. Next up the list was Jackie. Her husband died of cancer last year and she was still paying the bills. What would become of people like them? Although they could most likely find other jobs, once again they would be starting over in seniority and benefits. Something needed to be done about all this. She just wished she knew what.

———

Andie added a touch of shadow to the Ferris wheel. She leaned back, squinted, then touched up the right side a bit. There. Better.

She looked at the scene of the Fair. It was worth fighting for.

Tires squealed in the driveway. Andie looked out her open window to see Christi emerging from her car.

Poor Christi.

Andie knew she had a company dinner this weekend, yet she always felt she needed to make sure Andie was okay. Today should reassure her. She leaned toward the window. "Hey. Come on through."

Christi's eyes scanned the windows. "Where are you?"

"In my studio."

Christi looked toward the window, cocked her head. "Your studio it is."

Andie heard the back door creak open, followed by foot-steps—which stopped in the kitchen. The sound of running water soon followed. *What is it about control freaks? Let them control their own lives. I don't need one in mine.* "Christi, will you quit cleaning my kitchen and come on back here?"

Christi laughed. "Maybe if you did it yourself, I wouldn't have to."

"Why should I, when I have a friend like you to do it for me?"

"Annoyance. That's a good sign." Christi's voice grew closer in the hallway. "How'd you know what I was doing, anyway?"

"Experience."

"What's that smell?" Christi rounded the corner to the studio door and stopped in her tracks. She stared at the canvas, mouth open. "Wow! I'm speechless."

"That's a first."

"My, aren't we feisty today?" She walked up closer. "I'd be offended, but I'm too enthralled with this masterpiece to think straight."

Andie squinted, leaned forward. The lines weren't quite right, the colors a bit off. "Do you really like it?"

"You've got to know this is beautiful."

It needed work. A lot of work. "It's been too long since I've done anything. It looks amateurish."

"Are you kidding? I can't believe how talented you are. Why aren't you painting all the time?"

Andie shrugged and laid her brush aside. "Blair doesn't like it. It's wrong to spend time on art when there are people out there who need help."

Christi folded her arms across her chest and rolled her eyes. "Honestly, he can be such a pain sometimes."

"Well, he is right. There are more important things I should be doing."

"Humph. Maybe we'll show him—and you—how to combine your art and other things. We're going use this painting *of* the Fair *for* the Fair."

———

Melanie took another sip of coffee, still trying to sort through the week's events. Things were not looking good for Alfords.

"Morning, Mom." Sarah poured herself some orange juice and plopped at the kitchen table. "I called Beth and told her I didn't need a ride this morning."

Melanie turned the page of her Sunday paper. "Really? Why?"

"I told her I'd ride with you. It's silly, really, for her to pick me up when you're going anyway."

"Well, I . . . I have an appointment this afternoon."

Sarah's smile dropped slightly. "With that lawyer, right?"

"Yes." What was she thinking? Her teenage daughter actually *wanted* to go somewhere with her. Okay, so it *was* church, and Melanie *had* planned to stay home and catch up on the housework. And she *did* have an appointment with Les Stewart at one o'clock.

"You said this afternoon. You're still free this morning, right?"

She couldn't tell Sarah no. "I guess I better hurry and get ready." She put her coffee cup away and went to her room.

She pulled out her khakis again—they were the only pants that would work—then stared at the sparse row of shirts hanging in her closet, as if just the very act would make additional choices appear.

"Mom, aren't you dressed yet? We need to leave soon." Sarah leaned around the doorframe, her long blond hair hanging like a golden waterfall.

"I wanted to at least wear a different shirt this week. Everything I own is so out of style."

Sarah leaned over so far she fell onto the floor. She pulled her knees into her stomach and began rolling from side to side, groaning.

Melanie dropped the two shirts from her hands and ran to her daughter. "Sarah, are you all right?"

Only when she knelt over the bent and writhing frame did Melanie realize the truth. Sarah wasn't groaning. She was laughing!

"Young lady, what exactly do you find so funny in all of this?"

"You." Sarah sat up and wiped her eyes. "You've never—" Another round of laughter stopped her midsentence.

Melanie stood up and retrieved the two shirts she'd dropped in her panic. "Okay, if you can't speak, you can at least point. Are either of these appropriate to wear to your church?"

Sarah snorted and wiped her eyes. "You were there last week—you know people wear a little of everything."

"I know. But that's not how I was taught. What little I did learn about church in my childhood was that what people wear is second in importance only to staying awake during the sermon."

Sarah stood and put her arms around Melanie's shoulders. "I forget about all the stuff you went through when you were a kid. Jeff and I are so lucky to have a stable mom like you." She swallowed hard. "Jeff's nineteen years were better than most people who die of old age can claim." Sarah's voice caught on the last words. She pointed at the yellow shirt in Melanie's hand. "Wear this one. The yellow color brings out your pretty eyes."

"Like anyone will notice my eyes."

"Jake Sterling told me you had the most fantastic brown eyes he'd ever seen. Said he wondered how I got such light blue ones, when yours were so much to the other extreme."

It had been a long time since anyone noticed anything about Melanie. Did Jake Sterling really say that? Likely not. He probably asked Sarah how someone with such beautiful eyes got them from a mom with such plain dark ones. "Sarah, you're exaggerating."

"Am not. Those were his exact words."

A tiny spark of warmth lit, then quickly died inside of Melanie. There was nothing to it.

"Okay, Mom, we've got to go."

"Wait just one minute. I want to check my hair one more time."

Melanie shuffled out of the car, regretting that she'd let Sarah talk her into coming back. Then she remembered that Sarah was the main reason she'd come last week. She needed to remember her priorities, needed to do whatever it took to make certain her daughter was protected.

A crowd of people milled around in front of the glass doors. Melanie took a deep breath and prepared to breach the whale's mouth once again.

"Melanie, Melanie!"

Melanie searched through the dense crowd for the person attached to the shrill voice. A flash of blond curls emerged from the throng. Trish rushed over, waving. "I was hoping you'd come back!"

Sarah stopped walking and eyed the other woman with amused interest. "Trish, this is my daughter—"

"Oh, you don't have to introduce me to Sarah—I've known her for years."

"You have?"

"I was her Sunday school teacher back when she and Jeff first started coming here."

A mild shock coursed through Melanie. "Last week you knew I was Jeff's mom?"

Trish seemed surprised by the question. "Of course."

"And you still sat with me?"

Trish drew in her chin and scrunched up her lips. "Jeff was one of the dearest young men I have ever known. Why would I not want to sit with the woman who raised him to be so?"

"I thought everybody here was mad at me."

Trish's eye flashed. She leaned forward and kept her voice low. "Don't think that the rantings of a few misguided people represent the spirit of this church. We loved Jeff, we love Sarah, and we love you as part of their family and as a child of God."

Melanie grew uncomfortable. She wasn't certain that she qualified as a child of God, but she didn't want to bring it up.

A crowd of teenage girls giggled and chattered their way over. "Sarah, come on. We've saved you a seat over— Oh, hi, Mrs. Johnston."

Sarah looked at her friends and hesitated. "I, um, I came with my mom today."

Melanie watched her daughter look at the group of friends, then back to her. It was as if she had the impression that Melanie needed her help, and she couldn't abandon her. Melanie didn't want to hold her back—that'd ruin everything she was trying to accomplish.

"That's all right, Sarah. Go sit with your friends. I'll see you after the service."

Trish linked her arm through Melanie's. "Don't worry, I'll take good care of your mother."

"Well, if you're sure."

Melanie nodded. "Positive."

Sarah meandered off with her friends but kept looking over her shoulder as if to be certain that Melanie didn't make a break for the car. "I guess we'd better go inside and be seated so that Sarah can see I'm not planning to run away."

Trish laughed. "I was just thinking the same thing."

They walked in and sat toward the back again. The Dirty Dozen took up their posts and the music began. It almost felt...normal.

Several hours later, Melanie parked in the city lot behind Les Stewart's office. The white stucco walls and red tile roof of this building had graced State Street for almost a century. Les occupied a small office on the second floor.

As she climbed the staircase, questions rang through her mind, echoing and clanging against each other. It was too much. Too much to think about, too much to understand.

She walked into his office and saw him on his small balcony, talking on his cell phone. She sat in one of the wingback chairs across from his large mahogany desk, which filled about half the office space. A bookshelf lined one wall, spilling over with bound legal volumes and thick notebooks. Other than that, there was no sign that anyone worked here. Nothing on the walls. No pictures on the desk. Nothing.

He waved at her, flipped his phone closed, and came inside. "Sorry about that. Let's see, where were we?" He reached inside his desk drawer and removed a legal pad and pen. "Oh yes. Demurrer hearing next week."

Somehow it seemed too soon to jump into talk about the lawsuit. She wasn't ready yet. Maybe some small talk first. "Why do you have this office?"

He looked up, his eyes unfocused. "I'm sorry, what?"

"This office. I mean, I'm your only client. You don't have any kind of signage to let anyone know you're here. Why don't you just work out of your house?"

He pressed his lips in a straight line, but the corners curled up as if against his will. He leaned back in his chair and dropped his pen on his desk. "You don't miss much, do you?"

"It's an obvious question."

He rubbed the bottom of his chin and allowed the grin to cover his face. "I know you like direct honesty, so okay, I'll give it to you. I have vivid memories of my first visit to your house. Your reaction; Sarah's reaction."

"Big estate in Montecito, huh?"

"Not big by Montecito standards, but I thought this might be more to your liking."

Melanie leaned forward. "You must think I'm an idiot."

He shook his head and offered an ingratiating smile. "I know a lot of people don't like displays of wealth. I want to be sensitive to that."

"No, you don't understand. You must think I'm a fool if you think I don't have some idea of what the rent would be for an office like this, even though it's small. It faces onto State Street with a balcony. You think that's any different?"

He laughed outright. "I give up. From here on out, I'll lay it all on the line. Deal?"

She stared into his eyes and didn't respond.

He held her gaze for almost a minute, then looked down and picked up his pen. "You look nice. Breakfast date this morning?" His attempt at humor fell as flat as the rest of the façade he tried to create.

"Not that it's any of your business, but my *date* involved no one but me and a church."

He smiled and shook his head. "Brilliant. It will look good before a jury."

Melanie bit back a response. The man was doing his job. "What were you saying about the hearing?"

"Right. It's this Thursday—no need for you to attend. I expect it to be sustained and we'll go forward from there. I'll have twenty days to file an amended complaint."

"This could drag out forever."

"I'll serve the complaint much sooner than that."

"Then what?"

"We wait for their response. Things ought to start moving along after that."

Andie looked at the mountain of shopping bags at her feet. She shook her head and turned toward Christi. "Thanks for coming with me. I would never have been able to carry this alone."

Christi guffawed. "Are you kidding? A chance to get away from my in-laws *and* come to Saks? My kind of Sunday afternoon errand. Scott's been on my case to watch my spending there, but when I told him why we were going, even Mr. big-shot attorney couldn't come up with a rebuttal."

Andie laughed as she put one shopping bag under her right arm and picked up two more with her hands. Christi did the same and, as they walked out the door, she whispered, "Still, I hope he doesn't drive down State Street right about now. He'd have a coronary if he saw me with all this."

"Why? None of it's yours."

"By the time he remembered that, he'd be hooked to a ventilator at Cottage Hospital and our spring trip to New York would have to be canceled."

"Honestly, Christi."

"What?"

"The way you worded that. It sounded like you're more concerned about the trip to New York than Scott's life." Andie was teasing, but there was more than a little truth behind the words.

Christi shifted the bags in her hands. "Said I hoped he didn't drive down the street, didn't I?"

"Yeah."

"See, I thought of him first."

Andie laughed. It actually felt good, although she knew the guilt would come later. But it was fun to tease Christi, and besides that, she had accomplished something worthwhile today. The bags she carried were filled with over a thousand dollars' worth of donated merchandise. They would bring in lots of money at tomorrow's luncheon and silent auction for the Cancer Center.

She could work behind the scenes and still make a difference. Trouble still loomed about the Fair, but they wouldn't stop her from doing other things. And it was impossible not to like a day as pleasant and beautiful as this one. Andie swung her purchases a bit and looked around her. Life sometimes stole up on her with a reminder that not everything was misery.

She stopped.

There, across the street. A woman stood in the doorway of an office building. She remained stone still, staring at Andie.

It took only a fraction of a second before Andie realized who it was. She gasped and stopped walking. She willed her feet to move, her eyes to look somewhere else, but they would not obey. Even the wind seemed to blow harder, as if to push her forward and away from here.

"Are you coming or what?"

Andie could not answer, nor even acknowledge Christi's question. She could only continue to stare across the street at the hatred blazing from the woman's face.

"It's her, isn't it?" Christi's voice dripped disgust.

The bags in Andie's hands grew heavy as stones. She realized how this must look—like she was out having a great time shopping and spending money. Shame and embarrassment returned as quickly as the breeze that now snapped cold instead of pleasant, and bitter ache snagged her heart. How could she have forgotten Chad so quickly? How could she have been caught laughing on the street?

Christi rushed forward in typical Christi form. She went to the very edge of the curb and cupped her hands around her mouth. "Hey. What are you staring at?" Her voice echoed down the city block, bouncing off buildings and pinging off cars.

Even from this distance, Andie could see the woman's face flare red with embarrassment—or anger. Melanie Johnston turned and disappeared around the side of the building.

Andie breathed a sigh of relief and started walking again. Only then did she notice how many people had stopped to gawk at the scene Christi had created. She felt her face grow hot, but Christi walked on without seeming to notice the stares all around them.

She turned back toward Andie. "What a coward. How dare she stand there and try to intimidate you. Was she following you? Something needs to be done about her."

chapter thirteen

Jake coasted his motorcycle to a stop. He looked around the parking lot. No sign of Melanie's blue Civic. Good. His plan to beat her there had worked.

He pushed open the door and stood at the sign requesting he wait for the hostess. At three o'clock on Sunday afternoon, the restaurant was practically deserted. A full minute later, Jake still stood at the sign, wondering if the hostess had decided to take a midday nap.

A door behind the counter swung open. A short, tired-looking woman approached. "Sorry. Didn't see ya out here. One for dinner?"

"Uh . . . actually there will be two. Just for coffee." Why did he add that last part? This woman didn't care what he ordered.

She looked over his shoulder toward the parking lot and raised an eyebrow. "Blind date?"

Jake didn't answer. He'd already said too much.

"Right this way." She grabbed a couple of menus and led him to the nearest booth.

"Would it be possible for us to sit a little farther back? Somewhere with a little more privacy?"

She nodded, her eyes gleaming with a knowing look.

"It's none—" Jake started, a rush of anger and frustration surging at this woman who wouldn't mind her own business but then immediately regretted it. He wanted so much to live with the love of Christ evident in his life, but he always seemed to fail. His temper fought him at every turn. "I'm sorry. I didn't mean to snap at you."

The woman shrugged and escorted him to a corner booth. "Just trying to have a little fun." She placed a menu before him and another across the table. "Your waitress will be right with you." She walked away without further comment.

Jake could see out the window from his seat and knew the minute Melanie's faded blue Honda pulled into the lot. She sat in the car for a moment, as if gathering her wits about herself. Jake understood.

This entire situation was so emotionally charged it filled him full of fear. Fear that his quick mouth would make its presence known, fear that she would sense his idiotic attraction to her. Most of all, he feared he would do something so stupid she'd be forever turned away from God.

What was it she feared?

He watched her climb from her car and walk inside. The hostess approached her. A few quiet words were exchanged and she led her back to his table. "Here you go, hon. Enjoy your meal." She cut a glaring look at him, then walked away.

"You're not going to believe what I saw today." Melanie's face was flushed and her usual matter-of-fact manner had been replaced by an anger-fueled rawness Jake had not seen before.

"What did you—" Before he had a chance to finish the question, the waitress arrived at their table.

Melanie turned her face away from the woman. "Coffee, please, with cream."

Jake smiled, sensing the woman's irritation at having to work for such a small order. "Same. Oh, and maybe a piece of apple pie."

The waitress nodded her approval and lumbered away.

Jake turned his attention back to Melanie. She glared at the wall as if she might hit it. "Okay, what did you see?"

"I was just downtown at my lawyer's office. I walked out the door, and there, on the other side of the street, was Andie Phelps and another woman. They were both loaded up with bags from Saks Fifth Avenue, walking down the street laughing. Can you believe that?"

"Why wouldn't I?" In truth, Jake felt his hackles rise, but he didn't want to assume Melanie's thoughts were the same as his. He wanted to hear it in her own words. "Did it bother you that they were laughing, or that they had been shopping at Saks?"

"Neither." She put both hands on the table. "Both." She turned angry eyes on Jake. "Didn't her son mean anything to her? Can you believe she's out socializing, spending money on a bunch of high-priced stuff, when her son just killed my boy?"

The waitress plopped two steaming mugs on the table, then produced a bowl of individual-sized creamers. "I'll be right back with your pie."

Jake waited until she walked out of earshot. "Appearances can be deceiving, Melanie. You know that. I see the brave front you try to put on. You pretend like you are doing fine—especially whenever Sarah is around." He swirled some cream into his coffee.

"Maybe. But you don't see me out shopping."

"Here's your pie." The waitress set it on the table, winked at Jake, and pushed back into the kitchen.

Jake put his hand over Melanie's. The softness of her skin against the roughness of his palm felt so comforting. "That's not the lifestyle you have. Don't judge because it's hers."

She pulled her hand back, leaving a cold emptiness behind.

He wanted to make her understand his point. "When I'm really upset about something, I start designing something in my garage. It sort of keeps me too busy to think about the real problem. In this case, that other mother lives in a different world than you and me. Maybe her self-medication is to go shopping."

"She should at least be out doing something to help other people. Instead, she's wasting a bunch of money on nothing."

For the most part, Jake agreed. Still, he couldn't stop the urge to continue his course of thought. "If there's one thing I've learned over the years, it's that I can't judge another person by my situation. Perhaps it would be better if she was out doing charity work, but wouldn't you like to find the quickest, easiest way to ease your pain?"

Melanie didn't answer. Jake took a sip of his coffee.

She looked at him, her face a little less flushed. "You didn't stir that."

Jake smiled. "I like it shaken, not stirred."

She laughed. "You've watched a few too many James Bond flicks in your time."

"Maybe." He took a deep, steadying breath. "I saw you at church this morning."

Her eyes opened a little wider. It intensified the copper sparks in the brown of her irises. "You did? I didn't see you."

"That's because you were surrounded by people the entire time. What did you think?"

"It was . . . interesting."

"I think you were very brave coming back a second time."

"I must say I've been pleasantly surprised."

"I'm not going to tell you that you won't ever hear an un-kind word spoken there, because it's not the truth. We're all human and full of faults. But I can tell you that everybody there knows you're in pain. They all wish they could do something to help."

She took a sip of her coffee and made an almost imperceptible face.

Time to lighten the subject. "Tell me again why we had to meet here instead of a coffee shop?"

"Because I'm not going to pay four dollars for a swallow of coffee, no matter how good it tastes, and I don't want to sit in the same room with a bunch of people who will."

He liked this side of her. "You don't have much patience with pretension, do you?"

"None. You know, that pie looks pretty good." She started to raise a hand to beckon the waitress, but Jake stopped her and split his piece, which he'd barely touched, in half.

"My treat."

Melanie gave him a look he couldn't hope to interpret—suspicion, gratefulness, exhaustion all seemed mixed up in it—before stabbing a bite for herself.

They finished the rest in silence, and Jake thought how tiring it must be for her. Not just the grief but the anger. He remembered what that used to be like. When the fight left you it felt like you could sleep for days.

After another five minutes or so Melanie balled up her napkin and stood. "Thanks for the coffee, Jake."

"Any time. I'll walk you to your car."

She moved quickly away from the table, and Jake knew if he paid the bill and stayed until he got his change, she'd be gone. So he waited until she had her back turned, then tossed a ten-dollar bill on the table. He took care that she didn't see it. He didn't want her to know he'd just paid four dollars for a cup of plain coffee.

Outside she stood with her face raised to the sun. When she heard him, she pointed toward the cycle he'd brought out for a ride. "Is that yours?"

"A client's. I can't afford my own work."

Her eyes lingered on the bike in a way that told Jake she'd ridden before. "So," he said, "you want to see how the other half rides?"

———

Sunday night, Christi Baur stood waving down the driveway to her departing guests. She continued to watch until the car was out of sight. She turned to Scott. "Nice seeing your brother and his family again."

She didn't have to speak the rest of the thought, but she knew he understood it was even nicer to see them leave. She loved them dearly, but they—and those kids!—were such a mess. You could teach an eighteen-month-old to drink without spilling and eat without grinding Goldfish into the Persian carpet. Christi knew. She'd done it. Three times.

Scott started toward the house. "I really need to go in to the office for a little while."

"On a Sunday night? Are you going to help Sam?"

"Christi, you know how important it is that I not get overly involved in that case. Blair Phelps has been a good friend and member of the same social clubs for years. I'm doing everything I can to help, but I can't put myself in the middle of it."

Christi folded her arms across her chest as her husband walked away. "Well, Andie Phelps has been a good friend and member of the same social clubs as me for years, and I *have* to put myself in the middle of it. That's what friends do."

Scott held open the back door. Christi walked through, fuming. The post-in-law house scouring would take days. The phone rang, but someone else could get it.

Kelly stuck her head into the kitchen. "Mom, call for you. Something-or-other Burridge."

Christi smiled at her sixteen-year-old daughter, happy that something was going right tonight. She reached for the kitchen phone. "Hang up the extension please, Kel."

Scott appeared at the door, scowling.

She ignored him. "Hello?" The news that followed brought pure joy. She set the phone on the counter and rushed to the nearest computer.

"Christi, why is a private investigator calling you?" His voice at her back shocked her. She hadn't heard him follow her into the family room.

"Told you, Andie's my friend. I'm going to do what I can to help her."

"You were behind that other story, weren't you? You and your investigator."

Christi shrugged, but couldn't keep the pleased smile off her face. "Maybe."

"Let her lawyers deal with this."

"Lawyers deal with law and trials; I'm dealing with protecting Andie. If that requires doing a little investigation on my own, then that's what I'm going to do."

She opened Outlook on her computer and scanned the list of e-mails.

There.

She double-clicked on the attachment. The screen glowed with the promise of new hope. She couldn't have been happier.

Scott leaned over her shoulders and stared at the screen, then glared at Christi. "I hope you're not planning to do what I think you're planning to do."

"The Santa Barbara court of public opinion deserves to know what kind of woman Ms. Melanie Johnston really is. Definitely not the grieving little mother she'd have everyone believe." She smiled. "Quite a bike."

"Those pictures prove nothing and could very well bring a libel suit if you take them to your friend at the newspaper."

Christi leaned back and smiled sweetly at her husband. "Of course I'm not going to take them to my friend at the newspaper. Mr. Burridge is e-mailing them—anonymously, of course. I'm not connected in any way."

"Christi, this is fighting dirty."

"That woman threw the first chunk of mud. I'm just making certain she gets what's coming to her."

"You are making a mistake, and by the time you realize it, you will have destroyed everyone in your path." Scott stormed from the room.

"Then stay out of my path!"

Scott slammed the door. His tires soon screeched in the driveway. Good riddance.

Now, back to the more pressing problem. Where had she left that old toothbrush? Time to scrub away all reminders of her previous guests.

chapter **fourteen**

Monday morning dawned dark and rainy. The weather was appropriate.

Jake looked at the pictures on his office wall. Did he imagine it, or did Jeff's eyes accuse him? He walked over to the wall. "I'm so sorry. I wanted to help her, to be there for her. Now I've made things worse."

He could still hear Jeff's voice, repeating as it had so many times over the years. "Please keep praying for my mom. She really needs Christ's love. Pray that she sees it in my life."

Jake slunk back to his seat, then looked toward the ceiling. "Why, God? It was such an innocent thing. Why would you let it get turned into this ugliness?"

Well, he needed to call her before she left for work. Best to get to it. He picked up the phone and punched in her number. Would she speak to him? Slam the phone down?

Melanie answered on the third ring.

"Hi. It's Jake."

"Well, if it's not the 'mystery man.'"

"I felt awful when I saw that in the paper today." He looked toward the offending article again. It showed Melanie standing beside him, looking at the new custom bike. A honky-tonk was visible in the background. The headline read, "Still up to her partying ways?"

She didn't answer for five full seconds. "It's not your fault."

"I know, but I really enjoyed talking to you like that. I felt good that you could open up to me, like I was actually helping in some small way."

Silence. Jake heard a sigh on the other end of the line. "You did help." Did her voice sound choked or was it poor reception?

An uncomfortable silence settled in. Jake wanted to say so many things, to ask so many questions, but none seemed appropriate. He knew he couldn't push her. She could build walls faster than he could climb them.

"I've got to go."

The line went dead before Jake could respond. He stared at the receiver in his hand and shook his head. Now what?

He set the phone back in the cradle and laced his fingers behind his head. Jeff would want him to do everything in his power to help her, wouldn't he? The fact that she was a vulnerable woman in need of help troubled him. A vulnerable woman and a lonely man often made for a bad combination. He needed to be careful.

Lonely man? Where did that thought come from? He wasn't lonely. Was he? For a short moment he tried to convince himself that he wasn't, but those arguments were hollow. He *was* lonely and Melanie *was* intriguing. But he couldn't allow himself to think about that.

Back to the thought at hand. What could he do to help her? The newspaper articles were making certain that not one shred of her dignity remained intact.

Then he remembered the kid from youth group three or four years ago. What was his name? Started with an R. Let's see, Robert? No. Randy. Randy Peterson. That was it.

His father was a reporter for the paper. Randy had gone back east to college, but Jake was pretty certain his parents still attended the church.

He flipped through the phone book until he found the *News-Press* phone number. "John Peterson's desk, please."

————

Friday morning, Melanie went to work early. She felt a renewed sense of satisfaction since Les let her know the good news about the sustainment yesterday. The case was finally starting to move along. She placed the price-break sign in front of the bran cereal, then moved toward the Toasty O's.

"Melanie, could I see you in the back office, please?" Mr. Mortensen stood behind her, his eyes averted.

"Sure." She gathered up the rest of her signs and followed him down the cereal aisle. What sort of bad news was coming? Whatever it was, she could take it. The case was moving forward, and nothing would get her down.

He walked behind his desk, but instead of sitting, he leaned across it, putting his weight on his hands. "Melanie, there are some problems that have arisen from all this. You know that."

He sighed heavily and dropped into his seat. With his left hand he indicated that she should do the same. "I called you in here to give you a choice."

"A choice?"

"I'm sure you remember at the last meeting we discussed the fact that layoffs were a possibility."

Her throat felt scratchy. "Yes."

"I got a call from the home office last night. They want the financial hemorrhage at this store to stop. Now."

Now? "What choice?"

"I can either lay off eight people, effective Monday, or you can transfer to our Thousand Oaks store." His face had gone pale.

Melanie knew he hated having to do this. Even if he loathed it, that still didn't make it right.

"Thousand Oaks? That's over an hour each way from Santa Barbara, and more in commuter traffic."

"It's the only store nearby with an opening for a pricing co-ordinator. You are guaranteed the position, and it would mean a slight raise to help offset relocating expenses."

"I can't relocate. That's not a choice for me."

Mr. Mortensen looked at her. "Why not? Thousand Oaks is a nice community."

"I won't do that to Sarah. She needs to be among friends." And she couldn't even think of leaving Jeff.

"I see. Well, then you have the weekend to decide whether you're willing to commute. If you choose to stay, I'll have to call the department managers tonight and tell them to prepare pink slips."

Melanie stood. "That young man took my son from me, and now his family is trying to get rid of me, as well. I've paid a price for what I'm doing, and I'm willing to continue to pay until justice has been done. The thing I'm not willing to do is to let any others pay, too. Jeff did that already. I'll take the transfer."

Mr. Mortensen nodded his head, his face grim. "I wish there was something I could do to change this. You've been a great employee. A great leader."

Melanie nodded and walked out of the office, choking on held-back tears.

Joe Server was putting his things in a locker when she walked through the back room. "Hey, Melanie, where you going?"

"I just found out I have the day off."

The scratching of pen across paper provided the only sound in the cemetery. Even the wind remained still and silent today—nature's own show of respect at the great loss.

Do you remember when you had your tonsils out? She paused, wishing for the response that would never come. *You were terrified about being put to sleep. Remember?* She could still feel the tight grip of his hand in hers. *I promised you I wouldn't leave. I promised I'd never leave you alone. Remember?*

She glanced across the lawn at the emptiness around her. *I keep my promises.*

She put the cap on her pen. "There. I think that's enough writing for one day, don't you, Jeff?" She stared at the silent ground, now completely blended with the rest of the area. "It says mostly the same thing every day. My son is gone. I can't comfort him...." She stopped speaking before she continued with the rest of what was in her heart—*it's too much to bear.*

She never spoke of her own grief to Jeff. A mother kept her own pain hidden from her children. They needed her strength.

The loud grinding of an engine filtered in from a distance, growing closer. It grew so loud, Melanie looked over her shoulder.

Jake coasted through the cemetery and parked beside her car. He looked toward her, nodded a greeting, and then removed his helmet and remained seated on his bike.

"See you tomorrow, Jeff." She stood and folded her small blanket.

Jake kept his head discreetly turned until she approached. He nodded again, his face grim. "Hi."

She loaded the blanket into the trunk of her car. "Did you come to see Jeff?"

"Umm, actually, I'm here looking for you. Sarah said I'd find you here. She, uh ... says you come out here a lot. She worries about it."

Melanie leaned against the hood of her car. "No need to worry." She looked him square in the face. This was none of his business. "Why are you here?"

He looked at his hands. "Stupid mistake. Forgive me. I wanted to talk to you about something, but I should have realized this wasn't the place." He looked toward the headstone, then down at his feet. The tip of his boot crunched an arc across the gravel, then retraced the path. Did his chin quiver? "He was such a great kid."

She wiped her eye with the back of her hand. "Yes, he was." She wouldn't cry; Jeff still waited too close. "What do you need to say?"

He took a deep breath and stared at the car trunk. "There's something I need to tell you."

"Well, tell me, then."

"You remember those pictures in the paper of us?" He looked at her, then quickly away. "I mean, of course you do, but I have a friend who's a reporter. I called him, and he interviewed me this afternoon. The story will run in tomorrow's newspaper."

There was something he wasn't saying. And that something was not good. "What did you say?"

"Nothing bad—don't get me wrong." Jake kicked a pebble and didn't look up. "I told him who I was, Jeff's mentor from church. Told him you and I had coffee in the little café and I showed you my bike on the way out. Explained to him that the honky-tonk was next to the café, and the caption beneath the picture was completely inaccurate."

"So is he going to run a story saying I wasn't really carousing in the middle of the day with a mysterious motorcycle man? Probably too late to stop the damage, but it couldn't hurt."

"Yes, he's going to say that. But . . . there's more."

"More what?"

"I don't know why this is so hard." He licked his lips. "Somehow, I feel like you might be upset by the rest of the story, and I don't want you to find out about it in the paper."

"Find out about what?"

"They are going to print a picture of Blair Phelps and me, shaking hands."

"Shaking hands?" A surge of heat coursed through Melanie's veins. "Shaking hands? With that . . . that . . . wrecker of lives?"

"I made a custom cycle for Blair Phelps' company last year. The picture is important, because it shows that I have ties to both families, and yet am sticking up for you. It shows I'm not just some wild 'mystery man' helping you cover your tracks."

"You mean to tell me that other family is paying your paycheck?"

"They did last year."

"There's some irony for you. The same family that just cost me my job financially supports yours. I guess we know where that leaves you, now, don't we?" She jerked open the car door. The key seemed to stick and would not slide into the ignition.

"Melanie, please. Talk to me." His face was inches from her window.

The key slid into place. She turned it, put the car into gear, and shoved her foot onto the gas pedal without ever acknowledging she'd heard him speak.

chapter fifteen

"Sarah, you're holding my arm so tight I almost think you're afraid I'm going to turn and run away." Melanie only half joked as she made her way through the parking lot. In truth, Sarah's grip was so firm it hurt.

"Maybe that is what I'm afraid of. Ever thought of that?" Sarah's grip eased a bit, but she did not let go.

A group of teenage girls stood huddled by the front door. "I see your friends ahead. You can go join them if you want."

Sarah looked at the group but did not release her mother's arm. "That's okay."

Melanie stopped walking and turned to her daughter. "Sarah, what's wrong? Did you have a fight with Beth?"

"Sarah, over here!" Beth's voice from the huddled mass of teenage womanhood answered Melanie's question. Sarah held up a hand in response but stayed at her mother's side.

"It's just that I know we've been fighting a lot this week, and I'm afraid you're going to turn your back on God forever because of me."

Whatever answer Melanie expected, that was not it. "Do what?"

"You know. I'm kind of like the only witness in your life, and I've been really bad at it, and I know you're only coming to church because of the mission trip thing, trying to get everyone to leave me alone and bother you. And now you're not going to really get to know God at all because I'm so bad at showing you what He's like." She blurted out the speech in one anguished breath.

"What makes you think it's your responsibility to show God to me, anyway?"

"That's what Jeff always said."

"Jeff?" Melanie's ribs suddenly pushed against her lungs.

"Yeah. He always said it was up to me and him to show you what God was really like, because you hadn't seen much in the way of true Christianity in your life. He said it was our responsibility. Now he's gone, and it's just up to me, and I'm not as good at it as he was."

"Oh, sweetie." Melanie wrapped her arms around Sarah's shoulders while blinking back the sting in her eyes. "You do a great job. It's my fault everything has gotten so bad. I'm—"

"Melanie, you're back. I'm so glad to see you. And, Sarah, don't you look lovely today." Trish moved up beside Melanie and hugged her arm.

"Sarah, are you coming?" The younger set stood waiting near the door.

Melanie nodded her head toward the group. "You go ahead. We'll talk more later."

Sarah nodded and shuffled toward the crowd. She looked nervously over her shoulder as she joined the group. Melanie waved some reassurance.

Trish grabbed her arm and started toward the building. "I hope you don't have any plans for after church, because I have a surprise for you."

"A surprise?"

"I'm not telling. You'll just have to wait and see."

Melanie sat through the service, but she was distracted and had trouble concentrating. She had never realized the burden that Sarah placed on herself for her spiritual well-being. She needed to do something to ease that burden from her daughter—she certainly carried enough without all that. She saw only one problem.

The only way she could think to help was to get more involved in the church and the study of the Bible. She wasn't sure she was ready to do that. When the Dirty Dozen walked forward for the final song, Melanie was relieved to be free of her own thoughts.

"You seemed a little fidgety today. Thinking about the surprise?" Trish stood smiling, waiting.

"The surprise. Yes." Melanie scanned the congregation, looking for a glimpse of her tall daughter's blond hair.

"We're going to lunch."

"Oh, I don't think I can. Sarah and I rode together, and—"

"She's coming, too. That's the surprise. A couple of other women and I have arranged the Johnston support group. We plan to take good care of Sarah and you, because we know this is a difficult time, and we know there have been some things said and done that make it even harder for you. So, right now, we're packing up our cars and heading to Lorenzo's. We have one table reserved for the women and another for the teenagers. We're planning to make this a tradition every Sunday from now on. We don't want the two of you thinking you have to face any of this alone."

Sarah came bounding down the aisle. "Mom, did you hear? We're all going to Lorenzo's. Won't that be fun?"

Melanie wasn't sure, but there was no way she could deny her daughter's enthusiasm. Especially after their talk this morning. A talk that still haunted her. Jake could probably help her understand, but she wasn't quite ready to turn to him again. She knew she was in the wrong treating him the way she did, but it was just another pain for her. And she had her share of those already without adding more.

———

Andie mixed the small bead of yellow into the brown until it became a tawny gold. She dipped her brush, worked the paint into the bristles, and began to painstakingly add the effect of sunlight to the portrait. This picture had formed in her mind and refused to leave her in peace until she committed it to canvas. She sat back and studied her efforts. The rust she'd felt earlier was beginning to disappear from her work. Her fingers and wrist remembered their dance, and she actually liked what emerged before her.

The garage door squeaked open. *Oh, no.* Blair was home. She didn't have the energy to face the fight that would ensue if he found out how she'd spent the last few hours.

She jerked the painting off the easel and rushed to hide it in the tiny closet, tossing in her old denim smock in one fast movement. A quick hand wash later and she pulled the door shut behind her.

By the time Blair opened the door from the garage, she had managed to throw herself onto the couch and grab the remote. Somehow, he never seemed to mind if she watched television, but painting seemed to be another matter. It was absurd. He came and went whenever he pleased—why should she be denied a few hours of enjoyment?

"Andie?" He appeared at the door of the living room.

She pretended to be absorbed in the news channel and acknowledged him with a silent, upraised hand. He sat in the chair closest to the door and settled into the silence. When she chanced a glance toward him, he was staring at the television as if transfixed by rumors of the newest diet breakthrough. She knew that he, too, was grateful for the excuse not to talk to each other. Things had gotten progressively worse until even civil conversation seemed beyond their reach.

Blair finally stood. He picked up the sandals she'd been wearing. "I'll put these in the closet on my way to the study."

Andie trembled. She was so sick of hearing about her failures. Maybe it was time for counseling. No. That would just give him the opportunity to criticize her in front of someone else. Maybe separation was the only answer. Then she thought of her father.

If she walked away from Blair, would she let him down the same way she had her father? Was she doing that even now, by her surly attitude? A chill ran down her spine.

The loud buzzing sound cut through the brooding air. Andie's anger dissipated as annoyance began to grow. Who would be stopping by uninvited on Sunday evening? She pressed the button. "Yes?"

"Andie? It's Kyle Ledger. Can I come up and talk to Blair and you for a minute?"

Oh no. Kyle was not only a member of their church but also a member of the Santa Barbara police force. "What's wrong, Kyle?"

Silence. "Um, I'd prefer to talk in person."

Andie buzzed him in, her fingers already growing cold. This scene felt a little too familiar. She thought of Sam Campbell's unexpected visit and the news it brought. Kyle's visit could mean no less. But how? Chad was gone. The toxicology tests had already been reported.

Andie opened the door and stood watching as headlights pushed closer to her. She wanted to send them back.

Kyle parked in front of the house and climbed from his car, carrying a bag in his hand. Even with only the porch light on his face, Andie could see the firm set of his jaw, the way he looked not at her but at the house. Bad news was definitely coming.

"Who was at the ga—?" Blair's voice trailed off behind her. A groan like that of some wounded animal escaped his throat. Still, he stepped out onto the porch to greet their guest. "Kyle, what brings you here?" His voice sounded strangled.

"Blair, Andie." He nodded at each of them. "I've got something to show you."

Blair gestured toward the open door. "Come in."

Kyle followed them into the living room but rejected Blair's offer of a seat. "You two go ahead. I think I'll stand."

Dizziness swam in waves through Andie's head.

Kyle gestured to the bag he was carrying. "I have something that I think you'll want. Something that belonged to Chad."

"Chad?"

Andie was glad Blair could ask the question, because she could not.

"The ranger at Lake Cachuma was doing a little cleanup yesterday. He found this washed up on the shore. He called us because he remembered from the paper that Chad had apparently been out there the night of the accident. He thought it might be important."

He reached into the bag and pulled out what at first appeared to be old, wet newspaper. When Andie realized what he held, the room began to spin around her. Dark spots swam before her eyes, and then the room faded into blackness.

————

Blair paced the study and looked once again at the antique clock above the mantel. Ten minutes after midnight. He felt no desire to go to bed. He couldn't imagine closing his eyes, facing the ever-increasing nightmares since Chad's wreck. Now a new one had been added.

He looked at the filthy Tyvek envelope that sat on his desk, still damp with Lake Cachuma's water, almost wishing the police had kept it as evidence. Kyle said photographs were sufficient since this was not a criminal case. Now it sat there, condemning Blair. He had seen it hundreds of times over the last few years.

The words, written with black Sharpie in all capital letters, were still legible despite their time in the lake. *A DIPLOMA FROM A PRESTIGIOUS UNIVERSITY HELPS BRING SUCCESS. CHAD'S ACCOMPLISHMENTS TOWARD HIS GOAL.* Inside were report cards, articles about service projects, award certificates.

Blair had come up with the idea to help Chad stay on track and motivated. The theory was, when he felt unsure of himself or thought he couldn't handle something, he could look at all he had accomplished already. He could achieve his goal by taking one step at a time. *Chad, it was supposed to encourage you. Not stress you to the breaking point.*

This envelope took Chad's life—there was no hiding from that now. Blair knew it, and knew the blame could rest nowhere but on him.

He could still remember the last time he'd held it in his hand. He could still hear the sound of his own voice, raised in anger. "Young man, a C minus is not acceptable. What about your goals, your dreams? You are going to spend the weekend reviewing every single problem that you missed on that test, then write Mr. Moore a letter of apology and ask for a chance to retake this exam."

Chad's voice returned, high-pitched with anger. "Dad, I studied hard for that test. I did my best. Isn't that what you've always said you wanted? For me to do my best?"

"I know that C minus is not your best."

"Yes it is. I spent hours preparing. I just don't understand trig. I start working with a tutor next week; I'll review the test with him. I can't do it myself and not this weekend. We've been planning this trip to Magic Mountain for months."

"I'll call the church myself and let them know not to wait for you. You've got more important ways to spend your Saturday than riding roller coasters."

Chad glared with just a hint of tears in his eyes. "I hate you!" He ran back to his room and slammed the door.

Why hadn't Blair gone after him? Why didn't he go back to Chad's room and talk to him, make him understand? He would explain the importance of a good college, the problems he had faced because he didn't get the educational opportunities Chad now had. But that's not how he'd handled it. Instead, he'd dressed in his finest and left for the black-tie event without even saying good-bye. He'd planned to leave Chad to stew, and talk rationally with him in the morning.

A morning that never dawned for Chad.

The clock gonged the half hour. Twelve-thirty.

He thought about Andie, upstairs asleep. After she'd fainted, she'd awakened only long enough to take a tranquilizer or two then cry herself to sleep. She'd be out for the rest of the night, but not him. He couldn't face the long blackness.

He picked up his keys and tiptoed to the garage, thankful the bedroom was on the far end. Andie would never hear him leave. He drove away, a single destination on his mind.

chapter sixteen

Melanie's clock radio started pumping country music into her bedroom at four-thirty in the morning. She reached across and slapped the snooze.

Nine minutes later, a salesman from the local used-car lot urged her to "Come in today—don't delay. Prices this good won't last forever."

She sat up in bed and turned off the offending noise. Today, for the first time since KTPC had started airing that annoying commercial, Melanie actually wished she could go to that old car lot. Anything rather than face the day ahead.

There was no time for self-pity in the life of a single mom. She swung her legs over the side of the bed and stumbled into the shower. Half an hour later, she kissed the still-sleeping Sarah on the forehead, poured a travel mug full of coffee, and forced herself into her car for the first of what would be many long days of commuting. Maybe someday she could make use of the time, but this morning's trip offered only ninety minutes to think and worry about the new job, with new people, in a new place. It had been fifteen years since she'd experienced that sensation.

She had gone to work at Alfords within a week of moving to Santa Barbara, and although she had transferred to the new store last year, so had many of the other employees, as well as the customers. Now she would be walking into a store full of strangers, having no idea what they expected of her, or what she could expect from them.

At 6:33, she pulled into the mostly empty parking lot. She sat in her car, trying to collect her thoughts.

The avocado green façade of the strip mall housed an Alfords, a drugstore, and about a dozen other businesses. The A and L in the sign needed bulb replacements, as it now simply read *FORDS*. A hanging banner across the front announced the store was open twenty-four hours—a fact for which Melanie was grateful. She would be able to start at seven and work until three-thirty, hopefully skirting most of the rush-hour traffic heading into Los Angeles for the day.

Something rapped suddenly against her passenger window, and a deep voice asked, "Melanie Johnston, is that you?"

In the dim light, she could only hope that the face belonged to Carl Brown, the store manager, and not some deranged killer who happened to know her name.

She opened the door and stood to peer over the roof at the man on the other side. "Yes, I'm Melanie."

"Glad to see you're early. Nothing sours my milk like tardiness. Personally, I like to get here while things are still quiet and plan out my day. I can see you and I are going to get along just fine." He walked toward the store, a box under one arm, a huge ring of keys in the other hand. "I'm Carl Brown, by the way."

He was no taller than Melanie's five feet six, but he was almost as large around. He had large rectangular glasses and a handlebar moustache that curled up at the ends. Something about the way he seemed totally at ease with himself gave Melanie the sense she was going to like him.

He headed toward the nondescript back door. "I like to go in the back way. I can put away my things and get organized before I make my first walkthrough of the store. Come on in, and we'll go have a little chat in my office before I throw you to the wolves."

Although she knew it was a joking expression, something about the way he said it made her apprehension ratchet up a notch.

Carl fumbled through his keys before finding the correct one and soon had them inside.

The first thing Melanie saw was a tiny cubicle off to her left that barely managed to contain the sparse furnishings. A rusty metal desk and double set of filing cabinets shoved against each other, leaving just enough room for a desk chair and a stool across from it. "That's the managers' office," Carl said, and Melanie noticed three different family portraits set on the filing cabinets. Carl appeared to have three children and a pleasant-looking wife.

"I'm sure this isn't exactly like that new store you came from, but we've been here for a while. We were due a remodel about five years ago, but corporate keeps dragging their feet about it. Too busy pouring money into fancy stores in high-dollar areas." He cleared his throat and turned red, then began to unload the contents of his box. He motioned toward the old stool. "Have a seat if you want. Sorry there's nothing more comfortable, but nothing else will fit in here."

Melanie sank onto the stool. "This is fine."

He walked around and sat at the desk chair. "There's something I think you need to be aware of." He laced his fingers together on the desktop and exhaled slowly.

Oh no. Perhaps the wolves comment wasn't such a joke after all. "Okay." Funny how her voice sounded so calm.

"We have an employee here who's been with the company a long time. Everyone expected her to get the promotion to pricing coordinator, and quite frankly, if you hadn't come along, she would have."

The lines around his eyes suddenly seemed more pronounced. Did stress or regret cause the change? Either way, it didn't bode well for Melanie.

He began to twiddle his thumbs. "When headquarters called about sending up someone from Santa Barbara, it didn't sit well with a lot of people."

"I had no idea."

"I'm sure you didn't."

Melanie saw no reason not to ask the next question. "What's your position?"

"I need someone here who can do the job. I gather from the rave reviews of your past supervisors, you are that person." His thumbs moved faster.

"But?"

"Candace is a hard worker, too. She's been with us several years, and she's a single mom. I know she could use the extra money. But, as I understand it, you also are a single mom."

"Yes."

"As far as *I'm* concerned, you're the person for the job. End of story."

"What about everyone else?"

"Candace won't give you any trouble. She's a hard worker and a great person. But . . . there are a couple of others who might try to make your time here a bit...*uncomfortable*. I may be overthinking it to warn you like this, but I don't want you caught unawares."

"Thank you for the warning, Mr. Brown. I'm glad to have the heads-up."

"Carl, please. We don't stand on formality in this store."

Melanie was even more convinced she was going to like this man.

He stood. "Are you ready for a tour?"

The store was old and in need of some upgrades, but it was clean and well kept. Melanie's desk was wedged into a dark corner, surrounded by nonperishables. Her new home away from home.

When the other employees began to trickle in to work, they all greeted her in a friendly manner, some more reserved than others. An attractive woman in her early thirties entered, and a sudden hush fell onto the group. Everyone in the building stopped what they were doing and followed her progress through the storeroom. Melanie assumed she was Candace.

Her short brown hair bounced when she walked; her cheeks seemed to glow with some hidden joy—or malice. She walked directly over to Melanie.

The backroom crackled with the tension passing from one employee to the other. Candace extended her hand. "You must be Melanie. It's nice to have you on board. Let me know what I can do to make your transition go smoothly." She smiled what appeared to be a genuine smile.

In her eyes, Melanie saw something else, something she recognized very well. Weariness. The bone-tired weariness of a single mother. If circumstances had been different, Melanie would have sized her up as a friend immediately. Given what she knew, she remained wary. Time alone would tell if she was right.

The staff dispersed, and Melanie soon lost herself in her work. Some aspects mirrored her last position exactly, but in the details she found differences and had to remain alert. Yet she found she could never completely concentrate, and as the morning drew on, Melanie finally realized why. She always had the feeling that someone was watching her—someone unfriendly.

Nothing happened though, and she chided herself for being paranoid.

Even so, she'd never been happier for a lunch break in all her life. It'd be nice to have some time to regroup. She went to her locker and worked the combination of the built-in lock. She pulled open the door but quickly drew back her hand. A dead rat lay on top of her lunch sack.

———

Andie awoke, groggy and confused. Something seemed wrong, but she couldn't remember what it was. She sat up in the king-sized bed and stretched. Blair's side was empty. In fact, it didn't look like he'd slept in it at all.

She tried standing but immediately felt wobbly and had to sit back down on the bed. Something happened last night. What was it?

A vague feeling of discomfort grew into a pressing, suffocating pain, but its source seemed out of her reach just yet. Once again, she pushed to her feet. This time, she managed to walk through the room, but grasped the doorframe for balance when she reached it.

Something about Chad. Something was wrong with Chad. But how could that be?

Chad was dead.

Then a fuzzy picture of Kyle Ledger standing in her driveway seeped into her memory. Kyle had been here last night. He brought bad news. What was it?

The envelope.

When memory broke on her, Andie rushed down the stairs, although her disoriented state made it difficult. She had to stay in a slightly bent posture trying to keep the dizziness from taking her. "Blair. Blair!"

He was nowhere to be found. She searched the entire house, then sank down onto the couch as the room swayed around her.

The memories flooded back with increasing clarity. She remembered how thankful she'd been to still have a few of the tranquilizers that Dr. Cutcliffe had prescribed just after Chad's death. Last night's sleep of oblivion made today's grogginess more than worth it.

She looked at the clock. Ten o'clock. No wonder she couldn't find Blair—he'd been at work for hours by now. She lay on the couch and allowed herself to fall back into a woozy sleep.

The brown waters of Lake Cachuma flowed before her. "Get it back, Mom, get it back!"

"Get what back, Chad?"

She waded into the water, toward her son's voice. She saw him bobbing in the water, struggling to stay afloat. He disappeared below the surface, but this time he didn't come back up. "Chad! Chad! Where are you?"

Loud sirens drowned out the sound of her screams. They rang and rang and rang. Her feet began to rise out of the water. She could hear a phone ringing somewhere in the distance.

The phone.

She shook herself awake and rushed to pick it up. Maybe Blair was calling to check on her.

"Mrs. Phelps? This is Neil Parker. Is Blair there?"

She sank into a barstool, her fuzzy mind beginning to clear with the panic. "Isn't he at work?"

"He hasn't come in yet. We thought maybe he was still at home."

Blair never went into work late. "Have you tried his cell phone?"

"He's not answering." Neil paused and cleared his throat. "Mrs. Phelps?"

"Yes."

"If you should see him, will you remind him we have that meeting with the people from Vitasoft this afternoon?"

"Of course."

Andie hung up the phone with an entirely new sense of dread creeping up her spine.

chapter **seventeen**

Jake Sterling turned his chopper onto Interstate 5 as the day's first light cut through the morning fog. A long drive stretched out before him. He was thankful for the time to collect his thoughts.

God, I'm in over my head here. You called me to work with teenage boys, Father, and I've done that. Now you've brought this woman into my life, and I feel like you're telling me I'm supposed to help her. But I can't. God, you know I'm not able to help her.

Jake accelerated and enjoyed the feel of the wind on his face. It felt like freedom. Freedom from the responsibilities of running his own business, from shepherding a group of young boys, from trying to avoid his past.

He shouted over the roaring wind. "That's not true. I don't hide my past. I'm very open with the boys about my time in prison and my lapse into sin."

Yes, but there's more to the story, isn't there? The part of the story you're afraid Melanie Johnston will force you to confront.

Jake didn't like where his thoughts were going. And they were just that. His own thoughts. It was not God talking to him. Couldn't be. He saw an exit up ahead. Maybe coffee would help.

He parked his bike in front of the convenience store and walked in. A teenage boy stood behind the counter of the otherwise empty store. His face was thick with acne, his hair short and spiked, and he wore a black shirt advertising a death-metal band in script made to look like bones.

"Dude, that is a totally sick bike."

Jake wasn't in the mood for small talk. "Thanks." He poured coffee into the largest cup they had.

"Looks custom."

Jake walked to the counter with his cup. "It is. I built it."

The kid dropped three swear words—the first two in disbelief and the last in admiration.

The boy's reaction was crude but honest and enthusiastic, and Jake couldn't help smiling. "I have a shop in Santa Barbara. Been doing customs for almost ten years now."

"How'd you get started? I'm stuck here behind the counter of Loserworld right here in the middle of Nothingland. I wish I had my own bike shop."

"Then work hard and save your money. Learn about the business. And don't forget the most important part of starting your own company."

"What's that? Advertising?"

"Prayer. Spend hours and hours down on your knees, asking God if that's really what He wants you to do. He'll answer."

The kid's jaw dropped. He looked out the window as if confirming the rider of that awesome motorcycle could really be the same man talking about God.

Jake smiled and picked up the Styrofoam cup. It was a common reaction. "Have a nice day. Remember. Prayer."

He walked out the door, laughing under his breath. Three long swallows finished off the coffee, and he tossed the cup in the trash before he climbed onto his bike. As he kicked down the starter, he looked back through the window and saw the kid, still baffled, mouthing something that Jake guessed he was better off not hearing.

Four hours later, he arrived at his destination. He drove his chopper slowly past the entrance to Folsom Prison, pulled to the side of the road, and killed the engine.

The gray walls, dotted with towers, still looked the same. Even from this distance, Jake felt the jolt of memories. He'd wasted—no, not wasted, spent—two years of his life behind those bars. And those two years had turned his life around. He found God through Prison Fellowship ministries. It made him the man he was today. A man with meaning, purpose—and regrets.

He kick-started the engine and drove on. Forty minutes later, he drove past the place where his first apartment had been. The old building had been torn down, and the new building now housed a dress shop and a Starbucks on the ground floor, and what looked like fancy condominiums on the upper ten or so floors. Even his old apartment had moved on to a better life.

The next two stops were going to be the hardest. He saw a McDonald's at the next intersection and decided he could use some extra time to prepare for what lay ahead.

Although it was past his usual lunchtime, he sat picking at his fries without a hint of hunger. He did not want to face the memories, but he needed to deal with them. They were a big part of the reason he didn't want to help Melanie Johnston, and yet he knew he had to.

Finally, he put the half-eaten burger and barely touched fries into the trash. He needed to get on with it.

First, he stopped outside the small home that had belonged to his ex-wife. He remembered the restraining order that had forbidden his presence here, the screaming, the anger. She had ridden into the sunset on another man's bike years ago.

Funny, that didn't really bother him anymore. The rest of the story did.

The biggest regret of his life remained here. Not only was she gone, but his kids were gone with her.

A crushing weight pushed against his chest. He couldn't stay here and wallow in this pain. He needed to move on. Yet he couldn't.

God, I know you've forgiven me my past sins, but why doesn't it feel like it? Why can't I forgive myself? Please keep Kara and Jenna safe, wherever they are now. Let them learn about you and know how much you love them. I know they'll never understand how much I love them, so you'll have to be the one they feel it from, for both of us, okay?

His vision blurred. He blinked hard and started the engine. One last stop to make.

The old house still looked much the same as it did the last time he was here. It appeared freshly painted, but surprisingly in the same ugly shade of bright green it had been some fifteen years ago.

The regrets from this house were not as apparent, but were in some ways more powerful than the others. The loss of his children burned like the scald of hot grease or searing exhaust, but that occurred before he knew the Lord. In this house, he deliberately and knowingly sinned. It had, of course, led to another, then another, almost pulling him into the same pit he had started out in. All it took to drag him down was a pretty face who wanted him. Which led to the first, second, and third snort of cocaine, the raging temper, the same life he thought he'd left behind.

Only the help of a strong Christian mentor who refused to give up—even when Jake screamed, "Get out of my life"—saved him from the depths. It was in this house that Jake had learned that there was no room for sin indulgence, no matter how small.

There was no gray area, only black and white. He knew that now and closely followed it with all the strength he possessed. That was another reason Melanie Johnston bothered him.

Something about her drew him to her in a way he hadn't felt in years. He couldn't afford to accommodate that feeling in any way. Yet why couldn't he get her out of his mind?

He pulled the digital camera out of his pocket and snapped several photos of the house. They would serve as a reminder of what taking one wrong step could lead to. He would not make the same mistake twice.

———

Andie paced while she watched the evening lights disappear into the darkness of night. When Blair's car appeared in the driveway, she opened the door that led to the garage and waited. Her agitation barely allowed him to park his car and open the door before the questions burst forth. "Where have you been?"

Blair looked at her and tilted his head as if confused. "What do you mean, where have I been? I've been at work, of course."

"Not until almost noon today. They called here looking for you and said you hadn't been in yet. I thought something terrible had happened."

His eyes focused just to the side of hers. "Well, everything's fine. See?" He reached across his car for his briefcase.

"Blair, I was frantic. I thought you'd . . ."

He stood and waved his hand in a circle. "Look at me. Look at my car. Not a scratch on either. I said I'm fine—now let it go!" He started toward the house, his eyes still averted.

What was he not saying? "They said you were about to miss an important meeting."

"Well, I didn't."

"Where were you?"

Blair pushed past her into the house. He didn't bother to turn as he answered.

"Research."

"What kind of research?"

This time he did stop. He turned on his heel, his face tinged with red. "What do you mean, what kind of research? What is it that you think I do, Andie? I work in a high-tech industry that is constantly changing. If I don't stay on top of things, we get left behind and no one could care less. I've got enough on my plate right now without having to answer to you about every minute detail of how I spend my workday."

The warmth of a single tear rolled down her cheek. Maybe she shouldn't push him like this, but he was lying. She felt it. "Where did you go to do your research?"

Blair turned his back to her and walked down the hall. "Somewhere that I could get a little peace and quiet, which is more than I can say for this house." He went into his office and slammed the door.

She stared behind him. Her body trembled—whether from rage or fear, she couldn't say. She slowly became aware of her subconscious thoughts. Something about Blair was different. He smelled different. What was it? A hint of smoke perhaps, but something sweet, too. It took another minute before she recognized it. Perfume.

chapter **eighteen**

Day two on the new job, Melanie watched everyone around her with renewed resolve. Whoever it was that didn't want her here was smart enough not to be public about it. Still, if she waited patiently, she might catch someone in the act. And she knew whoever it was hadn't finished harassing her. The uneasy feeling of being watched by unfriendly eyes seemed to press against her back wherever she went.

When it was almost break time, Candace sought her out. "Do you want to go to lunch together? There's a great little deli a few doors down with fast table service, and they make a mean BLT. I'm having one of those days where I just need to get out of here for a while. You know what I mean?"

Leaving the store with Candace could very well be a setup. It could also be the perfect opportunity to get information. "Sure. Sounds great."

Melanie went to her locker and worked the combination. She opened the door slowly, dreading what she might find.

Nothing.

Maybe yesterday was meant as a one-time statement, and now things would settle down. She slung her purse over her arm and followed Candace to a little place called Angie's Café.

Several quaint tables filled a small outdoor dining area. With the warmth of March in the air, it looked inviting. They found an empty table along the outer edge, placed an order, and within minutes their chips and sandwiches arrived. Candace nodded her head toward the waitress as she walked away. "See what I mean about the fast service?" She pulled open her bag of chips. "So how are things going so far?"

Legitimate question, or bait? Melanie hadn't told anyone about the rat episode. If Candace didn't know about it, telling her would serve no good purpose. If she knew and approved, then Melanie wouldn't give her the satisfaction of hearing about it from her. "Fine."

Candace tilted her head and looked at her as if waiting for more to the answer. She finally shrugged. "I'm glad to hear it." She popped a chip into her mouth and played with the bag. The crinkling sound filled the silence for a while, then stopped. "I'm sorry." The words sounded thick and choked. She stared at her sandwich, but a trace of moisture filled her eyes. "About your son, I mean. It must be horrible."

Melanie swallowed hard and tried to decide what game this woman might be playing. She sounded so sincere. But Melanie wasn't ready to trust her. "Thanks." She stared out at the cars circling the parking lot and forced down a sip of water. Time to change the subject.

Perhaps now would be a good time to bring up the obvious. Be honest. Maybe learn something in return. "Listen, I know that everyone around here expected you to get this job. I'm not here because I wanted to take it away from you—that's for sure. I just don't have a lot of other choices right now."

"I know that feeling." Candace blinked fast several times, then looked away. "There's a lot in life that doesn't leave us with much of a choice, isn't there?"

Melanie couldn't help but nod. The lunch continued in almost complete silence. Although it grew awkward, in a way it seemed almost companionable. As if each woman had her own wounds and hurts, and they were dealing with them.

When the waitress brought the check, Melanie reached for it. "The least I can do is buy your lunch." She opened her purse and barely managed to stifle the gasp. The contents of her wallet had been dumped haphazardly throughout the purse, her credit cards had been cut to shreds, and her money was gone.

"Is something wrong?"

"I . . . uh . . ."

Candace leaned across the table and looked into the bag. "I can't believe them." She threw her wadded napkin onto the table and shook her head. "Please accept my apologies. I've tried to tell everyone that I'm okay, but some people just won't let it go. You know?"

She pried the lunch bill from Melanie's hand. "I guess the treat's mine today, huh?" She put some money on the table and stood.

"Don't let them get to you. It'll stop. Eventually."

They walked down the sidewalk toward the store, Melanie fuming. "I'm not real impressed with the security of the lockers around here."

Candace laughed. "The last person who had your locker used it to run a betting business on the side. He eventually got fired, but I'm afraid his combination was common knowledge. I'm sure if you tell Carl about it, he'll have the lock replaced."

"I don't want to do that. Not if I can avoid it, anyway."

Candace stopped and looked at her. "Why don't you start leaving your things in my locker? Nobody else knows the combination."

Melanie hesitated. "Why would you do that?"

"Because what they are doing is wrong."

"But what they are doing will help you, if they get me to leave."

"I believe it's more important to do the right thing than the thing that most benefits me."

An uneasiness seeped through Melanie's skin. Why? Candace sounded sincere, and Melanie agreed completely. What was that feeling? Suddenly, she recognized it. Guilt.

————

The end of the workday at last. Melanie retrieved her purse—from Candace's locker—and started back toward Santa Barbara, an uncomfortable feeling still gnawing her gut. The commute gave her too much time to think about it.

After Ventura, she turned her attention on the Pacific Ocean—calm as a lake today. The surfers would be bummed; the whale watchers, however, would be thrilled.

She finally arrived in Santa Barbara, drove through downtown, and headed north toward Goleta. Instead of taking the Patterson Avenue off-ramp toward home, however, she kept going. There was something she needed to do, and waiting wouldn't make it any easier. She exited at Glen Annie Road and drove toward the mountains, rehearsing what she needed to say but never getting it to her satisfaction.

It was just after five o'clock when she pulled into the parking lot. As she hoped, the employees' cars seemed to be gone for the day, but the door was still open. She walked through the cavernous silence, hearing occasional squeaking sounds from the office. She walked toward it.

Jake sat at his desk, a pile of invoices to his right. He looked really busy. She shouldn't stay long.

"Knock, knock." She knocked on the doorframe as she said the words.

He turned slowly in his seat. "Melanie?"

Her mouth didn't want to speak, but she forced it to move. "Do you have a minute?"

He jumped to his feet. "Sure. Please, take a seat." He pointed her toward the vinyl chair and waited until she sat before he did the same. "What's up?"

She fidgeted with the hem of her denim shirt. "I came to apologize." She studied a loose thread. "The article was really nice. Besides, you've got a business to run. There's nothing wrong with you working for that family. I overreacted."

Jake nodded. "Thanks."

"Thanks for doing the story." She twiddled the thread through her fingers. "Well, that's what I came to say. Have a nice evening." She stood to leave.

"That's it? You came all the way out here for that?" Jake followed her out of the office and pointed toward one of his creations. "Come on. Let me at least take you out for a ride."

She looked at the gleaming work of metal and art. For a moment she let the thrill of the thought take her. No. She needed to stay on task. "Can't. I've got another stop to make."

"I'll take you."

"I don't think so." She hurried toward the door before she changed her mind.

"You're going to the graveyard again, aren't you?"

She glanced around at him. "And if I am?"

"Do you think it's healthy to spend so much time there?"

"You don't know anything." She shoved past him, but he followed her through the empty parking lot.

"Jeff would want you to move on with your life. I know you're grieving, but going to his graveside every day is only going to keep you back. You know that."

"I know my visits to Jeff are none of your business."

"Jeff's not there, Melanie. He's somewhere better. He'd want you to know that."

"I *don't* know that. And I'm not taking a chance that he's out there all alone. I promised him I would never abandon him, and I intend to keep that promise."

———

Andie paced the entryway and looked at her watch. Again. Only five minutes had passed. Ten-thirty. Where was Blair?

He'd been working even later than usual for the past two nights, with plenty of excuses about research and job pressure. He couldn't even look at her anymore.

Maybe she should go to Blair's office, pull up a chair, and talk things out. She could beg him to forgive her, plead for their marriage. Would that make Blair think her weak? Probably, but she had nothing to lose.

She pulled her black leather jacket out of the hall closet— Blair always said it looked nice on her. A quick peek in the hallway mirror showed her hair frizzing due to the night's mist. She smoothed it with her hands. It didn't help much.

As she pulled out of the driveway, she felt a strange sense of lightness. Finally, she was doing something. She'd spent too long waiting for life to happen to her. Now, she was taking charge of her situation. It felt good.

The Santa Barbara streets were dressed in eerie shadows, broken at intervals by the orange glow of streetlamps. She turned into the company's parking lot, noting only a few cars.

Several of the programmers were getting advanced degrees from UCSB by day, so they worked long and late hours. Blair's car would be parked in one of the reserved underground parking spaces—no need to look for it.

She walked to the back door and pulled. It rattled in her hand, then slipped from her grip. Locked.

Through the glass, she saw Neil Parker peek around the wall of his cubicle, squinting with furrowed brows. His smile grew wide when he recognized her. He jumped up and ran to open the door.

"Hey, Mrs. Phelps. Sorry about having you locked out, but I didn't know you were coming. Did Blair forget something? Need me to get into his office for you?"

"I . . . uh . . . well, isn't he here?"

Neil looked over his shoulder toward the hallway that led to Blair's office. "Don't think so. Come on in—we'll take a look."

Andie followed Neil past the row of cubicles, down the long hallway, and up the stairs to the second floor. Blair's office was dark. She must have passed him somewhere on the road.

When they started down the steps, another young programmer, whose face Andie did not recognize, was climbing up. He carried a steaming cup of coffee and had bleary eyes with dark circles underneath, a badge of honor in his field.

Neil stopped. "Hey, Gary, is Blair still around somewhere?"

"Blair? Nope. Saw him loading up in his car just as I was coming in."

Andie's heart thumped inside her with a new kind of dread. She tried to force a conversational tone from her terrified lips. "What time was that?"

Only then did Gary seem to notice that Neil wasn't alone. "Let's see, I drove through Burger King after my last class, so it must've been around six." Joe nodded and continued up the stairs, seemingly unaware of the blow he'd just dealt Andie.

Neil shifted his weight to his left foot and turned for a final glance up the stairs. Andie could almost hear him willing some logical explanation to spring to his lips. She held her breath and waited. She was out of excuses.

His face lit. "I remember now. That weird-looking guy who serves all the legal stuff was in today. When Blair left, he was carrying an envelope with him. I'll bet he was going to your lawyer's office."

What legal papers would have been served today? Andie did remember Sam had said something about an amended complaint, but she hadn't wanted to think about it. As much as she tried to ignore it and hope it would go away, the lawsuit was moving forward, ripping apart any shreds of hope in her life.

"He must have forgotten to call you."

Think, Andie, think. Whatever is going on with Blair, you don't want all his employees gossiping about it. You have enough problems without taking private matters public.

She forced herself to smile, although she suspected Neil saw it for the weak imitation it was. "He probably tried. I was out with friends and the battery in my cell phone is dead. That's what I get for not keeping it charged."

Neil nodded, and the crease across his forehead relaxed. "He's probably worried sick." He walked Andie to the door. "Have a nice evening, Mrs. Phelps. I'll watch to make sure you make it to your car."

"Thanks." Andie walked through the parking lot, concentrating on taking deep breaths. She'd held it together this long, she didn't want to lose it now. When she reached her car, she exhaled slowly and turned back toward the building. Neil waved. She returned the gesture. *Just a few more seconds of control. You can do it, Andie.*

She dropped into the driver's seat and closed the door. As she drove toward her empty home, she wondered what to fear. The thought of Blair meeting with Sam renewed her dread of the upcoming lawsuit. The thought of him somewhere else altogether frightened her even more.

chapter **nineteen**

Jake paced through the workshop, watching for the telltale flash of headlights. He hadn't been able to concentrate since Melanie called and asked if she could stop by on her way home from work. What was it about her that kept him so off-balance?

He knew he needed to stay away from her, but what would that do for her renewed interest in God? He couldn't let her stray because he didn't have the fortitude to resist a few adolescent hormones. No, he could, and would, control his emotions. It would pass soon enough.

A flash of headlights scurried across the walls, then went dark. Tempted to pretend to be working on a bike, Jake thought better of it. He walked to the door and stood waiting for her as she climbed out of her car.

Her feet appeared to be heavy as she trudged toward him. When she got into the light, he could see the lines of fatigue on her face.

"Come in. I've just made a pot of decaf, if you'd like some."

"Sounds good." She followed him back to his office. He suddenly felt the emptiness of the building around them, and for the first time he could remember, it felt oppressive.

"First off, I'm sorry about yesterday. I have no right telling a grieving mother that she shouldn't be spending so much time at her son's grave. That was out of line."

Melanie lifted her left shoulder and tilted her head. Subject closed. "Don't worry about it. So is that what you wanted to talk to me about?"

"This meeting was your idea."

"I know, but when I called earlier, you said you wanted to talk to me anyway. Was that it?"

"Uh-uh. You first." He smiled. "That way, if you get mad about what I say, we'll at least have both conversations out of the way before you race out of here."

Her head began to slowly nod, then faster, until a burst of laughter erupted. "I like the way you lay it all on the line. Don't find too many people who do that these days." She took a sip of the coffee, still nodding her head. "You've got a point. Okay, I'll shoot. Something Sarah said has been bothering me. I meant to ask you about it last night, but . . . well . . ."

No need to say more on *that* subject. "Bothering you how?"

"I'm afraid she's putting pressure on herself where it shouldn't be, and I wanted to hear your take on it." She spent the next few minutes telling of the conversation she'd had with Sarah at church last Sunday. "She just lost her brother, and at her age, she's under enough pressure. I don't want her all worked up about my soul when she has so many other things to deal with."

Jake prayed for wisdom in his answer. He didn't want to say anything to offend Melanie, but he wanted to answer with full truth, as well.

"That is part of the teaching of the Bible, you know. We are supposed to make disciples, tell others, spread the Good News. It's a big part of what Christianity is about."

"Yeah, but I'm her mom. *I'm* supposed to be the one worrying about *her*. She's got enough of her own problems."

"Doesn't the fact that she's still concerned about your soul, in the midst of her own troubles, give you an inkling of how important this is to her? Most teenage girls are so wrapped up in the here and now they wouldn't think of such things. This shows me the depth of character and commitment that Sarah has—not that I've ever doubted it. She's a remarkable young lady."

Melanie nodded and swirled her cup in her hands. "Yes, she is. What I need to know is, how can I take this burden off her? What would I need to do to set her mind at ease—you know, close this page in her book? I'm a good person. I don't know why she is so concerned about my soul."

"We believe there is more to it than being a good person. Salvation is a deliberate choice, and no one can make that choice for another. Only when you decide to confess your sins before God, ask forgiveness through the shed blood of Jesus, and accept Him as your Lord and Savior, would that 'page of her book,' as you call it, be closed. Now and forever."

"That's more than I want to do at this point."

"Maybe if you let her know you're giving the matter some thought, it would help ease her mind, huh?"

"Yeah, I'll do that. Now, what was it you wanted to see me about?"

"I've been thinking about our last conversation."

She grinned at him. "You mean fight."

He shook his head and laughed. "Disagreement."

Her eyes almost danced when she smiled. "Whatever. What about it?"

"Well, it seems to me—and correct me if I'm wrong—that you are very concerned that Jeff will not be remembered. That his legacy will be forgotten. Am I right?"

Her eyebrows lifted and the corners of her mouth curled down. "Very perceptive."

Jake's pulse raced. *Okay, your suspicion is confirmed. She's prepared for some form of judgmental response; proceed with caution. Remember what you planned to say.* Why did it seem so much harder than he had expected? *Deep breath. Press forward.* "The kids from youth group all loved Jeff. He touched several of their lives in ways you probably don't even know about. I'd like to plan a memorial service."

Her face brightened and she leaned forward in her seat.

She doesn't think it's pushy—she likes the idea. "Most of our college group missed the funeral because they were back at school. If we do it during spring break, many of them will be home. We could do it at the beach. I'd like you to come and just listen to the legacy your son has left behind. I think you'll be amazed."

"You would do that?"

"Say the word, and I'll make the arrangements. I think it will be good for everyone involved, but I need to start now. College kids, you know. They plan their spring breaks in advance."

She appeared to study her empty coffee cup, and when she looked up her eyes were pink. "I would love that."

"Consider it done."

She rose to her feet. "I need to get back. Sarah might need help with her homework."

Jake walked her to her car. "Thanks for coming."

She started the ignition. "Thanks for not giving up on me."

Jake watched the headlights disappear down the drive and into the street. No, he was not going to give up on this one. He would stay the fight.

———

Christi drove through the gate at Andie's house. What would she find today?

The amended complaint was served to Blair yesterday—although Scott said it was expected, it would feel like one more blow. This would be a bad day.

It seemed like Andie had made real progress in the past weeks—at times somehow finding a sense of distance from her grief, but those moments had been so fragile. Her moods could crash with the speed of a falling soufflé: from creative fighter putting her soul into a painting to despondent, wounded animal huddling from the world. Hopefully, the fighter was out today.

Christi climbed out of her car and looked toward the kitchen window. Dark. Better try the door.

"I'm back here." Andie's voice carried across the lawn. Christi turned to see her putting something behind the garden gazebo. She walked back to a chair and sat directly across from a large canvas propped on an easel.

Christi felt the smile creeping up her face as she walked toward her friend. "Painting another one?"

Andie shrugged. "It helps."

Christi walked around to take a peek. She looked at the canvas, amazed by the beauty her friend had created.

She recognized twinspurs and bergenia and spurge and all the blooms from around Andie's winter garden strung into a garland around a window, which looked out onto the Pacific Ocean. "Oh, Andie! It's so realistic I'd swear I can smell the flowers and the salt of the ocean."

"Take a deep breath. That's not my brilliant painting. You *can* smell both those things."

She's in a feisty mood. Good. This ought to be easy. "Glad to see you out here painting in the middle of the day, because I came to talk to you about just that—your painting."

177

Andie set her brush aside and picked up a rag to wipe her hands. "My painting? What about it?"

"Took it to an appraiser."

"You did what? You told me you were going to use it for advertising."

"And I am. But what if we could do even more with it? He said it was worth close to a thousand dollars. Said you have a lot of talent and he knew of several galleries that would be happy to carry work of that quality."

"Why did you do that?"

"Because I've always known it was something you liked to do and never would take the time to do it. I know that Blair's never been overly supportive of it—or much of anything you do for that matter."

"He—"

"Let me finish. I thought maybe if he saw that you could earn some money for your charities by your hobby, and it would make you happy in the meantime, maybe he'd quit being such a...jerk about it."

"He was just raised by an old-fashioned mother."

"You mean a woman who let her husband steamroll her into whatever he wanted. A woman with no choices, no self-worth. That's probably what led to her heart attack."

"Christi!"

"True, and you know it. Oppressed women live shorter lives."

Andie picked up a brush and rolled it between her fingers. "Well, at least she was good at something. I don't think she would have approved of me." She dipped the bristles and flecked the ocean with traces of white foam.

Andie's self-doubts never failed to irritate Christi. Today was no exception. "If Blair wasn't so critical, you'd know better than that."

"But he's right. I'm not very domestic."

"That's why you should hire more help."

Andie shook her head. "His mother—"

"I know, I know. 'My mother did it without any help, and there were four of us kids.' Honestly, Andie, how many charity boards, how many school projects, how many fundraisers did Blair's mother run?"

Andie shrugged.

"See? Besides, you're good at lots of things. The best listener, the biggest supporter, and the kindest-hearted person around."

Andie shook her head in her slight way. "All of that is stuff anyone can do. All it requires is sitting around and listening. I want to be good at *doing* something."

"You're terrific at painting. Just look at what you've created on this canvas."

"But that's worthless. I need to spend my time doing something productive, not playing."

Christi bit back the comment she wanted to make. Losing her temper now would also lose her point with Andie. "This is a talent, and it's a mistake to waste talent. I'm going to sell your painting of the Fair at this year's Fair. It'll bring enough money to make you rethink your version of playing."

She seems to be considering this. Better get out of here now, before your temper gets the best of you. "Got some other stops to make. You think about what I've said."

"Sure."

Christi hopped into her car and sped down the driveway. When she got to the bottom, she realized Andie hadn't been wearing her wedding band. Odd. *Maybe she takes it off when she paints.*

chapter **twenty**

Andie sat up in bed and rubbed her face. A vague sense of anticipation began to grow. Something exciting was going to happen today. What was it?

Oh yes. The Fair. Today was the board meeting.

Since the media maelstrom over the lawsuit had begun to diminish, she was confident they would decide to move her back into a leadership position. Yes, today was going to be a great day.

She strolled down the stairs and into the kitchen. The paper was neatly folded on the table, a sign that Blair had risen extra early and gone into work. After a bumpy week, even he seemed to be back on track.

She poured herself a cup of coffee and looked at the clock. Forty-five minutes until her favorite spinning class at the gym— plenty of time to make it. But somehow she wasn't quite ready for that yet. The idea of being packed in a close space with so many watching eyes did not appeal. At all. No, today she would ride the exercise bike in the den and read the paper.

A few minutes later, she unfolded the paper and started pedaling. After perusing the local and national news, she skipped the sports as always, then looked into the Life section. She was just about to put it away when some photos caught her eye. She looked again.

In Vanessa Phillips' pretentious gossip column, *Santa Barbara Chic*, the headline for today was "Out and About With the Fabulous People." Beneath the heading were candid photos of some of Santa Barbara's most famous and wealthy residents driving their expensive cars, wearing their outrageous jewels, doing their extravagant things. In the very center of the spread, there were two pictures of Andie. One of Christi and her walking out of Saks with the bags for the silent auction. The caption below it read, "Apparently Andie Phelps and Christi Baur are taking matters (and several bags of delights) into their own hands." The next picture was of her walking out of church in one of Mattilda Plendor's outfits. The caption read, "Andie demonstrated heavenly style at church."

The paper shook in her hands. How dare they print these pictures? If the members of the board saw this before the meeting, her chances were over.

She jumped off the bike and walked to the phone. The white pages stuck together and seemed to fight her as she flipped through. At last, she found the number, stabbed it into the keypad, and waited. The other end clicked after the second ring. "Vanessa Phillips."

"Yes. This is Andie Phelps—"

"You didn't need to call and thank me. I should be the one thanking you—for the killer pictures, I mean."

"I didn't call to thank you. I want to know where you got those."

"You sent them to me."

The dark hues of anger disappeared into bright shades of alarm. "I did what? Ms. Phillips, I've never seen those photos before in my life."

"That's odd. They arrived in an envelope last week with your return address on them. In fact, it was those photos that prompted the whole idea for that column. Oh well, no harm done. The article turned out great, didn't it?"

"Those pictures were taken out of context. One was me carrying *donations* from Saks, the other was me doing a favor for Mattilda Plendor. You made it appear that I am having one big shopping party since my son's death. I want you to print a retraction."

"I didn't make it appear anything. Those photos were completely unaltered. Mrs. Phelps, if you don't want people to see you out shopping and wearing designer outfits, then I suggest you don't go shopping or wear designer outfits. As it is, you've left yourself wide open. I'm not going to print a retraction of *pictures*."

Andie steamed. "Thanks for all your *help*."

"You're more than welcome." A click sounded at the other end, and the line went dead.

The phone rang again while it was still in her hand. "Yes?"

"Andie, this is Carolyn Patterson. In light of today's paper, the board has agreed to postpone the final vote until our meeting in two weeks."

"But that's only two weeks before the Fair."

"Would you rather resign now?"

———

"I suppose you want to go to lunch again today?" Melanie called down the hall as she walked toward Sarah's room.

"Yep." Sarah's voice sounded strangled.

She stood at the wall, her fingers tracing the picture of Juanita. The dark eyes smiled back at her from beneath long bangs. Sarah sniffled once and shook her head. "She was the coolest little kid."

Melanie nodded. "I remember all the stories. Sounds like a real firecracker."

"Yeah."

Melanie put her hand on Sarah's shoulder. "I really do hope things work out for you to go."

Sarah turned toward her and smiled, her eyes red. "I know you do." She touched a crayon drawing of kids on a soccer field and shook her head. "I don't know how I can live with myself if we don't."

The aroma of garlic and fresh-baked bread filled Lorenzo's parking lot. Melanie's stomach growled.

"I don't have to wonder whether or not you're hungry." Trish laughed and rushed ahead to hold the door for the group.

While last week's gathering had been a bit reserved and tense, this week the women began to feel comfortable with one another. And with Melanie. They asked after her new job, her recovery after Jeff, how Sarah was dealing with everything. By the time they were halfway through their meals, even the subject of the lawsuit came up.

There were four other women besides Melanie and Trish. Two were mothers of Sarah's friends, the other two were new to Melanie.

Rennie Micheel had short brown hair and no distinct features at all. Not unattractive, not displeasing in any way, just nothing that stood out. Melanie suspected that she could sit in a room full of people, and an hour later very few of them would be able to describe her, or even remember her presence. Melanie identified with that. She, too, was one of the "invisible people." At least she had been until the lawsuit.

Margaret Foreman, on the other hand, could only be described as severe. From her tightly wound hair to the starched stiffness of her clothes, everything about her looked like the stereotypical "church lady" of years past. Yet, her eyes put off a warmth that almost seemed gentle. Melanie wondered at the apparent contradiction, and wasn't altogether certain she liked Margaret.

"Did you see those pictures of that Phelps woman in the paper? Can you believe her, out carrying on like that?" Trish took another slurp of angel-hair pasta, then continued. "You'd think she'd show a little more discretion."

Rennie set her fork down and glared toward Trish. "She's not that 'Phelps woman.' Her name is Andie Phelps, and since you've never experienced her grief, how can you condemn anything she does? You speak about her like she's not even a real person."

So much for Miss Average. She had a big mouth and put it in the wrong place as far as Melanie was concerned.

"She's not much of one, if you ask me. A real person, I mean." Trish looked toward Melanie, obviously gauging her reaction to this conversation.

She tried to appear unaffected. These women were speaking their minds. If she gave any sign of being offended, they would shut down and she would never hear the truth.

"That's not for you to decide." Rennie picked up her fork and began to twirl pasta.

"You're right, it's not. It's for the court to decide." Trish lifted her water glass, extending her pinky in triumph.

"Shouldn't be." Rennie stuffed the forkful of pasta into her mouth and looked away. Her face began to glow with a light pink color.

Maybe she was wishing she'd kept her mouth shut, about now. She wasn't the only one.

"Excuse me? And why shouldn't it be?" Trish set her glass on the table so hard, drops of water splattered the red tablecloth around it.

"Christians aren't supposed to take each other to court."

"Says who?"

"Paul, in First Corinthians. He said Christians shouldn't take other Christians to be judged before the ungodly. He said to appoint men from the church to settle the dispute."

Trish's face flushed red and she nodded toward Melanie, as if trying to remind Rennie that she was present. "Well, times were different then."

Margaret smoothed an imaginary stray hair. "Besides, the Phelps family doesn't attend a church. They attend a country club. Have you ever seen that place?"

Although Melanie had been uncertain of how she felt about Margaret before, she now sized her up as a sister. Yep, this was a woman she wanted to get to know.

Her curiosity forced her into the conversation at this point. "Really? What's it like?"

"It's in the heart of Montecito. They have a gym, incredible landscaping, and a newly remodeled sanctuary. All the 'beautiful people'—so called—go there. If you drive by on a Sunday morning, I bet you wouldn't find a single American-made vehicle in the parking lot. Besides that, you saw the pictures in the paper. You know the kind of clothes those people wear."

Trish nodded. "Even their name is stuck-up."

"A name can't be stuck-up. The United Church of Montecito, what's stuck-up about that?" Rennie said.

"Have you ever heard one of the members refer to it as The United Church of Montecito? They all call it Uni-Mon. Like it's a sorority."

Margaret smacked her hand against the table. "Or better. It reminds me of those weird Japanese cartoons all the little kids love these days. Frugy-Mon…or Kooky-Mon… Well, you know what I mean."

Beth's mother, Christine, spoke up. "That's not entirely fair. I've been there for a couple of different events. There is a lot of money floating around at that church, but look where it's located. People who live in that area have a lot of money. Do you think any of them would want to learn more about a God who provided a little shack in the middle of their oasis?

"I think there are different styles of worship for different people, and I don't think we're the ones to judge. I'm sure some of them would be offended by our casual Sunday services, but we wouldn't attract the working class and the surfer kids if we tried to be all fancy. Maybe their ministry is to the jet set. You know, those people need Jesus just as much as anyone else. We each have our place in the Plan."

Margaret lifted her left shoulder in partial defeat. "Maybe."

Melanie finished her meal and stood to leave. She nodded at Rennie. "I guess I'm okay, even in your book. You said two Christians shouldn't bring each other into court. I'm not a Christian, and have never claimed to be."

She watched Rennie's mouth fly open and savored the victory. That would teach her. "See you next week, ladies." She tossed the money to pay for her and Sarah on the table, walked past the stunned faces, and retrieved her daughter. As she pushed through the door, she wondered if anyone would show up next Sunday.

chapter **twenty-one**

Blair leaned his elbows on his desk and stared at the closed door. Thankfully, he'd made it through the house and into his office without encountering Andie. Her questions only fueled his guilt. Besides, she didn't seem to want to see him, either. Time apart was better for both of them right now.

He reached for the clasps on his overloaded briefcase. They sprang open, revealing a gigabyte's worth of paperwork that needed his attention. At least it would keep his mind off everything else.

The phone rang. The light blinked atop the handset, working in time with the sound.

He had spent the last couple of days dodging calls from a paranoid Mike Daniels. He wouldn't call at home, would he? Most likely one of Andie's friends. She could answer it; he had work to do.

"Blair." Andie's voice called from the hallway. "Blair. Phone."

Oh no.

She opened the office door. "It's Sam Campbell."

Didn't lawyers ever take a rest? Sam called at least three times a week. What more could he possibly need to know?

At least it wasn't Mike.

Andie didn't leave the office. A call this late meant something was happening, and she would not leave until she found out what it was. She leaned against the wall and watched.

The paperwork from Parsons Bank and Trust sat on the top of the stack. Blair casually tossed an empty file folder over it before answering. "Hello, Sam."

"Evening, Blair. Sorry to call so late, but there's something I think you need to be aware of."

Blair looked toward Andie. It had been little more than a week since her fainting episode; he tried not to show alarm. He forced a casual tone. "Really? What is that?"

"The police department didn't exactly volunteer every scrap of information they had about Chad. They didn't hide anything, mind you. They just didn't advertise. You know what I mean?"

Blair knew what was coming. He sank back into the seat behind him. Just when he thought things couldn't get any worse, they always did.

Sam cleared his throat. "Today it became clear that Les Stewart's investigator has uncovered Chad's two previous pullovers before the ticket. Knowing the way he works, I won't be surprised to see it in the paper in the next couple of days. Maybe even tomorrow. I thought that you should be prepared."

"Then they'll be printing a lie, and we'll sue them for libel. There weren't two previous pullovers, only one. It happened in November, just after he'd gotten his license. Anything they say beyond that is fabrication."

Across the room, Andie slid down the wall to the floor and pulled her knees up to her chest. "There were two."

"Sam, I'll call you right back." He hung up the phone without waiting for a reply. "What did you say?"

"Kyle Ledger called me in December and told me he'd caught Chad speeding. I promised to talk to him, and I did."

How could she have kept this from him? About his own son? "You mean to tell me there was a second time I didn't even know about? Why didn't you tell me?"

Andie's eyes narrowed. She looked at him, and in her eyes Blair saw pure contempt. "I knew you would hit the roof. Chad was having enough problems at the time without having to deal with all that."

He stood, and by sheer force of will restrained himself from grabbing and shaking her. "If I'd known about it, maybe I could have stopped the accident."

A glimmer of moisture filled her eyes, but these weren't the tears of grief he'd seen so much of. These were the tears of hatred. "Really? What good would a week of berating have done? It was just a few weeks later that he got the ticket that cost him his license—because you refused to take him to traffic court, remember? You said a six-month suspension would stop his recklessness." She pushed herself back up the wall. "Your methods didn't stop it, either. I'm so sick of everything being my fault."

She ran out of the room, and the sound of her footsteps pounding up the stairs echoed through the house. Finally, a loud bang shook the walls. She had slammed the door to their bedroom.

Blair knew where he wasn't welcome tonight. Just as well. He picked up the phone.

Sam answered on the first ring. "I take it there *was* a second incident."

"I can't believe she kept that from me. If I'd known, I could have done something."

"Perhaps. I'm sorry to have made more trouble."

"No, you were right in calling. Better to find it out from you now than to learn about it in the paper tomorrow."

"That was my thought. Blair, can I make a suggestion?"

"Sure." What could it hurt?

"I've seen lots of similar cases. These situations can tear the healthiest of relationships apart. I know you have a marriage worth fighting for. Get to work on it now—before it's too late."

Blair didn't answer, just hung up. How can you rebuild a marriage after something like this? Andie blamed him for Chad's death. How could he look at her, knowing how she felt?

A dark emptiness surrounded him. Maybe Sam was right, but at this point, he didn't have the strength to fight anymore. He had lost his son. He was about to lose his house. It only made sense that he would lose his wife, too.

———

Andie heard the pounding. It wasn't so close, but near enough to be annoying. She pulled herself up from the depths of sleep and listened.

The back door.

Most likely Christi, since she knew the gate combination. She'd found the door locked and would assume Andie was not home when her knocks went unanswered. That was just fine with Andie. She closed her eyes and drifted back into the darkness.

The pounding was closer now—more insistent.

Andie opened her eyes again and looked around the room. The light splashed across the small sitting room, making it appear cheery and cozy. But what was the knocking?

When she looked through the door into the master bedroom, a shadow came from the direction of the door off the deck. It continued to pound, and though it was the last thing she wanted to do right now, Andie very slowly peeked around the corner.

Christi stood on her deck, knocking on the glass doors that led to the bedroom. A scowl scrunched her face. If she didn't show her face, Christi might just knock down the door.

Andie sighed. She shuffled over and slid the door open. "What time is it?"

Christi studied her, and Andie knew she couldn't approve. Still in yesterday's clothes, unbrushed hair, unwashed face. She was kind enough to bite her tongue at least. "Ten. What's up with you?"

Andie shook her head, still frazzled from her scare. "Been fighting with Blair. Spent all of last night in our sitting room with the remote. I must have fallen asleep on the couch sometime this morning."

"Men." Christi came inside. "Back door's locked. Took me a while to find you. Where's your Windex? I left marks on the glass." Without waiting for an answer she disappeared into the house. Several minutes later she reappeared, glass cleaner in hand. As she wiped the tiny smudges, she glanced toward Andie. "This ought to cheer you up. I come bearing good news."

"Good news?"

"Yep." She smiled with satisfaction—whether at her cleaning job or the weight of the upcoming news, Andie couldn't tell.

"Come into the sitting room." Andie led Christi into her favorite room in the house—besides her studio, anyway. Decorated in pale sage and gray, it had a tiny fireplace surrounded by a loveseat, a chair, and a small desk. It had always been her space. Even Chad had left her alone here. Maybe that was why it seemed a haven now; it was the one place in the house unhaunted by his memory.

Christi perched on the loveseat, Andie at the desk. "Okay. I'm ready for some good news."

"We can go back to Alfords." Christi smiled in victory and waited. Braced, it seemed, for shouts of triumph.

Andie flinched and felt something like nausea in the pit of her stomach. "What?" Her voice came out a raspy whisper in spite of her efforts.

Christi opened her eyes a little wider and leaned forward. "I *said*, we can start going back to Alfords. The Johnston woman was transferred to another store. I wanted to be certain before I told you. It's true. Everyone is thrilled. See what happens when we all stick together?"

Andie pressed her fingers against her lips and focused on deep breaths. *They did this for me. They ruined that other woman's job, for me.* "That's . . . great news."

Christi stared at Andie, silent. The clock ticked from the office wall, a bird chirped somewhere outside the window, and Andie's pulse thrummed in her ears.

When Christi stood, the hint of a frown formed on her lips. "Got to run. Promised Scott I'd meet him for an early lunch." She made a show of looking at her watch, although Andie knew it was an excuse.

"Don't keep him waiting, then. Men hate that." She smiled stiffly, glad that Christi had the perception to leave her alone.

Christi nodded. "I'll let myself out the back door."

"Okay." Andie collapsed across the sofa before Christi had closed the door behind her.

Andie's friends had forced that poor woman from her job. No. Andie had. Because she didn't have the nerve to stand up and tell them, "No, this isn't right." Because she had smiled and let them carry on. Because she was, and always had been, a doormat.

chapter **twenty-two**

Andie couldn't remember a Sunday when she'd been more miserable about pulling into the church parking lot. Blair rarely missed church, and for her to show up alone guaranteed that she would face inquiries. Or worse, knowing glances. Maybe she should just tell the truth. Somehow, she didn't think "We haven't spoken since Wednesday" would go over well with the ladies' group.

The parking lot ran along the side of the church, with four rows of spaces. She chose the very last spot in the very last row and backed her car in. She wanted to make the quickest possible escape. When she climbed out of her car to walk into the sanctuary, she realized the first of her errors.

She might be able to get quickly out of the parking lot from here, but she had a long way to walk in her latest dress à la Mattie. This one went almost to her ankles, in some new "fashion forward" fabric as thick and heavy as denim. Fashion forward or not, the kick pleat stuck together as she walked and she found herself having to take tiny steps. Even then the fabric whipped around her legs, chafing the entire length of her calves.

"Andie! Andie!" Christi's call made certain that everyone in the parking lot who had previously failed to notice her flailing presence was now well informed. Christi sprinted over, looking fresh and tailored in a rose-colored skirt and fitted top. "There you are. Been looking for you."

Great! It figured that Christi would choose to make her once-a-month appearance today.

"Been telling everyone about your painting and the appraisal. Everyone's so excited. They all want to talk to you about it."

Andie did not want to talk about it. She didn't want to talk to anyone about anything. "Maybe some other time."

"Come on, you modest thing. This way." Christi grabbed her arm and dragged her in the general direction of the foyer. Andie tripped in her efforts to keep up.

Only then did Christi turn and truly look at her. "What is that you're wearing?" She stopped walking long enough to give Andie a head-to-toe inspection. A smile twitched at the corner of her mouth and she bit her bottom lip. Although she managed to remain quiet on the outside, Andie could see the laughter dancing in her eyes.

"Oh, you know. One of Mattilda Plendor's things."

Christi appeared to be holding her breath. "Never thought you liked avant-garde fashions."

"I don't." Andie looked around to be certain no one in the parking lot might be overhearing the conversation. "I hate them. But what am I supposed to do? It makes her so happy to be helping that I just couldn't tell her no."

Christi erupted into laughter. "You've got to be kidding. You're wearing something you hate because you don't want to hurt someone's feelings?"

The words stung. "I thought it was the polite thing to do. She's still grieving, too, you know. I thought maybe by letting her help me, I could help her."

Christi shook her head and rolled her eyes, her laughter gaining volume. Suddenly, she seemed to become aware of the fact that Andie was not laughing with her. She took a deep breath and cleared her throat. She continued to giggle beneath her breath with every few steps they took. "You really shouldn't let her push you around like that."

Like Christi had room to talk. It seemed everyone wanted Andie to stand up for herself, except when that person was the one involved.

More and more Andie was beginning to see that her whole adult life had been spent trying to please others. She never did, or even said, what she really wanted.

Some things need to change here. She felt as though a beast had been caged inside her, and she couldn't continue to hold it in.

They approached the assembled group of women. As they drew closer the hum of excitement grew, until someone's voice rose above the crowd. "Andie, Christi just told us the exciting news. That is so great."

"Is it?"

The hum silenced. Andie's voice had escaped with more anger than she had intended. The now-mute group stared at her with wide eyes. *Better use care with this newfound independence.* Perhaps she should leash the beast, for now. "Do you really think so, I mean?"

The women's faces relaxed, and the excited murmurs rippled through the group once again. A chorus of "Yes" and "Wonderful" followed.

"That outfit is fabulous." More agreement chased around the circle. Carissa's averted eyes and Kendra's raised eyebrow told Andie that they might like the outfit, but they didn't think it worked on her. *I couldn't agree more.* The cage needed to open, and soon.

"How are things going for this year's Fair? I'm sure you've outdone yourself as always."

"I—"

"Organ's playing." Christi grabbed her arm. "We'd best get inside."

The women started walking toward the church, and the subject dropped. Andie would definitely thank Christi later.

Carissa stopped at the door to the foyer. "Where's Blair?"

Andie managed to smile sweetly. "He has a big project at work. He hated not to come but felt he just couldn't."

Knowing nods all around. Most of this group understood facing events alone when work beckoned the provider. Andie wondered how many of them had made the same statement she just made, knowing as well as she did now, it wasn't the truth. *It's time to make some changes.*

———

"I'm not going to take it, not anymore."

"Pardon me, madam. I could not hear you properly."

Andie spun around and dropped the bowl she had been scrubbing. It clattered across the floor, sending suds and water splashing. "Sorry, Silas. I was just talking to myself." She reached down to pick up the bowl, thankful it was plastic.

"So I presumed. Might I suggest that perhaps your words would be better directed toward God?"

"I'm sure you're right." Why did he have to put on such a superior air? He was one step away from homeless, dirty, and annoying in the way he spoke. Why couldn't he just leave her alone? She didn't want to listen to his nonsense.

Nonsense? Is that what talking to God has become to me?

She started to work on the next bowl. *Okay, God, this is for you. I'm not going to take it anymore. I'm tired of letting people "help me." I'm tired of a husband who treats me like a hired servant, or an errant teenager, or nothing at all. I'm tired of getting pushed around.*

There. Happy? As she dried the bowl she realized how pathetic her prayer life had become.

chapter **twenty-three**

Melanie lifted the clothes from the washer. Even laundry felt heavier today. Her bones ached with exhaustion, but more than that, her insides were numb. The stress of starting a new job, constant undermining at that job, and the hour and a half commute were taking their toll.

"Mom, are my shorts clean yet? The game starts in an hour." Sarah leaned her head into the garage, her face bright with teenage angst.

Pinpricks of irritation bit into Melanie's skin. "Maybe you should have thought of that sooner and washed them yourself, hmm?"

"Maybe I should have. Maybe I should have done that instead of making dinner for you!" She slammed the door and disappeared back inside the house.

Melanie's irritation disappeared behind a cloud of guilt. Sarah had always done her share of work around the house. It was all part of the single-parent gig. Now, with Melanie's commute taking up three hours a day, Sarah had been carrying even more of the burden. Melanie tossed the last of the clothes into the dryer, started the cycle, and went in search of her daughter.

She found Sarah in the bathroom, furiously trying to french braid her hair. A clumpy mess was the result so far. "I hate my hair."

Melanie stepped forward. "Here, let me do it." She undid the previous mess, brushed through it, and started to work. "I'm sorry, honey. I know you do your share of work around here. I just snapped because I'm tired, that's all."

Sarah shrugged. "I'm sorry, too. I know things are especially hard for you with the new job." She sighed. "Things aren't going so well with our fundraising, either. The last two car washes have been rained out and the bake sale didn't bring in as much as we hoped." She sniffed and wiped her left eye. "Juanita will hate me."

Melanie finished braiding one side. Before she started the other, she touched her daughter's shoulder. "She won't hate you. That girl probably understands lack-of-funding issues better than you or I ever will." She brushed out Sarah's hair and divided it into three sections. "I'm sorry. I know you're paying a price for something that I am doing. There's nothing fair about that."

A tear slid down Sarah's face. "There's nothing fair about my brother dying, either. It's not fair that Juanita lives in a rundown shack. Things are never gonna be fair, so we may as well make the best of it."

Melanie nodded at her daughter's take on the cliché. She hated that she'd had to learn the truth of it so young.

———

Andie paused just outside the shop. *Remember your resolve.* She shoved the door open and marched in. She would not allow herself to be pushed around this time.

"Andie, darling. There you are. We've got your dressing room lined with clothes. Come on back and we can get started." Mattie, dressed in a cream-colored pantsuit and high heels, floated across the floor with arms extended.

Andie accepted the brief hug. "Mattie, I need to talk to you. I . . . uh . . . can't keep taking clothes from your store."

"Not *taking,* dear, *modeling.* Do you realize that we've had several inquiries since you got started? Especially after that spread in the newspaper. Everything looks so good on you, especially since you've lost— Well, let's just say that every woman in Santa Barbara wants to look just like you. You're the perfect model."

"Yes, but, Mattie, I—"

"Now, now, dear, no need to thank me. Let's go find your next great look."

Two other women were in the shop. Chantal, the lead clerk, and her middle-aged client. Andie could see that they had both stopped what they were doing to watch the spectacle unfolding before them. She lowered her voice. "Mattie, could we talk privately, please?"

"Of course. Follow me."

She led the way past the dressing rooms, through a series of doors, and into her office. Decorated with an interesting mix of modern and antique furniture, the black-and-white room spared no space for any hint of color. Mattie motioned Andie into a chrome seat. "Color distracts me when I'm creating—works the same during purchasing. You're an artist, so I'm sure you understand that."

Andie was not here to discuss her status as an artist and did not want to be softened by mindless conversation. "Mattie, I'm not taking any more of your clothes."

Mattie's gasp told her that perhaps the words had come out a bit gruffer than she had intended. The familiar tingle around her neck and face made her wish the words back. *Stay true to your course.* "Thank you for all that you've done. It's been wonderful wearing the beautiful outfits from your store, and the heartfelt meaning behind them means more than I can say. However, I think it's time I return to the comfort of my own clothes."

"If you're certain that's what you want, dear. You always look fabulous. I only wanted to give you a little lift."

"And I do appreciate the thought. More than you will ever know. I suppose I'm just seeking familiar things right now. I've lost Chad; I can't lose myself, too."

Mattie's eyes looked moist, but the high arch of her newly lifted eyebrows made it impossible to know if she was hurt or simply suffering hay fever. She strummed her red nails across the white lacquer of her desk. "I'm glad you told me, dear."

"I brought my charge card. I want to pay for the three dresses I've already worn."

"Nonsense. I've written off the cost as advertising." She smiled; this time it seemed genuine. "And it was money well spent, too." She stood and gestured toward the door. "Thank you for letting an old woman indulge her fantasy for a while."

Andie walked out of the shop, the tingle of guilt still biting against her skin, but the thrill of having spoken her mind surpassed the discomfort. For the first time in a long time, she'd told someone no, stood her ground, and refused to go along with whatever. It felt good. Next on her list for this newfound strength was Christi. Then Blair.

———

Melanie looked at the sticky mess spilled on the floor all around her desk. She took a deep breath, rolled her shoulders, and stretched her neck. Slowly, she exhaled in a long puff, hoping it would take some tension with it. No such luck.

This week had been full of little "accidents" all around her. Missing paperwork, pricing signs incorrect or missing, "accidents" that only seemed to happen around her workspace. Only her personal items had been left untouched, and that was most likely because she was sharing Candace's locker.

She found herself constantly looking around, wondering where the next attack would come from and who would carry it out. On the surface, everyone seemed friendly enough. But she had seen several employees, when caught off guard, exchanging knowing glances. Candace was never among them.

What motivated her? She, of all people, had the most to gain if Melanie left, yet she continued to show support. Outwardly, anyway. Maybe that was all part of the plan—keeping her above reproach while the rest of them did her dirty work for her. Melanie didn't want to believe that, but life had shown her early on that people were not always what they appeared on the surface.

She grabbed a mop, scrubbed up the mess, and sat at her desk to complete her paperwork for the day. Surely things would calm down soon. How many more miserable days could they inflict on her before they grew tired of the effort, or at least felt she'd paid her dues? It had been more than two weeks. Enough, already.

She looked over the stack of signs for the next day's price changes. Another big day loomed ahead.

Forty minutes of hard work later, she completed the last of the day's tasks. She schlepped from her desk to the locker room and retrieved her things—thankfully still intact.

The crisp air energized her as she walked through the parking lot. Her little car sat in the corner, waiting to take her away. She smiled at the little heap of metal, then stopped. Something looked wrong. Her car seemed shorter than normal. She hurried forward until she drew close enough to see the problem. Then she stopped moving. All four tires had been slashed.

———

Andie paced the entryway and looked at her watch once again. Only five minutes had passed. Six-thirty. March 22.

Where was Blair?

He couldn't lay aside his long hours, his lingering anger, his—whatever it was he'd been spending so much time doing.

The thought chilled her. Their lives had grown so far apart since their wedding—eighteen years ago today.

Over the course of the last few days the tension had lessened more or less to the levels before the last fight. Andie had assumed they would at least keep up the pretense and have their annual anniversary lobster feast. By now the spiny creatures had surely died in their boxes.

In the early years of their marriage, Blair would take the day off, and they would drive to the marina together to pick out fresh lobster from the fishing boats. This was a twice-a-year event for them—their anniversary and Christmas Eve. After Chad was born, they brought him along.

She could still see his face, framed by short blond hair, peering into the portable tanks. "That's the one, right there. He's just my size."

The fisherman had lifted the lobster. "This one right here?"

"Yeah." Chad's voice sounded unsure. He looked toward Andie and blinked.

The fisherman squatted so that he was nose to nose with Chad. "You've got a good eye, little man. That's the one I was thinking of taking home myself. It's the best of the whole bunch."

Chad beamed. "Hear that, Mom and Dad? He said I got a good eye!"

This year, Andie had bought the lobster alone. Still, she had expected Blair to show up and help cook them. They always did it as a team. She sank into a chair.

Another glance out the window revealed nothing. She decided to swallow her pride and call his office. She didn't want to beg him to come home, but maybe their anniversary, of all nights, was the time to try a little harder.

Neil Parker answered on the second ring. "No, Mrs. Phelps, he's not here."

"Are you sure he's not in his office?"

"I saw him leave about two o'clock. I'm the last one in the building and am just about to lock up now."

"Oh, well, uh . . . thank you, Neil."

Andie hung up the phone and walked straight to her car. She needed to get out of the house for a while.

She drove along the coast, barely seeing the world around her. She looked onto the ocean at the lights twinkling from the offshore oil platforms. From her vantage point, they looked like glittering towers instead of the reality of steel and grease and rust. Just like her marriage. Blair had all but left her after Chad's death. Since the discovery of that envelope at Lake Cachuma, their relationship had become a sad husk of a thing, empty and dry.

She finally forced herself to drive back to her empty home. Maybe she'd pull out a DVD and spend the evening on the couch.

When the garage door opened, Blair's car sat parked in its spot. What excuse would he have this time? She steeled herself, prepared to let him know she knew the truth. No story about research was going to get him off the hook this time.

The sound of running water came from upstairs. He was probably in the shower. Another bad sign. What did he feel he needed to be cleansed of? The images the question painted across her mind left her nauseated. Time to confront this head on. But how? Maybe she'd start by playing dumb and go from there.

She walked up the stairs, sat on the chair beside the bed, and waited. She heard the shower turn off, then water running in the sink. Shaving? Brushing his teeth?

The door slid open and Blair walked through, wrapped in a towel. He stopped when he saw her. "There you are. Where have you been?"

Driving around wondering where you were, but that little admission won't get us to the truth, will it? "Doing a little shopping. How about you?"

He sauntered into his walk-in closet. "Doing a little working." His attempt at humor twisted in Andie's stomach.

"Just now getting off?"

Blair emerged from the closet, stuffing his leg into a pair of tan pants. When he looked toward her, Andie saw the alarm flick through his eyes. The question had been enough to put him on alert. "I had a lot to do." He continued to watch her evenly, obviously waiting to see if he got a reaction.

"That's what Neil said."

That got him.

His lower right jaw began to twitch, a sure sign he was under pressure. He stared at her for another moment, then walked back into his closet. "When did you talk to Neil?"

His tone was conversational—a little too much so. He knew he'd been caught.

"I called the office. He told me he was the only one there and about to lock up. Said you'd been gone for several hours."

Blair returned to his closet and came out pulling a sweater over his damp hair. "I'm going to have to talk to Neil. It's getting more and more difficult to surprise my wife these days."

Or lie to her? "I'm sure it is."

He walked out of the room. The sound of his footsteps faded down the stairs, then the door to the garage squeaked open.

Just like that. He had walked out.

Andie was too numb to feel anymore. She simply stared at the wall, the realization of what had just happened floating somewhere outside her immediate consciousness.

Then the door squeaked again and the footsteps retraced their path. Blair walked into the room and stood before her, hands behind his back. "I was planning to give you this later, but since you've caught me red-handed, perhaps now is a better time."

He pulled a small rectangular box from behind his back, wrapped in the Tiffany's signature light blue. "I left early and did a little shopping of my own. Here, this is for you."

Andie took it in her hands but did not open it. The white bow blurred into a blob through the tears that doused her eyes. "You didn't have to do that."

He came to sit beside her on the bed. "Yes. I did. I know I've been hard to live with for the last few months. I've lost Chad; I don't want to lose you, too."

Andie threw herself against his chest. How she had longed for some words of comfort—of love—from him. This moment was so sweet, she didn't want to disrupt it by opening the present.

He wrapped his arms around her and kissed her on the top of the head. "Open it up. When you go to your next charity meeting, your friends will be so dazzled, they'll go home and ask their husbands, 'Why can't you be more like Blair?'"

Andie laughed and wiped her eyes. "Somehow I doubt that." She opened the box.

Sparkles reflected through the room when the light hit the bracelet. Gold Xs linked together, with square-cut diamonds studding every inverted corner, effectively surrounding each X with diamonds.

Blair lifted it out of the box. "Which arm?"

Andie extended her right wrist and watched him latch the clasp. He twirled it once around her arm. "There. Beautiful."

"So beautiful." Shame squelched the joy of the unexpected gift. "Blair, I'm sorry. I shouldn't jump to conclusions."

"The last months have been hard for both of us. I know I'm not doing much to help matters. This bracelet is my promise that I'm going to try harder."

"I will, too." She held her hand aloft and watched the play of the light off the colorless stones. The gold looked so smooth she reached up to touch it. "We better get started on the lobster."

Blair smacked himself on the forehead. "The lobster! How could I have forgotten? So much for doing better, huh?" He ran his hands through his wet hair. "Do you think they're still alive?"

"Maybe."

"I've got an idea."

He led her down to the garage, opened the cooler's lid, and peeked inside. "Yep, they're still moving."

"So what's the great idea?"

He smiled and pointed inside the cooler. "To celebrate our anniversary, let's give these little guys their freedom. What do you think? They might be too far gone to make it, but at least we'll give them a chance—which is more than they would have had." He looked at her, his eyes twinkling with mischief.

Andie smiled, feeling a small warmth of hope begin to seep into her. She welcomed the reprieve from the chill. "Great idea."

They drove down to East Beach. The volleyball courts stood silent and empty in the glow of the moon and early rising stars.

Blair tilted his head toward the ocean. "Let's leave our shoes in the car." He removed socks and shoes, then rolled up his pant legs. "I'll take these guys into the water. No need for both of us to come down with frostbite."

They walked to the water's edge together; then Blair waded in up to his knees. He lifted the crustaceans high above his head. "Little lobsters, long may you live in harmony and freedom." He dropped them into the water and returned to the shore, then lifted his right hand toward the ocean. "Go in peace."

chapter **twenty-four**

"Melanie, I don't think we can ignore this problem any longer."

Melanie's arm stopped halfway through the sleeve of her jacket. Apparently she wouldn't be going home just yet. "What problem?"

She had not told Carl about any of the troubles she'd experienced over the last couple weeks. She hoped they would eventually die down and did not want to burden him with the squabbles of the employees.

"The price changes, the signage. I haven't said anything until now because I assumed you were just nervous and settling in. I hoped these issues would eventually come around. According to your references, your postings were flawless at your old position."

"And they are this time. I always triple check them. What errors have you found?"

"Come into my office."

Melanie followed the man into his office, wondering what form of sabotage had befallen her this time.

"I just made a walk through the store. Several signs were on the wrong items, and several more had the wrong prices on them. I know we've had several complaints from customers about prices incorrectly posted."

He lifted a sign from his desk. "Look. This was in front of the store-brand coffee. It says ninety-nine cents a pound."

Melanie leaned forward. "It also says Red Delicious apples at the bottom. Mr. Brown, I put that sign in the correct spot not more than two hours ago. Ask Freddy—he was stocking the apples when I did it."

"Why, then, do you suppose I found it four aisles over? Did it magically transport itself?"

"I don't know. The same way . . ." She stopped herself. She didn't want to go into all the other stuff now. It would seem like an excuse.

"The same way, what?" He sank down into his seat. "The same way someone got into your locker? The same way someone took a knife to your four tires?"

"How did you know all that?"

"I may not say much, but I am not deaf, and most certainly am not dumb. I've been seeing what's been going on here since you arrived. You never came to me about it, so I never broached the subject."

"Do you know who's doing it?"

"No. That's another reason I didn't bring it up. I've given repeated general warnings, but until I know who's doing this, there's not much I can do."

"If you know about all that, then surely you understand that I am not the person putting the signs in the wrong places."

"When this first started happening, I immediately suspected something was wrong. I called Mr. Mortensen at your old store, and he confirmed that your sign placement was always perfect. So that tells me we have a different kind of problem on our hands. I'm not sure what we can do about it."

"I'm hoping that whoever is behind all this will eventually tire of it and go on about his or her business."

"That was my hope, as well, but I don't see that happening. Do you?"

Melanie shook her head. "Mr. Brown, when my son died, the worse thing that could possibly happen to me happened. Having to change jobs, driving extra, putting up with someone's vicious pranks is not fun, but I can handle it. Maybe after I've been here long enough to establish friendships, we will find out who's behind all this. I'm prepared to stick it out, though."

Carl nodded, his eyes drooping. "I'm sure you are. I know the past couple months have been a nightmare for you. And the way you have been treated by some of your co-workers has not helped. But . . . I can't have my entire store suffering for it. I've talked to upper management about our situation. Alfords is opening a brand-new store in Orange County next month. I've recommended they hire you as a floor manager. It has been approved."

He looked at Melanie with the glow of expectation in his eyes. The job offered would mean a promotion and more money. Of course he expected her to be excited. Thrilled, even. She wasn't. "I don't know what to say."

"Words always escape me in the face of good news, too."

"Carl, I appreciate very much the way you looked out for me. But I can't take that job."

He sighed. "You're surprised, that's all. Don't make any decisions now. Take a little time and think about it. The pay would be better; Alfords would help with moving expenses. There is an excellent public school system there. I think it is the opportunity of a lifetime for you."

"But I can't move."

"Change is hard, but sometimes it is for the best."

"Sometimes it's not."

His head snapped back. He stared at her evenly, then began to speak in a soothing voice. "Of course no one wants to relocate their school-age children, but sometimes it can't be helped. I want you to think about it. Things may get worse around here. Eventually I may have no choice but to take some sort of action. Make this move now while you have a brighter opportunity to replace it. Hmm?"

When Melanie stood, the walls of the room seemed to spin around her. She held the chair-back for support. "I'll . . . I'll think about it."

"Good. We'll talk more in a few days, then. Have a good night."

Melanie very much doubted that would be the case.

The long drive home was a welcome relief. It gave Melanie time to think. Alone.

She couldn't relocate.

It wouldn't be fair to Sarah. It wouldn't be fair to Jeff—no matter what Jake and the others thought about it. Jeff was still in Santa Barbara, and that's where she needed to be. With her son. She kept her promises!

Still, she doubted her job would last for long in Thousand Oaks, not the way things were going. It wouldn't be long until she was forced to move on, whether or not she wanted to. Better to act now while she still had choices.

If she could hold out until the lawsuit was resolved, she would have the financial ability to wait and think things through. But what would she do in the meantime? What had Les told her? This was a "fast-track" case, and the trial should be held within a year. Well, that still left the next ten months.

She picked up her cell phone and called a number she now knew by heart. This surprised her, but so did a lot of things these days.

Les answered on the second ring. "Melanie, I was just about to call you."

"You were?"

"Yes. Things are starting to move along now."

"Really? Has something happened?" Relief flooded her. Perhaps it wouldn't be even ten months. Perhaps her freedom would come much sooner.

"Yes. The Phelps' attorney filed a cross complaint today."

"Cross complaint? What's that?" Funny, it didn't sound too much like something that was going to end all this.

"It's the legal process in motion."

The fact that he answered in vague terms rather than specifics let her know this was something she was not going to like. "You didn't answer my question. What does that *mean,* a cross complaint?"

"Well, basically, they are saying that their son was not at fault."

A car horn blared from behind her. Only then did Melanie realize she had stomped on the brakes.

"How could they say that? Of course he was. What do they think happened, an earthquake shoved the two cars together?"

"Well, that's what a cross complaint is. They say it wasn't their son at fault; they say it was Jeff."

The silver Corolla pulled up beside her. A middle-aged man in a short-sleeved button-down screamed through his closed window. His face glowed red and his lips kept moving, even as he started to pass her.

Melanie was grateful for the glass that separated them. She knew plenty well what he was saying, but at least she didn't have to hear it.

She pulled over to the shoulder, slammed the car into park, and flung the door open. "Jeff?" She walked around the car and found a large rock and flung it against the steep embankment.

"Jeff? They are trying to accuse *Jeff* of this?" She picked up another rock. Then another, each time picturing some fancy house belonging to the Phelps family as the target.

After about the fifth rock, she had released enough anger to realize she'd left Les hanging on the phone—the phone still in her car. She kicked up a cloud of dust and pebbles, screaming words not unlike those the Corolla driver had used. "How could they do this?" She climbed back into the car and picked up the phone. "Les, are you still there?"

"Melanie? Are you hurt? Do I need to call for help?"

"No, there wasn't an accident. I pulled over and let off some steam." She banged her hand against her steering wheel. "You know, I actually had a little bit of sympathy for that family until now. Now I want to take them to court and take away everything they've ever had. How dare they even imply that Jeff was at fault?"

"You need to calm down. I told you, this is the way the game is played."

"So you're saying this is just a bluff? They won't really try to prove Jeff was at fault?"

"It's a bluff, more or less. But they will come up with highly qualified experts to back up some portion of their cross com-plaint. It's just part of the process."

Melanie took one last deep breath. "The process stinks. If you ask me, the Wild West had a better system. They just took out the bad guys and strung them up."

"Yes, but how many innocent people do you think got strung up before they realized they should have maybe had a bit more discussion? Don't worry. We'll make it through all this. We'll prevail. We just have to stay the course in the meanwhile."

"Yeah, well, I've got to get back on the road. I'll talk to you again in a few days." Melanie pulled back onto the 101, still shaking. She couldn't believe how warped the whole process had become.

She approached the Santa Barbara city limits. *The transfer.* She'd completely forgotten to ask Les about the time frame. Maybe this new development would grant her financial independence a little sooner.

Melanie's stomach cranked on something bitter. Financial independence?

This was not about the money.

chapter **twenty-five**

March 24 dawned clear and warm. Andie wandered the halls of her empty house. Alone. The sheer size echoed with the quietness all around. She finally found her way to her little studio and collapsed in a seat.

Blair's anniversary commitment—made two days ago—had lasted only a few hours. He'd worked until late last night, and today, Saturday, he had gone in again. On Thursday he had promised to take her out for a nice dinner tonight to make up for the lobster. She wondered if he would forget this dinner, too.

She stared sightlessly at the art supplies lining the walls. She thought of years past and began to cry. Blair had moved out of her reach. Finally, she ambled into the kitchen.

The piles of paperwork from her various charities gave her more than enough to keep busy. She picked up a stack concerning the Fair, but it only depressed her. The Fair was the only thing that mattered anymore, and she was banned from doing anything. She couldn't even honor Chad or her mother now. They had taken that from her.

Several hours later, a gnawing hunger called her attention to the fact that she had not eaten all day. She glanced at her watch. Two-thirty.

Blair had left that morning without eating breakfast or packing a lunch. He must be hungry. She would make sandwiches, cut up some fruit, and take a small quilt. They could have their own picnic on the floor of his office. Maybe it would be just the thing to begin to work through the barrier between them. Maybe he would remember about his promise.

Maybe she just needed to prove to herself that he really was there.

When she arrived, the empty parking lot didn't surprise her. It was Saturday, after all. The door was locked—as she'd expected.

She knocked. Then again. The doors shook from the blows, but still nothing.

Blair probably couldn't hear her from his upstairs office. She pulled her cell phone out of her purse and dialed the direct line to his desk. The call was transferred to voice mail.

Maybe he was working in the computer lab or the conference room. She dialed the main number, and this time she could hear the ring of the phone inside the door. Still no answer.

She walked down the outside steps and peered through the bars of the underground parking garage. Empty.

The metal bars of the gate seemed to expand and shrink in time with her pulse. She focused on deep breathing and looked away. *Think.* Okay, they had been through this kind of misunderstanding before, and she knew there had to be a logical explanation. Blair wouldn't lie to her.

She called his cell phone, anxious to hear the answer. He picked up on the second ring. "Andie. Hi. I'm glad you called. Listen, don't wait dinner on me, I'm plowing through the pile on my desk. I don't think I'll be home until late."

"So you're still at work? At your office?"

"Of course at my office. Where else would I be?"

In the background, Andie heard a female voice purr, "Who's that you're talking to?"

Blair quickly cut in. "I've got to get back to it." The phone went dead.

———

Jake leaned forward in an effort to get the broom farther beneath his desk.

"How many times you gonna sweep that floor tonight?"

He jumped at the sound of Tony's voice behind him, causing the broom handle to snap against the underside of his desk. It jerked from his hands. "Ouch."

"Jeff's mom must be coming, huh?"

Jake picked up the broom and scowled. "I don't know what you're talking about."

"Oh, come on. Every time you know she's coming, you clean everything ten times and make a fresh pot of coffee. Last time you even changed shirts. You can save that 'I don't know what you're talking about' noise for some other sucker. I know better."

Jake leaned against his desk. The papers there suddenly seemed to demand his full attention. "Get out of here. I've got work to do." He leaned the broom against the wall and forced himself to leave the pile of dust in the middle of the floor. He flopped into his desk chair and stared at his antagonist, daring him to say more.

Tony walked away from the door, but the sound of his laughter lingered far behind him. *Darn that kid!* Only when he was certain Tony was out of sight did Jake pick up the dustpan, sweep up the mess, and take the broom out to its hook in the shop.

Before he made it back to his office, she arrived, looking tired.

"Let's go back to my office. Do you want some coffee? I always make a pot of decaf this time of the afternoon."

Unfortunately, since they were in the middle of the shop, Tony witnessed their interchange. He had his back turned to them, working on some engine part, but Jake could see his shoulders heave and the redness of his ears. "Tony, why don't you go clean up the back workshop?"

Tony's face was bright red when he turned around. He nodded but didn't respond. Jake knew he was holding his breath to suppress laughter. He hoped the kid made it to the back room before he passed out from lack of oxygen.

Melanie walked into the office and sat down. "You get a new chair?" She leaned into the padded back and rubbed her hand across the textured fabric.

"Nah, just had this one stuck back in a corner somewhere—decided I'd pull it out." Thankful that Tony was out of earshot for the second of his little fibs, Jake vowed to stick with the truth from here on out. "Sarah tells me you're having some trouble at work."

Melanie sighed and suddenly looked ten years older. "Yes. They want me to transfer to a store in Orange County."

"Really? Do you want to go?"

"Can't. I'll have to try and find something else around here, I suppose."

"Why? Maybe it would be good to make a clean start—for you and Sarah, too. She'd make new friends. Your grief might be less if you couldn't—"

Her head snapped in the direction of the door.

"Sorry. I don't mean to keep bringing that up. I just wish I understood it more." The muscles in his legs tensed, prepared to make chase.

The seconds ticked past as she continued to stare at the door. Then she leaned back against the seat and folded her arms. "I was abandoned." The words hung in the air, thick and raspy. She turned toward him, her eyebrows raised, waiting for a response.

He felt his head fall forward, his eyebrows knit, but he couldn't stop either. "Excuse me?"

She leaned toward him. "When I was two years old. I was left on the front steps of the Tennessee Children's Home. They never found out who my parents were."

He let her words tumble through his mind, hoping eventually the spinning would stop and they would fall into an order that made some sort of sense. Hoping he would have some words of wisdom to make it seem okay. "Wow." It was the only thing that came out.

The left side of her mouth twitched in wry humor. "Speechless? This is a first."

The lightness helped him regain his composure enough to ask the next question. "As tragic as that is, I still don't understand what it has to do with Jeff's grave."

Her jaw dropped, and she shook her head as if he were a total nincompoop. "I will never, *ever*, abandon my kids. I want Jeff to know I'm still here for him." She leaned back and folded her arms. "Now you know. Happy?"

"Melanie, he's not abandoned. He's with God."

"So *you* say."

"It's true! Just let me tell—"

"Time for a change of subject." She pulled one knee up and wrapped her hands around it. "I've told you my story, now let's hear yours. You keep alluding to this *past* of yours, but I don't see any evidence—except for the fact that I'd expect someone like you to be married with kids."

"Well, I . . ." He shook his head. "It's a long story."

"Fair is fair. Let's hear it." There was no teasing in her eyes. She was testing to see if he would be as open with her as she had been with him. If he failed now, her time of trust was over.

"I was. Married . . . I mean." He looked at her, then at his hands. "Same as you, I guess—we were young and wild. I got sent to Folsom for a few years. She cleaned up her act, met someone else. She wanted a divorce and . . ." *Okay, we don't need to go any further with this story.*

"And what?"

He knew he needed to tell her the truth, but his throat had gone so dry he didn't think he could speak.

"We all make mistakes in our lives. I've made some really big ones."

"And what?"

"Custody."

"Kids? You have kids?" He watched her eyes dart toward his desk, then the walls, looking for evidence. She wouldn't find any. There was none to find.

"Yes. When I had over a year left to serve, I signed papers authorizing their stepfather to adopt them. I knew I had messed my life up in a big way and hoped maybe this new guy would be better for them. It was before I learned about grace, forgiveness. Before I could forgive myself."

She stood, her arms stiff at her side. "You abandoned your own children?"

"I did what I thought was best for them."

Tears spilled from her eyes. "I can't believe I actually admired you." She jerked her purse from the floor and stormed out the door. She slammed it so hard behind her the entire garage shook.

Jake buried his face in his hands. This time he had blown it for good. *God, why? Why would you keep bringing her around, just to have me mess things up a little more every time I'm near her?*

The heaviness of loss pressed against him with new weight. He couldn't lift himself above it this time. He was sinking. *God, I can't do it anymore.*

"Guess it didn't go so well, huh?" Tony stood smiling at the door. He took one look at Jake's face and turned around. "I'll just get back to cleaning the warehouse."

"You do that."

———

Melanie couldn't believe she had actually admired Jake. What a fake. The man had abandoned his own children, just like her parents had left her on the steps all those years ago.

She drove into the cemetery and parked in the usual spot. As she walked toward Jeff, the view blurred through tears. She sank down onto the ground beside her son's headstone. "How're you doing, bud?"

She reached out her hand and touched the cold granite. "Oh, Jeff. How I miss you. How I—" A sob worked its way up from her heart and out her throat. She'd always made it a point not to cry in front of him. This time, she couldn't stop herself.

"I'm sorry, Jeff." The tears continued, blurring her vision into a blob of green that might just have easily been a meadow on a spring day. But that's not where she was. She sniffled. "I'm weak, Jeff—always have been, if you want to know the truth. I tried to hide that from you in your life, and even since your death. But you might as well know it now. Your mother is a weakling and a coward."

She wiped her eyes, but the tears continued to pour. "Don't worry, though. I'm still working for you. I'm taking this thing into court to save the life of another child. You'd want that, wouldn't you? To have your death work good for someone else?"

She traced the letters on the marker with her index finger. JEFF JOHNSTON. She looked at the dates—entirely too close from the beginning year to the end. Her gaze wandered farther down at the verse inscribed on the bottom. Although she had seen it many times, she'd never thought much about the words. To her, it was simply Jeff's favorite verse and the way he would want to be remembered. *That our God may count you worthy of his calling, and that by his power he may fulfill every good purpose of yours and every act prompted by your faith. 2 Thessalonians 1:11.*

Every good purpose, every act prompted by your faith. "What would those be for you, Jeff? Why would God, if there really is a God, take you out of this world before you had a chance to fulfill your purpose?"

She stood to her feet and stumbled back to her car. There were no answers for her questions.

———

Andie drove away from Blair's office thinking of all the times he'd berated her for questioning his absences due to "research," and even the time he'd supposedly been shopping for her. Shopping. She looked down at the bracelet on her wrist, and it suddenly became clear exactly what it was. A guilt offering. She reached down to rip it from her wrist.

She held the steering wheel with her elbows and began to work the clasp. A teenage boy on a skateboard darted in front of her. She jammed her foot against the brake and grabbed the wheel with both hands. The scene slowly unfolded before her as her car moved closer and closer to the oblivious boy. Her tires squealed to a stop not six inches away from him. Only then did he look at her, wires from hidden earbuds visible for the first time.

He flicked up his middle finger and screamed at her. "Watch it, lady. You'll kill someone driving like that."

She had almost been responsible for the death of another teenage boy. *Oh, dear God, help me.* She pulled into the closest parking lot, a hardware store, and laid her head against the wheel. She needed to regain her composure before she attempted any more driving.

Oh yes. The bracelet. She lifted her head and completed the removal. There was no doubt now. Blair had been caught. The only question that remained was what she was going to do about it.

Remembering her resolve to quit acting as a doormat, she decided to confront him. She would demand the complete truth. Was Blair in love with someone else, or was he using this other woman to numb his grief? Did he blame Andie and want to punish her?

She drove home, her eyes constantly scanning the side of the road for pedestrians—that was one near-miss she didn't plan to repeat. When she parked in her garage, she'd never been so thankful to arrive safely home.

The sun set and the full moon appeared in the star-filled sky. Their beauty would normally inspire her to want to paint something. Tonight they screamed at her like a lie. Tonight she just saw how tiny they were. A pinpoint of hope in a void so big she couldn't help but get dizzy beneath it. She'd never really looked into the emptiness before, truly looked, but tonight when she did, she recognized it. It was her. Her home. Her marriage. Her life. Empty and cold, and not even the glint of Blair's gift could warm it.

Sometime during the 2:00 a.m. movie she fell asleep on the living room sofa. At six, she awoke to the sound of movement. The door from the garage squeaked open. Andie turned her back to the hallway. She heard the sound of Blair's footsteps going up the stairs. In a few minutes, she heard them return. "Andie?"

She didn't answer. She heard his footsteps growing closer. He touched her shoulder. "There you are. Must have been a good movie."

When she opened her eyes and looked up at him, he raked his hands across his bloodshot eyes. "Sorry I'm so late getting home. I worked until almost two o'clock, then fell asleep on the couch in my office. I'm going to get some sleep. You can make it to church without me today, huh?"

"Sure."

He stumbled from the room, apparently unaware—or perhaps he just didn't care—that she was angry. *Okay, time for a new plan.*

chapter twenty-six

"You'd better hurry and get dressed or we'll be late." Sarah looked across the breakfast table, hope shining in her eyes.

Melanie took a sip of coffee. "I'm kind of tired. I think I'll skip church today."

"Mo-o-om." Sarah drew the word out into three syllables to fully demonstrate her displeasure.

"Sa-r-rah." Melanie lifted the paper so she didn't have to see the spark fading in her daughter's eyes. It would only fan the flames of guilt. The story on the latest natural disaster in Africa looked interesting, but Sarah's sad face superseded it.

"You've been up for three hours. How can you suddenly be too tired to get ready for church? This is not about tired."

"I said I'm tired, and that's the end of it."

"Sure it is." Sarah shoved her chair back from the table and stormed from the room, leaving her half-eaten bowl of cereal behind.

Melanie bit back the demand that her daughter return to the table, finish her breakfast, and clean up the mess. As much as she wanted to do it, the feeling that she was somehow the one at fault kept her quiet. Still, there were ways to behave. Proper ways. And Melanie had seen too often what happened when children got to act any way they wanted.

She stood and walked to the closed door of Sarah's room. She raised her hand to knock, but couldn't bring herself to do it. That nagging guilt wouldn't let her. You couldn't punish someone for pointing out your lies, and Melanie knew it wasn't exhaustion that kept her from church. She was hiding. Resigned, she turned and walked back into the kitchen, where she picked up Sarah's bowl, washed it out, and put it in the dishwasher. A peace offering. Satisfied that she'd done her part, she sat back at the table and made a point of looking at the paper when Sarah came through a few minutes later.

The unmistakable beep of Beth's mother's car sounded in the driveway. Sarah must have called her from her room.

"Have a nice time."

The door squeaked open. "Yeah, whatever."

Melanie's mouth opened, but she clamped it shut. One thing she had learned in dealing with teenagers was that sometimes it was best to let things cool down for a while. She would *not* tolerate sass, but she would postpone a little mother-daughter talk until Sarah returned home.

She wandered around the house aimlessly for a while after Sarah's departure, feeling miserable for reasons she didn't fully understand. The pile of laundry overflowing from the hamper pulled her back into reality. There were plenty of things that needed doing. One thing a single mother was never allowed was time to mope.

She dove into the pile of laundry, cleaned the bathrooms and the kitchen, then ran the vacuum. Last, she picked up a dustrag and walked into Jeff's room. *Two months.* Actually, it had been two and a half months since her son last set foot in this room, yet the memories were so strong she still expected him to come walking through the door at any minute, declaring the whole thing a bad joke or, perhaps, a terrible dream.

His lanky frame would saunter in any minute now, just like he had at Christmas.

She could still smell the cinnamon candles, still see his boyish face, hear the happiness in his voice. "Merry Christmas, Mom." He held out a package wrapped in red paper. "Sorry I didn't have any money to get you a real gift." The lights twinkled on the tree behind him.

"Oh, Jeff, you know I don't need anything." She had opened the oblong package and found a framed 8 x 10 photo of Jeff and Sarah standing in the surf at Goleta Beach. Tears stung her eyes. "Oh, this is perfect." And it was.

Jeff hugged her, then whispered loud enough for Sarah to hear. "It'd been a lot better without the chick, but I couldn't get rid of her. You know what I mean?"

Sarah had thrown a stuffed reindeer at him—a leftover from her childhood that she still carried around all through the holidays. A full-blown pillow fight had ensued, until all three of them had collapsed in laughter.

Melanie looked at the picture of them at Knott's Berry Farm from last summer Jeff had kept on his desk. So much joy and hope. So much love. So much *faith.*

The word startled Melanie because she realized what a big part of Jeff it was. And she'd been forgetting it.

The sound of a car in the driveway forced Melanie from the room. She closed the door carefully behind her and dumped the dustrag in the laundry pile on her bedroom floor. She steeled herself for the battle ahead with Sarah.

The doorbell rang. The front door was not locked, and even if it was, Sarah had a key. This was a step too far. Melanie had given her space and time to settle down, but now her daughter pushed her too far. Melanie rushed down the hall and jerked the door open, her face heating. "Sarah Johnston, this is not—"

Trish's eyes startled at Melanie's outburst, but she quickly recovered her composure.

Melanie's face flushed hot, this time from embarrassment. "Trish. I thought you were Sarah."

The corner of Trish's mouth twitched. "So I gathered." She stood, waiting.

"What brings you here?"

"Lunch."

"What?"

"Lunch. The other women are going to meet us at the restaurant. I gave them my order, and since you always eat the same thing, they are placing yours, too. Chop, chop. We've got to get moving or our food will get cold."

"Trish, I didn't come to church today."

"Well, duh. I wouldn't be standing on your front porch right now if you did, now, would I? A deal is a deal. We've made a vow to hang with you every Sunday until the trial, and I, for one, intend to keep my end of the bargain. Now, come on. You can ride with me."

Melanie looked down at the old T-shirt and pair of sweats she was wearing. "I'm not dressed."

"I'll give you one minute. After that, I'm dragging you out, regardless."

"But I—"

"Fifty-five seconds." Trish put her hands on her hips and tapped her foot.

"But, Sarah—"

"Already at the restaurant with her friends. Fifty seconds."

"Okay, okay. Come in and have a seat while I change." Trish followed her inside while Melanie rushed back to her room in search of jeans and a decent shirt. She threw on a button-up shirt and her favorite pair of Levi's. What was it about these people that they wouldn't take no for an answer? They just kept coming around trying to help, no matter what she did. Didn't they ever give up?

The realization hit her. They were like Jeff. He always saw the good in people. Always went the extra mile to support someone he felt needed help. Maybe there was something to that faith thing after all.

———

Blair woke, groggy, eyelids heavy as granite. His face felt hammered in, his tongue was dried to the roof of his mouth, and the slightest movement twisted his stomach with nausea. A small joke from his fraternity hangovers resurfaced; guys would ask, "You get the license plate of the truck that ran me over?" His stomach surged. How could that have been funny?

He sat up and rubbed his head. What time was it? He looked toward the clock on the bedside table. One-fifteen.

Andie must be home from church by now. He lowered his legs over the side of the bed, planning to go talk to her.

No. Wait. Better to shower first. Two staggering steps and his foot snagged on his shirt, hastily discarded in the middle of the floor. He stumbled, and this time the motion was too much. He ran to the bathroom and emptied the contents of his stomach, praying Andie wouldn't suddenly decide to come check on him.

After a minute or three on the tile, he stood, splashed cold water on his face, then brushed his teeth. When he looked at the mirror, his reflection shocked him. Pale and stubbled, he looked like he belonged on lower State Street, cup in his hand, a sign on his lap. He stumbled into the shower, letting cool water wash over him. Slowly, his mind began to rouse, but as it did, the shooting pain in his head worsened. Maybe getting up was a mistake.

Eventually he got out, managed to throw on a pair of jeans and a T-shirt, then edged down the stairs, one step at a time, clutching the rails for support. The floor below appeared almost fluid, undulating like the waves on a shore.

When he reached the bottom, he took a cautious step. Solid. Good. He practiced his excuse for Andie and walked in the general direction of the coffeepot. The kitchen, along with the rest of the house, stood dark and apparently empty. Andie must have gone to lunch with some friends after church. Just as well. It would give him a little more time to get his act together. He'd microwave some leftover coffee and be good to go by the time she returned.

He picked up the carafe. It was empty. Odd. Andie never went anywhere without at least one cup.

An engine revved up the drive, intensifying the pain in Blair's head. Only one person screeched like that. Great. Andie must be bringing Christi home with her from church. All he needed right now was to listen to incessant female chatter. Maybe he'd make up an excuse about having to get to work.

He watched Christi's car skid to a stop outside the kitchen window, his plan of escape slowly pulling together in his mind. She climbed out of the car. Alone.

Unnoticed in the dark kitchen, Blair watched her stride toward the back door. Her rapid steps caused the scarf she wore around her neck to flap behind her, like the Bloody Red Baron in his flying Fokker. Yep, it fit her. Even the car was the right color. She tried the lock, then pounded on the door with a bit too much enthusiasm. The sound shot pain through his skull.

He would have ignored her knocks and stayed hidden in the darkness, but he knew better. Christi would knock on every window and door in the house until either someone answered or she was satisfied there was truly no one home. Better to get her out of here as quickly as possible. He eased himself forward and cracked the door.

"Oh," she said, seeping with disapproval. "There you are."

"Yes, here I am. What do you need?"

"Came to check on Andie. She sick?"

"She hasn't made it home from church yet. Must have gone to lunch."

"Hasn't made it home from church? She didn't *come* to church. *That's* why I'm here. Made my random appearance, and no Andie. She okay?"

He wasn't ready for this. Dread tugged at his stomach, which wasn't even close to strong enough this morning. He winced. Meanwhile, Christi stood on her toes and strained to look over his shoulders. She was one pushy piece of work. "Christi, I told you, she's not here."

Christi continued trying to look around him. "Well, where is she?"

"I'm not sure."

For the first time since this conversation started, Christi actually looked at him. Her lips scrunched together and her eyes narrowed. "You sick?"

"I worked late." *Not that it's any of your business.*

She lifted an eyebrow and folded her arms across her chest. "Um-hmm. Tell her to call me when she gets home."

"Yep."

She pivoted on one foot and stalked back to her car. Her engine roared to life and she screeched down the drive.

Blair walked back into the kitchen, picked up the phone, and dialed Andie's cell. It connected immediately to her voice mail. He hung up without leaving a message.

He walked over to the message board. As with most of her things, it was so cluttered he couldn't tell if a note had been left for him or not. He thumbed through the assorted notices tacked to the corkboard, his hopes dying with each layer. Nothing.

Her studio. He rushed down the small hallway, the apprehension mounting, and looked into the room. Empty. Its usual state of disarray proved totally uninformative. He searched every room in the house. "Andie?" The door to the hall bathroom was closed. He knocked. "Andie?"

No answer. He tried to slide the door open, but it was locked. Panic zoomed through him at full speed. What had she done?

"Andie!" He pulled against the door, but it was useless. He ran into the kitchen, got a knife, and used it to trip the latch. He flung open the door, his heart pounding, dreading what he was about to see.

Empty.

Only then did he remember Andie's comment earlier in the week about that lock sticking. His heart rate surged, the excess blood crushed his head like a mallet. But at least the adrenaline finally snapped his mind fully into gear.

If she's not here, and she didn't go to church, where is she?

A piece of a thought began to nag at the back of his mind. His feet walked of their own accord up the stairs and back to their bedroom. He opened the door to Andie's closet. Scattered shoes filled every inch of the floor, shirts hung sideways, purses bulged over the top shelf—Andie's usual state of disorganization. How could she stand to live this way? A single bare spot drew his attention—a space just big enough to have held her small carry-on case. A space that stood vacant.

Andie had left him.

chapter **twenty-seven**

Andie had no idea where she was headed. The fact that she didn't want to see Blair right then was her only clear thought. Where could she go?

All the major hotels in the Santa Barbara area would be booked solid on such a beautiful spring weekend. But today was Sunday. Maybe she could find something. But which hotel?

More than anything, she wanted time alone so she could think. This made it necessary to get out of the downtown area. Still, she didn't want to go too far.

What about those cozy little cabins she'd seen out by El Capitán State Beach? She could rent one, take long walks on the sand, and think about what to do. It offered the privacy she needed.

She turned north onto Highway 101 and prayed they had availability. She arrived twenty minutes later and walked up the plank steps to the registration office.

"Yes, we have a lovely creek-side unit available for the next three nights. Mrs.—"

"Smith. Andrea Smith. I'll pay cash up front if that's okay."

The twentysomething girl behind the counter smiled. "Cash works for me." She typed into her computer screen, then placed the money in a drawer that had popped open. "Okay, here's your key. There's a small shop that serves coffee, and you can buy any sundries you might need there, as well. Our restaurant serves breakfast, lunch, and dinner. Drive across the bridge and park your car in the creek-side lot. Someone will pick you up in a cart momentarily. Enjoy your stay, Mrs. Smith."

"Thank you." Andie drove her car across the bridge and pulled her suitcase out of the passenger seat. Before she'd even closed the door, a golf cart drove up behind her. The young man behind the wheel appeared only a few years older than Chad, had the same intense blue eyes. Did he play baseball? Love the Dodgers? Hate school dances?

Drive too fast?

A sharp pain shot through her chest. *How many wounds can it take before it finally goes numb?*

"I'm Bruce. I'll get you to your cabin." He took the bag from her hand, oblivious to her state of mind, and tossed it in the back. "We drive these things around here all the time. If you ever want a lift back to your car, or to the restaurant, just flag one of us down." Andie took the passenger seat next to him, and the cart shot forward, winding its way over a packed dirt path through a wooded glen.

A minute or two later, they stopped outside a small wooden cabin. Only the wheels behind the bottom latticework revealed the truth. These were nicely dressed trailers.

Bruce carried her suitcase up the steps and opened the door to her unit. "There's your coffeepot and fridge. Thermostat's on the wall. The fire ring out front is all ready. Just strike a match and you're good to go. More wood is available for purchase at the general store if you decide you want to keep it going."

"Thanks."

"No problem. Have a nice stay." Bruce hopped back into the cart and sped away.

Andie collapsed into one of the rough-hewn wooden chairs on her front porch. She listened to the gurgle of the creek somewhere below, heard the chirping of the birds, and wondered what she was going to do now.

Should she leave Blair for good? She didn't have anywhere to go. And if she left, what would she do for a living? Her last paying job had been over seventeen years ago.

What could she put on a résumé? Three years working in an insurance office straight out of college? She had left that job over a year before Chad was born and didn't have the slightest idea about insurance workings these days.

She could stay with Blair. Stick it out. Seek counseling.

No. She would not stay simply to pay the bills. She knew too many women—businessmen's wives in town, politicians' wives on TV—who put up with cheating husbands for security and the promise of paid credit card bills. No, she would not do that.

She needed time to examine all the layers of issues involved. And she didn't want to talk to Blair at this point. She'd spend the next couple of days hidden away. Think. Pray.

Pray? What good has prayer ever done? She'd prayed for Chad every day of his life—that life had been cut much too short. She had prayed for her relationship with Blair, and he was having an affair. The realization began to slowly dawn on her. She was mad at God. Maybe she had been all along.

———

"Suppose you two better go to dinner without me." Christi's declaration irritated her more than a little. Sunday night was family-dinner-out night, with a careful rotation schedule of who chose the restaurant. She had endured the last two weeks, through Kelly's sushi and Scott's steakhouse. Tonight should be her turn.

Just thinking about Tupelo Junction made her mouth water. The gourmet Southern food was her favorite in all of Santa Barbara. Fried green tomatoes, squash hush puppies, free range fried chicken! In her tightly controlled menu of the regular week, Christi looked forward to her once-every-three-weeks deviation into the sinful. She sighed.

Kelly's face lit up. "Does this mean we can go to sushi?"

"Work that out with your father. But next week it's *my* turn."

Kelly shook her head. "I don't think so. When I missed a week because of the ski trip, I didn't get my time back."

"That was for pleasure. This is different."

Scott lifted some grapes from the fruit bowl and popped two into his mouth. "I'd be willing to bet that she's checked into the Bacara and is having a facial by now. I don't know what you're so worried about. It's not like Andie's the wild, adventurous type." He popped in three more grapes. "Either that, or she's back home by now, and she and Blair are so busy making up for whatever it was they fought about, they forgot to let you know."

"No. Blair's frantic. He's called me at least five times. He knows I'd kill him if she showed up and he didn't call."

Scott picked up his jacket from the chair in front of him. "What do you think, Kel? Shall we go get some California rolls?"

"Woo-hoo." Kelly danced out the door behind her father.

Christi picked up the phone and dialed Andie's cell, again. And as before, she got voice mail. She needed to do something—to get in her car and start looking for her friend. But where should she start?

She picked up her keys, determined to systematically drive to the most likely places. She'd start with the beach, then drive through the parking lot of all the nice hotels in the area. It was an inconvenience she wouldn't have to suffer if the desk clerks had been more helpful on the phone. All that blah blah about confidentiality made her sick.

No matter. Andie's car in the parking lot would tell the tale.

An hour into her search, Christi was driving toward the Bacara when her cell phone began playing jazz. She flipped it open and looked at the caller ID. "Andie, where are you? I've been worried to death. Gave up my Tupelo Junction night to go looking for you." Although she'd meant the last part as lighthearted, she realized how shallow it sounded as soon as the words were out.

"I . . . I've left Blair. Do you want to come talk?"

"Yes, I want to come talk. Where are you? Might take me a while—I'm all the way out at the Bacara, looking for you."

"You're pretty close, then."

Andie gave directions and hung up the phone. At least one thing was going right she wouldn't have far to drive. Five minutes later, Christi pulled into the parking lot. Before she stepped foot out of her car, a gorgeous young thing in a golf cart pulled up behind her. "Need a lift?"

Christi fluttered her eyes, a habit ever since Kappa Phi, and floated into the seat beside him. "Your place or mine?"

He laughed but didn't answer.

"Actually, I'm here to visit my friend. She's in 113."

"Oh, Mrs. Smith. I drove her to her cabin a while ago. She seemed melancholy."

Mrs. Smith? Apparently she's more upset than I thought. "Melancholy? Well, aren't you the poet. Either way, I'm here to cheer her up."

"Good deal. She's such a classy-looking lady."

Classy-looking. Lady. Those words summed up Andie quite well. Although she never seemed to see it in herself. "Don't worry. An hour with me and she'll be begging you to drive her around the facilities at top speed."

He smiled as the cart squeaked to a stop. "I look forward to that." Christi climbed out, and the dreamboat disappeared into the night, the gentle hum of the electric motor fading as he went.

"Were you flirting?"

Christi whirled around, startled. Her eyes adjusted to the darkness, and she could see Andie sitting on the front porch, rocking. In spite of her teasing words, there was no mistaking the tears in her voice.

"How could I help it? He's so adorable." Christi climbed the steps and squatted beside her friend. "So . . . what's up?"

"I've left Blair."

"So you said. Mind telling me why?"

Andie's chair creaked as she began to rock. "He's having an affair."

"Bull."

"Excuse me?"

"You heard me. Bull. Blair would never cheat on you. Every woman in town envies how much he loves you."

The chair stopped moving. "Let's go for a walk." Andie clomped down the stairs, leaving Christi no choice but to follow.

As they walked the dark gravel pathway, Christi made it a point to take high steps. It kept her from stumbling over the bigger rocks, and who knew what kind of critters might be lying around out here after dark? "Don't you want to go back to your cabin?"

"I've spent almost the whole day walking. Talking to God. Questioning Him. I don't understand any of it, but I keep feeling like He's telling me to trust Him."

"You'd know more about that kind of thing than I would. Tell me what's going on with Blair."

Andie told the story of the unexplained absences, the late nights, the blatant lie. "I heard another woman's voice. He came in at six o'clock in the morning, then said he'd been at the office the whole time. There's someone else." Andie's voice seemed filled with the same gravel that lined the road. "I've never been what he needed anyway. I'm a terrible housekeeper, I'm not very organized, I'm not particularly good at anything."

Christi stopped and dug in her feet. She grabbed Andie's arm and jerked her around. "That's a lie! Don't ever let me hear you say that again."

Andie pulled at her arm. "Every time you come to my house you either clean or organize something. I know I've never measured up to anyone's standards."

"Someone like you single-handedly came up with the idea for the Fair for the Cure. Someone like you has been on every committee for the school, church, and charity league that no one else wants to be on. Someone like you is the first to come around with chicken soup when I'm feeling sick."

"Don't you get it, though? I bring you Campbell's soup. You make a gourmet chicken stock with your own homegrown spices. I don't measure up."

"Andie Phelps, tomorrow I will deny I ever said this, but, well, we both know I'm way too uptight. I need someone like you to remind me to never sweat the small stuff, because to you, almost everything is small stuff. Usually, even when I'm doing something to help someone else, I'm thinking of what I'd rather be doing, while you give your undivided attention to anyone who has a need."

"Something else you'd rather be doing, like eating at Tupelo Junction?"

Christi knew she should be embarrassed by the truth, but it was what it was. "Exactly. See how shallow I am?" They both laughed, and it felt good to release the tension. "Have you called Blair to tell him where you are?"

"No. I don't want to talk to him. I need to sort some things out on my own."

"He needs to at least know you're safe. He's been a madman all afternoon, calling all over town."

"I'll just bet."

"Andie, he's called me half a dozen times wanting to know if I'd heard anything. I'm not exactly his favorite friend of yours, so you know he's got to be worried crazy if he's calling me."

"Kind of like I was at about two this morning, huh?"

"At least let him know you're alive."

"That's more courtesy than he showed me."

"Yes, and you're a bigger person than he is."

For the next half hour they walked and talked. They were all the way back to the cabin before Andie acquiesced. She opened the sliding glass door and walked inside. Christi stayed on the porch, to allow privacy.

Andie leaned out. "Come on in. I'm not going to talk to him long."

As Andie punched in the numbers, Christi could see her hands start to shake. She put the phone up to her ear and stared at the wall. The look in her eyes scared Christi. It was the same dead, flat expression she'd had after the accident.

Andie flinched. "It's me."

In a flash, her eyes took on some fire. Andie shook her head at whatever was being spoken on the other end. Christi was glad to see it. Better for her to rage against her husband than curl up and shrivel on the inside.

"You weren't so worried about where I was yesterday, were you?" Andie spat. She twisted her hair around her finger. "Really? Busy at your office? So was I. In fact, when I called you yesterday, that's where I called from."

She looked at Christi, rolled her eyes, and shook her head. "It's a little late for that. I'm taking a few days to think." She punched the button and flipped the phone shut. It began to ring again almost immediately. She hit the off button.

Wow. This was a new empowered Andie. "That was a thing of beauty. Let him twist awhile."

Christi looked around at the cabin. Some might call it charming, but she preferred more of a five-star version of charm. "Listen, if you want to spend a few days away from home, how about coming to our guesthouse? It's just sitting there empty."

"Blair might come looking for me there. Besides, I've already paid for three days."

"Don't you want to come back with me now?"

Andie shook her head. "No. Thanks. You get on home. I need some time alone." She slouched down on the bed. "Please don't tell anyone where I am."

"The one thing I *can* do is keep a secret. I'll be by to check on you tomorrow, okay?"

"You don't have to."

"I know. I want to." Christi hugged her friend with more emotion than she'd felt in a long time. She planned to go home right now and get started doing a little extra cleaning on the guesthouse. She would come back tomorrow and wouldn't leave until Andie agreed to stay there.

chapter twenty-eight

Melanie stole a quick glance over her shoulder at the assembled employees sitting in four rows of folding chairs. None of them knew what the big announcement was, but she did. She dreaded what was about to happen, but welcomed it, too.

Carl Brown walked toward the front of the room. He straightened his tie and cleared his throat. "Okay, everyone. Thanks for coming in early for this meeting. We have a few important details to discuss.

"By now, you all know Melanie Johnston. She's been with us for the last several weeks and has done an outstanding job. In fact, she has done such an outstanding job that Alfords has offered her a promotion to another position in Orange County."

A murmur went through the crowd. Were they angry that she got offered a promotion, or happy at the thought of getting rid of her? She wanted to look over her shoulder and see their faces, but pride wouldn't let her. No. She would pretend like everything was just fine.

Carl called the group back to attention. "I was saddened to learn that she has chosen not to accept the offer."

The resulting murmur this time was much louder. Melanie allowed a quick backward glance. Candace sat directly behind her, smiling. She patted Melanie's shoulder. "Good. I'm glad you're not going to leave us."

"People, if you would be quiet, we could get on with this." Carl waited for the crowd to settle. "I am sorry to report, however, that she has turned in her resignation. She plans to look for something closer to home, and I wish her all the best in this endeavor. She has recommended Candace as her replacement, and I plan to accept that recommendation. So, congratulations, Candace. Melanie will help you get started over the next three weeks, and then you'll be flying solo."

Melanie turned to offer congratulations, but Candace did not look pleased. She stood, her face grim. "I will *not* accept this position."

Carl straightened his tie. "We'll talk about this later, Candace."

"No! I want to talk now. The only reason Melanie would give up this job is because of the harassment she's been getting around here. I will not accept a promotion for any reason other than I am the most qualified. I certainly don't want a position that my predecessor has been bullied out of."

"Candace, you are plenty qualified."

Melanie looked in the direction of the voice. A hard-faced woman sitting three rows back folded her arms across her chest and glared at Melanie. "Everyone knows the position would have been yours anyway if *she* hadn't started making trouble in that other store. Now you'll get the position you deserve."

"Wrong." Candace shook her head. "She didn't make trouble for anyone. She saved a bunch of people's jobs by transferring here. She *is* more qualified for this job than I am, and it was only fair that she take it."

Candace looked around the room at each of her co-workers, then let her gaze come to rest on Melanie. "I think she's done a fabulous job, in spite of all the efforts to make trouble for her.

I know you all think that by doing these things to her you are supporting me, but that's not true."

She looked at Carl Brown. "Mr. Brown, if Melanie doesn't withdraw her resignation, then I'll put mine in, too. I absolutely will not work in a store where a perfectly nice woman has been treated so badly and in a position that has been gained in such a way."

A collective gasp went through the crowd—none louder than from Melanie's own mouth. She reached back and squeezed Candace's hand. "You can't do this. I'll be okay. You need this job."

Candace shook her head. "So do you."

Melanie couldn't believe what had just happened. Never had she seen anything so selfless, or maybe just plain crazy. What was Candace thinking?

Carl called the meeting back to order. "Seems to me, the rest of the group needs to have a little powwow. What's it to be, folks? Do we lose both of these fine women, or are the rest of you ready to accept Melanie as pricing coordinator and stop all these shenanigans?" He looked at Melanie and Candace. "Ladies, if you two would be so kind as to go out front so that we may speak plainly, we'll call you back in a few moments."

The two women walked through the swinging door of the back room. Melanie turned on her heel. "What are you thinking? This is the chance of a lifetime for you. You're a single mom. The difference in income is a big deal."

"You're a single mom, too. One that has recently lost a child. How could I forgive myself if I took what was rightfully yours? Jesus would never have me do such a thing."

Melanie started. "So you're a Christian?"

"Well, I try. And the one thing I know is that it means trying to do the right thing, no matter what. I don't want to sell that out for a little extra money."

"That's why you've been so supportive all this time. It's been about your faith."

The door swung open behind them. Carl Brown emerged. "Ladies, will you please come back in?"

The two women walked back into the room, facing the stares of every single person. "It has been unanimously agreed that we will not accept the resignation of either of you. We want you both to stay at your present positions for as long as this store stands."

Melanie took a backward step. She looked around at the faces, some still rife with hostility. What kind of respect did Candace garner if they were willing to accept Melanie because of her? The concept seemed out of her grasp.

———

Andie awoke to the sun streaming through the windows. She buried her head under the pillow and rolled over. With the return of wakefulness came the return of the pain. She needed to get up and moving.

She threw her legs over the side of the bed and forced herself to stand. She stumbled over to the coffeepot and followed the instructions to brew some caffeine. While she waited for the machine to do its work, she threw on an old pair of sweats and sat. Soon the room began to take on the aroma of fresh coffee. She picked up a white ceramic mug, poured it full, then walked out toward the beach. *Okay, God, where did we leave off yesterday?*

Several hours later, she saw a woman waving at her from the far end of the beach. Christi. She groaned and walked toward her friend.

Christi put her hands on her hips. "About time. I looked for a good half hour before I found you. Had me worried you'd run off."

"Just thinking."

"Get your bags together. You're thinking at my guesthouse from now on. Even Scott agreed."

"He'll tell Blair where I am."

"Oh, please. Scott can keep a secret better than anyone else on the planet."

The two women started back toward the cabin, although Andie preferred to stay on the beach. "Maybe so, but if Blair goes looking for me, that's where he would start."

"Even if he did, what's he going to do—break down the door? Come on, Blair's not the type. Eventually you're going to have to let him know where you are, anyway."

"Maybe."

"Maybe, nothing. I'm right and you know it. Get your bags and let's get moving."

Christi took a few steps before realizing Andie was not following her. She turned, puzzled.

Something in the way Christi demanded her obedience had finally pushed Andie too far. "No." She took a deep breath and straightened her shoulders. "Thank you for your offer. But I've paid for three days, and I plan to use them."

Christi cocked her head to the side. In spite of the fact that she bit her lips together, they still curled up at the corners. "Listen to you. Who is this, and what have you done with Andie?"

Andie smiled. She liked this newfound independence. "Thanks for checking in. I'll be in touch. Be careful driving home."

Christi's mouth actually dropped open. "I do believe I've just been invited to leave. My, my." She held up her hand to flag an approaching golf cart. "Why, Bruce. How nice to see you again." She smiled back over her shoulder. "Call me when you're ready."

Andie watched her friend drive off, and could hear her clear laughter over the hum of the electric engine. The renewed burst of adrenaline could best be put to use by making some calls now. Maybe she could set a few other things in order, as well. She dialed Carolyn Patterson's number.

"Hi, Carolyn, it's Andie."

The other end of the line was silent for just a second too long. "Oh. Andie. I was planning to call you later."

"Well, here I am."

"Yes. Here you are." She paused. "The board met this morning, and it was determined that you should relinquish your duties for the Fair—for this year only, of course. Next year we hope to have you back on board."

"But, Carolyn, I—"

"I know this is your baby, Andie, but you of all people should understand that we don't want to do anything that will hurt the effort. The majority of people who participate in the Fair are families of middle income. That demographic is strongly sided with the Johnston family and will do whatever it takes to show support. You understand that, don't you?"

Andie felt the morning's coffee churning inside her stomach. She climbed onto the porch and collapsed into a chair. "Yes. I understand. Thank you, Carolyn." She managed to flip shut her phone and jump to her feet in time to vomit over the rail.

———

Voice mail answered before the first ring. As usual. "Andie, turn on your phone!" Blair threw his handset against the wall and watched a chunk of plastic break free and skitter across the floor.

He kicked over the stools from around the kitchen counter. She was not going to simply run out on him. Who did she think she was?

He shoved through the door into the garage, fired up his car, and skidded down the driveway. After his spending the last two days leaving humble, apologetic messages, she hadn't even bothered to return his calls. This was going to end. Right now.

He crossed Marina Drive and nearly hit an idiotic tourist. The fool was walking backward into the street, camera on his face turned toward the ocean. Blair blasted his horn. Why they didn't gate off this entire neighborhood, he would never understand. Tourists ruined everything.

He took the next turn, and then the next, until he pulled into the Baurs' driveway. He didn't know the gate combination. He'd have to buzz.

"Yes?"

"Christi, it's me. I need to talk to you."

"What do you need?"

"To talk to you in person. Now!"

"Don't think that's such a good idea. You sound a little upset."

"Of course I'm upset. I know you know where Andie is. Tell me or I'm going to break this gate down!" As soon as the words came out, he realized he had lost his best chance of gaining her help. She'd keep it from him for pure spite. "Look, Christi, I'm sorry. I'm just worried, that's all. All I want to do is talk to her."

"Maybe you should have been thinking about that on Saturday night, hmmm? If you had, you wouldn't be having this problem now. Would you?"

Control freak.

Unwilling to listen to her condescending tone one more minute, he shoved the car into reverse and stomped on the pedal. There was work to do, anyway.

He drove to his office, his veins burning with increasing indignation at his ungrateful wife and her hoity-toity friend. Yeah, he'd forgotten to call, but was that a crime worth *this*? He had been working his backend off, trying to save the company, their house, what was left of their lives, and this was the thanks he got. He slid his card key into the parking garage, but by the time the gate lifted, he had thrown the car into reverse.

Work was not what he needed. He needed some comfort—and knew just where to find it. He whipped the car around and made tracks.

chapter twenty-nine

Jake sat at the desk in his office, planning what he might say to the boys tonight. He was supposed to be their spiritual mentor, guide them in the right ways. Yet he had abandoned his own children. Abandoned.

Yes, he had thought it was for the best at the time—maybe it was. Truth was, though, he had no idea. He had signed away his rights without any concept of where his daughters might end up or what man might enter their life. He had prayed for them over the years. Wasn't that all he could do?

A burning guilt told him there was more, that he should go look for them. But another voice told him, "No, they're over eighteen now—they can find you if they want to."

He realized then there was a new direction he should be taking his prayers. Not only about keeping his children safe and drawing them to God, but also about whether or not he should seek to make contact. Could he even get that information if he wanted to?

He looked down at his notes for the group and realized he had nothing left to give the boys in his group. It was time he stepped down from his position. He was too old.

"Hey."

The voice behind him startled him, and for just a second he thought it might be Melanie. When he swung around he realized why. Sarah Johnston leaned against the doorframe, her arms folded across the oversized sweatshirt she often wore. He hadn't realized how alike they sounded. "Afternoon, Miss Johnston. What brings you here?"

Sarah slumped into a chair without being invited. "My mom."

A spark of hope ignited. "Your mom sent you to talk to me?"

Sarah's lips scrunched together on one side and she appeared to be trying very hard not to roll her eyes. "Are you kidding? You obviously don't know my mom very well."

"Well, that's definitely true. What then do you want to talk about?" He tried to put on his best Sunday-go-to-meeting smile. He was a leader for the youth group—he couldn't afford to let them see that he struggled with doubt and pain. If they realized how poorly he handled things, how could he possibly be the example they needed?

"I know you two had a fight. She won't tell me what about, but I'm sure it was something to do with *Jeff's legacy.*" She lifted both hands and made air quotation marks as she said the words, as if she were tired of hearing the phrase.

"Jeff's legacy?"

"Yeah, that's all she ever thinks about. She has this idea cooked up in her head that the only way Jeff's life will have mattered is if she makes a big deal of all this stuff in court."

"I take it you don't agree."

"No, I don't." She bit her bottom lip and stared at the floor. "In fact, I think Jeff would hate that she's doing all this. I think he'd tell her to go on with her life and remember the good times. He'd tell her not to dwell in the past 'cause it won't change anything."

"I understand what you're saying, but what does any of that have to do with me?"

"She likes you. She'll listen to you."

"Likes me? I hardly think so. Sarah, it was more than a fight. I told her some stuff about my life, and she hates me now."

Sarah shook her head. "I don't buy that. She wouldn't be in the terrible mood she's been in for the last three days if she hated you. Nope. She likes you, but she's mad."

"Regardless, I don't see what all this has to do with me. She's not speaking to me—she's not going to listen."

"You're planning the memorial for spring break, right?"

"I don't know. I was just sitting here thinking about canceling it. I thought it might be easier for her."

"Don't you dare. She needs to hear from the other kids what Jeff meant to them. She keeps saying he'll be forgotten, but we both know dozens of people who couldn't if they tried."

Jake studied the eyes across from him, pinched in earnestness, still gleaming with moisture from the mention of her brother's name. Sarah needed his help, and he was going to give it as best he could. "Okay, I won't cancel it. Do you think your mom will still come?"

"Are you kidding? She wouldn't miss something honoring Jeff even if Jack the Ripper was hosting it. No matter how mad she might be at you, I'd say you're still a step or two above him."

"I'm not so sure."

Sarah sprang to her feet, seemingly brightened by the idea of the memorial. "Thanks. You're the best."

"Where are you hurrying off to?"

"Girls' group. We're meeting a little early tonight."

"Why?"

She grinned and looked at him, her head tilted. "Promise not to tell?"

Jake put his hand over his chest. "Cross my heart."

"We're going to hide, then throw water balloons at the boys when they come for their meeting." She giggled as she turned to go.

Jake watched her sashay out the door and thought about the poor guys who would arrive at his shop in the next forty-five minutes. Okay, he'd promised not to tell, but that didn't mean he couldn't help them fight back.

He walked to the back of the shop, unlocked the cabinet, and began to assemble the arsenal of assault water rifles he'd accrued over the years. He'd get these babies loaded and ready for action. After the boys took the first round like gentlemen, they would be ready to go on an all-out offensive. He took the first weapon to the sink and began to fill it.

There were probably some church members who would be upset at the frivolous use of youth group time, but he believed a little frivolity was one of the things that kept them coming back. It wasn't all fun and games, but it wasn't all study and rules, either. He suddenly felt ashamed of himself for his earlier thoughts about giving up this job he loved. The job God had called him to do.

———

Bruce put Andie's suitcase in the trunk. "This it?"

"Yes." She handed him a folded bill. "Thank you."

"Thank *you*, Mrs. Smith. Please stay with us again soon."

Andie nodded and climbed into her car. The turn of the key felt so permanent. This place hadn't been paradise—no place could be under these circumstances—but it had been a haven, a safe retreat for the last days, and she knew that reentering the world would bring everything back down on her. Likely more, once Blair found her. Still, she'd already extended her stay one night past her intentions, and it was too easy to imagine continuing on. And since part of what she realized during her days in seclusion was that she needed to stand up for herself, that meant she couldn't run away anymore. It was time to make the next move.

She drove south on Highway 101. The Pacific Ocean lay smooth and sleek, mirroring the sky above, and the sun shone a blanket across the blue. Yet beneath the surface, there were many things that could hurt—kill, even. The great whites that occasionally went after surfers. Jellyfish, whose sting paralyzed you far from shore. Even stingrays, like the one that killed that alligator wrestler last year. Things that looked calm and serene on the surface could still wound you deeply. Just like Blair and all his apologies.

She dialed the number to her house, knowing Blair would already be at work. She needed to make certain. No answer. Good. She could stop by her house, pick up some clothes, and make it to Christi's without a confrontation. She planned to spend the next week in her guesthouse and reevaluate from there.

Thirty minutes later, she pulled into her driveway, relieved to see the house quiet. This shouldn't take long. She avoided the garage, in the unlikely case Blair should come home while she was still in the house.

Over the last four days, she had spoken to him only briefly. It would be just like him to block her car in with his own as a way of forcing her to stay and listen to his excuses—excuses she wouldn't believe anyway.

She climbed the stairs, not bothering to turn on lights—the sunlight through the windows provided more than enough illumination. When she reached her room, she started across the space toward her closet, then stopped. There, lying sprawled out on the floor, was Blair.

He wasn't moving.

chapter thirty

When she walked into Les's office on Saturday morning, Melanie found him looking at a large rectangle wrapped in brown paper. He quickly closed the flap and set it against the wall when he saw her. He cleared his throat and looked down at his legal pad. "Now, let's see, where were we?"

As he studied his notes, Melanie looked at the large object leaning on the wall—obviously something in a frame. She knew that he was no longer married but had been a time or two. Maybe this was a family photo of his children and grandchildren—dressed in white shirts, blue jeans, and bare feet, standing on the beach. That was the way all family photos seemed to be made in Santa Barbara.

"Oh yes, the case-management conference. That will happen week after next."

Melanie nodded. "And that's—"

"You jerk! Get out of my face before I smack you one!" Shouted words blew into Les's office through the open balcony doors.

He jumped up, glared toward the street below, then slammed the door shut. A gust of air whooshed through the room, causing the flap of brown paper to fly up. It came to rest slightly askew.

Melanie saw the words *Los Angeles* across the top. She remembered that he'd said something about being interviewed by a magazine a few weeks ago. Still, he wasn't mentioning it now. Back to the subject at hand. "So . . . a case-management conference is when they set the trial date, right?"

He nodded. "And some other things. They'll send us to mediation in the meanwhile. Also, they'll set the date for the mandatory settlement meeting."

"Mandatory settlement? Nothing doing. I'm not going through all this just to settle."

"It's all part of the procedures. The meeting won't even happen until right before the trial. The judge will call everybody in and try to make each side believe their case can't possibly win, so we'd all better settle."

"But—"

"Don't worry. He can make us attend the conference. He can't make us settle."

"So do I need to attend the case-management thing?"

"No. I'll call and let you know our pending dates. After that, we'll go into the discovery phase. We'll talk more about that as we go along."

Melanie nodded and looked at the brown parcel. "Anything else we need to talk about?"

He shook his head. "That'll do for now."

She walked from his office, down the sidewalk toward the parking lot. A small magazine shop caught her attention. She went inside and looked for a copy of the most recent issue of *Los Angeles* magazine. She flipped through profiles of movie stars and restaurant reviews until page twenty-seven, where she found Les's picture, along with those of three other men who looked equally distinguished—or inflated, depending on your view.

"Today's Power Players," the article was entitled. Les's picture showed him in khakis and a button-down, standing at the rail of a yacht. "Lawyer with a heart," said the caption under his name.

> Les Stewart moved to Santa Barbara last year, with plans to sail, travel, and enjoy his retirement. However, after a grieving mother asked for his help, he gladly postponed his hard-earned retirement.

The rest of the article talked about his life, career, and the basic skeleton of the case.

An uncomfortable sensation that felt a lot like betrayal began to chew at Melanie's gut. Nothing in the article was false—the paper presented Jeff in a good light. But this lawsuit was supposed to be all about Jeff. Somehow, this made it seem like it was a lot about Les Stewart.

———

Andie walked down the long corridor in the hospital's rehab wing noting that the smell of disinfectant—strong though it was—did not quite manage to mask the other scent. Vomit.

When she reached the next-to-last door on the right, she saw *Kathleen Griffin, M.A.* in bold white letters on the nameplate above the door. Yes, this was the place. She knocked gently.

Maybe if no one heard her, she could turn and leave. She could say she tried, and no one answered. Her hopes disappeared when the door opened.

"Andie? I'm Kathleen Griffin. Thank you so much for coming." She extended a hand, which Andie took. The warmth of Kathleen's hand drew her attention to how cold her own had gone. "Please, come in, have a seat." She pointed toward a chair covered in faded gray vinyl. "We've been taking good care of your husband for the last two days."

"Good." She looked around the room.

Kathleen Griffin appeared to be about fifty. Broad-shouldered and heavyset, her hair was black-and-gray-streaked twigs of frizziness. She looked like a reformed hippie who'd gotten stuck having to find a real job but couldn't quite leave the sixties behind. Andie looked around the office, searching for posters about Woodstock or something similar. Instead she found framed verses. *"I can do all things through Christ who strengthens me."* Then, *"I have told you these things, so that in me you may have peace. In this world you will have trouble. But take heart! I have overcome the world. John 16:33."*

Kathleen cleared her throat. "That one almost sounds a bit pessimistic, doesn't it? You have trouble; you'll keep having trouble." She had obviously seen the direction of Andie's gaze.

"Why is it on your wall, then?"

"Mrs. Phelps, the people who come through these halls need to understand that staying with us a couple of weeks is not going to solve their problem. It is a lifelong problem. One which your husband has dealt with very effectively for the last twenty years, I gather." She flipped open a chart on her desk. "In that respect, you're lucky. A lot of our patients have to go through a long detox process before they even make it to this point. All your husband had to do was sober up."

"Lucky us."

Kathleen tapped a pencil on her desktop and frowned at Andie. "Mrs. Phelps, an alcoholic relapse is a serious issue."

Andie thought back to her father's suicide. "I want to help him—I really do. But there are lots of other issues here besides Blair's relapse."

Kathleen's expression softened. "I know this is a difficult time for your family. Losing a child is more than anyone should be asked to withstand. It's important, though, that the two of you get to the very root of your problems, hold nothing back, deal with all the ugliness. If your husband tries to cover up his feelings, he is sure to relapse again. He cannot begin the healing process until he is completely honest."

"Okay." Nothing was mentioned about the danger of smothering Andie's feelings. She realized what she'd stepped into.

In the name of healing, Blair would come in here and vent at her for an unlimited time. She was expected to be a good wife and take it all, then beg forgiveness for her failures. It would be called therapy. If that was therapy then her daily life was therapy enough. What about *her*? What about her therapy? A spark of anger lit inside her.

Kathleen went to a side door and opened it. "You can come in now."

Blair's face was pale, his eyes puffy and dark. He wore a T-shirt and jeans. He didn't look at Andie as he shuffled to a chair and stared at the floor, like a condemned man before the executioner.

Kathleen closed the door and returned to her seat behind the desk. "Blair, let's begin with you. What do you need to say to Andie?"

Andie felt the muscles in her neck tighten. *Here it comes.*

Blair shifted and crossed his left ankle across his right knee. "I'm sorry."

Andie blinked. He had rarely spoken these words in their marriage. Still…their effect was diminished by too many other factors. They served only to provide an added second before the condemnation would start.

He cleared his throat. "I know I've never done anything quite good enough for you. I've always tried to be a good husband and provide for you like you needed and wanted, but somehow along the line I've failed you."

The words hit Andie like a slap across the face. The spark of anger blazed. "What do you mean, you've never done anything quite good enough for me? You make it sound like my high expectations caused this. I've never demanded anything of you, Blair. Well, nothing more than coming home from work now and then."

Blair's gaze jerked up toward Andie in obvious surprise.

The long-repressed emotions inside her would not be held back any longer. Words began to spew from her, even as she knew she should be holding them in. "I've never been good enough for *you!*"

Blair's mouth dropped open, and he looked toward Kathleen. Kathleen flipped another page on the chart. "Mrs. Phelps, I think—"

"You think what? Blair's the one who decided to drink away his problems, leaving me to deal with all the resulting garbage. But since he has the *problem*, I've got to sit in here and listen to him rag on me for all the supposed pressure I've put on him over the years? Well, I won't."

Andie jumped to her feet. "I've spent the last twenty years listening to constant criticism because I was not the person he wanted me to be. I accepted him fully for who he was, but he could never do the same for me."

"That's not true." Blair stood, as well.

"Oh yeah? How many times have I berated you for playing the occasional round of golf? How many times have I railed at you for half an hour for being compulsive about your sock drawer. Huh? But my painting and messy closet have been the target of hundreds of your rants."

She could see the hurt on Blair's face—a face that was so wounded and broken now—but she was beyond remorse. "I've listened to it every single day of our marriage. The only thing I do for the pure joy of it is painting, and you tell me it's a selfish use of my time. Things always have to be your way, and my way is wrong, and I'm sick of it."

Kathleen stood and leaned across her desk. "Could the two of you please sit down? This is not accomplishing anything."

Blair dropped back into his seat. Andie sat, but she stayed on the edge of her chair and turned her anger on Kathleen. "What *would* accomplish something? Me sitting here and taking it? Listening to Blair say the words he hasn't had the courage to say up until now, but that he's been throwing in my face with everything he does?"

Kathleen picked up her pen and scribbled something in the chart. Doubtless something about Blair's crazed wife that drove him into the arms of alcohol and another woman. "What, exactly, is it that he hasn't yet said?"

"That Chad's death is my fault."

"Your fault?" Blair leaned forward in his seat, looking as though he were ready to pounce.

"Yes. I'm the one who should have made certain that his grades were perfect. It was my responsibility and I failed. I have to live with that every single day of my life. I see the way you look at me. I carry enough guilt without having to listen to you spit my failure back at me." Andie stood and walked to the door. "I'm sorry. I want you to recover, but I can't be the beating post in order to make you feel better. I just can't take it." She turned the knob and ran from the room.

"Mrs. Phelps." Kathleen's voice sounded somewhere down the corridor behind her, but Andie would not turn. She fled the rehab center, jumped in her car, and drove away.

God, I blew it. I mean, there's no reason to tell you that—you know it already—but maybe it'll make me feel better for saying it. Andie drove down the freeway with no clear destination in mind.

Why did I blow up like that at Blair? He needs me now. He needs me to help him heal. What do I do? I kick him when he's at his lowest point. I'm no more good to him than I was to my father.

She drove south for a few more minutes, until a feeling began to gnaw at her gut and would not let up. Finally, she gave in, turned around at the next exit, and drove toward downtown. She knew where she needed to go, but had no idea why. Still uncertain, she parked in the lot and knocked on the back door of the soup kitchen.

Silas opened it. "Madam, what brings you here again today?"

"I . . . uh . . . I felt bad because I had to leave my shift early, and thought I might see if I could do a little extra now."

He nodded, and the lines on his leathery, sun-baked skin crinkled together. "Actually, I was just preparing to mop. I could use the assistance."

She nodded, grateful for the distraction.

He handed her a mop. "I assume your appointment did not go well?"

Her fingers gripped the handle for support. "No." She dipped it in the bucket of soapy water. "I stormed out."

"You, madam? Storming? I have never seen you storm."

"Well, I stormed today." She swished the mop across the floor. "It's not my fault. If he hadn't been so critical for all these years . . . But still, I'm sorry I did it."

He flipped his dreadlocks over his shoulder. "Perhaps not sorry enough."

"Excuse me?"

"My father used to say, 'You are not truly sorry if you are still blaming someone else for your actions.' " He put his mop into the wringer and squeezed.

Andie looked at the formerly homeless man, who still never bathed or washed his clothes. Why should words from him—any words—make her feel guilty? He didn't know what he was talking about.

But somehow, even hours after she'd left the soup kitchen, his words still rang through her mind. *"You are not truly sorry if you are still blaming someone else for your actions."*

She drove to the beach and sat on the sand, warm beneath the late March sun. She watched the froth churning in and out. She understood how it felt.

A crushing weight seemed to settle on her chest. A memory formed in her mind, still so powerful, she could smell the charred bread.

Blair was once again late coming home from work and hadn't bothered to call. Chad, maybe five years old, had been crying for an hour that he was hungry. She hugged him. "I guess we'll eat without Daddy tonight. Again." She handed her son a banana and put the bread in the oven.

Maybe a quick walk to her studio while the bread was browning. Her once-a-week class at the Santa Barbara Museum of Art was coming up, and her landscape still needed something. When she saw it this time, the answer was obvious. It needed a touch more red. She picked up the brush.

Blair came through the door just as the smell of burning bread filled the kitchen. He took one look at the soggy, over-cooked vegetables and the rubbery pot roast, and his face glowed brighter red than her painting. "Andie, I've spent the entire day working like a dog. When I come home the least I can expect is a nice meal and a picked-up house. Your painting is nothing but a selfish use of your time. Look at the pantry—it needs to be cleaned. You have a pile of paperwork on the kitchen counter from one of your charity events. It's ridiculous that I work as hard as I do and have to live like this."

Chad had heard the commotion and walked into the room. "Mommy, I'm hungry."

"You're in here painting while your son is wandering around the house hungry? Andie, this has to stop. I want you to stop taking that class and get refocused."

The fact that his son was wandering around the house hungry because he arrived home an hour late seemed lost on him. The fact that it was the same reason for the overcooked vegetables and meat had also escaped notice.

The anger welled up in her again. She'd had enough of Blair and his criticism.

"You are not truly sorry if you are still blaming someone else for your actions."

The voice in her mind came from nowhere, and only fueled her anger. "Why should I be sorry? He's the one that's been so mean."

A woman jogging down the beach in shorts and a sports top glanced sideways and ran faster. Andie realized then she had been speaking aloud. She didn't care. For the first time she could remember, she didn't care what anyone thought of her.

Did you carry no blame?

"Okay, I was painting, but only for a second. Well, long enough to burn the bread. But . . . I've never really painted after that. I've done more than my share of penance."

She pictured the times she'd spend the entire day cleaning out kitchen cupboards, scrubbing baseboards, organizing shelves. Blair would walk through the door and smirk. "We'll see how long this lasts."

Why couldn't he ever be proud of her? All he cared about was his work.

Why does he work so hard?

Pride.

Or maybe his family?

Andie stood up and walked knee-deep into the surf. She did not like the questions forming in her mind. She needed to be up and moving.

Okay, I'll go back and apologize to Blair. But not today.

Use your gifts.

"I don't have any."

Painting.

"Nothing good comes from painting. It's a waste of time." A thought began to pull at the back of her mind. Her paintings could be used for good. She could think of several charities and mission groups that could use visuals for their publicity. She thought of the picture she could never clear from her mind. "I … I'll try."

Chad.

"Chad? What can I do … ?" The answer was buried deep in her gut. As much as she didn't want to acknowledge it, there it was. She knew that everyone in her life would be angry at her. But she knew peace would not find her until she did what she'd wanted to do all along.

chapter **thirty-one**

Sarah slipped through the front door without a word, her face lined with sadness.

Melanie looked up from the pile of laundry she was folding. "Sweetie?"

"It's official. Our trip has been canceled. The deposit's due, and we're not even close." Sarah flung a neon yellow paper with her right hand and wiped her eyes with the left. "Poor Juanita."

Melanie picked up the paper.

> *Due to lack of funding, our mission trip to Mexico will be canceled. We will put the money raised so far into a special account, and hope to make the trip next summer.*

"I am sorry, Sarah. I know this is my fault." She rubbed her hands across her forehead and wished she could wipe away the hopelessness that clung to everything around them.

"Jake says it's not." Sarah didn't sound as though she believed him, but she sank down onto the couch beside Melanie. "He gave us a big talk about how people can't stop God's plans, and if God had meant for us to go on this trip it would have happened." She stared at the wall as she recited this information, and somewhere in the process her expression softened, as if she were convincing herself just by repeating the words. "He says we don't see the big picture, and we've got to trust, or something like that.

"Jake said that?"

"Yeah." Sarah reached her hand into the laundry basket and pulled out a towel. She put her face into it. "Nothing like the feel of towels warm out of the dryer." She began to fold it. "Love the smell, too."

Melanie shook her head, amazed. How could Sarah move so easily from disappointment to the joy of the warm smell of laundry? How did she bear up under the burden of all that had been taken from her? Her daughter possessed an inner strength Melanie knew she lacked. Where did it come from?

She knew the answer, but would not allow herself to admit the truth. As long as she didn't acknowledge it, she wouldn't have to do something about it.

———

On Saturday morning, Melanie pulled into the parking lot at East Beach. She put two dollars in the appropriate slot of the parking honor box and moved toward the crowd of teenagers already milling around. She wanted to find Sarah, who'd come early with friends, but at the same time wanted even more to avoid Jake. In the end, she chose to take a seat on one of the benches lining the walkway.

"Hey there." Tony dropped down onto the bench beside her and leaned his elbows on his knees. He twisted his neck around so he could see her. "How ya been? We've missed you at the garage."

"I've missed you, too, Tony. It's just that I have been really busy, and . . ." She stopped herself from adding more to the lie.

He nudged her with his elbow. "Yeah. Jake's been bummed out, too. I figure maybe today you two can settle whatever it was that's been bothering you, and you can start coming around again, huh?"

"It's not that simple."

"Never is. At least that's what we always think. Truth is, it usually is that simple."

Melanie laughed. "I didn't realize you were such a philosopher."

"What can I say? We all have our hidden talents." He nudged her again and stood. "I see someone I need to talk to. I'll catch you later." He walked across the sand toward a pretty young woman. The two of them talked, shoulder to shoulder, then put their arms around each other.

"There you are. I've been watching for you." Sarah swung her foot out and shoved her mother's. "What are you looking at?" She turned to see for herself.

"I didn't know Tony had a girlfriend. I guess I never talked with him that much during my visits."

Sarah sat on the bench. "That's not his girlfriend."

"Then why are they hugging?"

"They're not hugging, Mom, they're praying."

Melanie felt her face flush. She supposed if she was going to hang out at these kinds of events, she would have to learn the way the church crowd did things.

"Okay, everyone, let's get started." Jake's voice shouted above the crash of the waves and the voices from the neighboring volleyball courts. They assembled in a blob roughly shaped like a circle. Melanie sat on the sand in the midst of the group.

A couple of the boys brought out guitars, and the kids began to sing songs of praise. They were songs Melanie vaguely recognized from the Dirty Dozen. Their musical selections surprised her. This was a memorial service—why would they be singing such upbeat songs? Didn't these kids understand what they were here for?

Finally, Jake stood up. "Thanks for coming, everyone. As you all know, it's been almost three months since Jeff changed his address."

For a moment, Melanie had no idea what Jake meant, but it dawned on her as he continued.

"I know his new home is beautiful and perfect. But I think we can all agree that we are selfish enough to wish he were back here, in this not so perfect and not always beautiful place. Today we want to celebrate his memory once again. To take time to reflect how his life touched ours. To give thanks to God for giving us the time with him that we had. Who wants to share first?"

Tony hopped to his feet. "I'll go." His Adam's apple bobbed, and when he swallowed, he seemed to almost choke. He looked down and worked his toe in the sand.

"Some of you've known me a long time. You already know what a loser I was. I s'pose it's time the rest of you find out, too."

What an odd way to start a tribute to Jeff. Melanie leaned back, her hands sinking in the sand.

"I started giving Jeff a hard time in junior high. I'm not sure why I liked to pick on him so much, but for whatever reason he became the chief target of all my pranks. I'd walk past him on the sidewalk, try to push him into the mud."

Melanie's stomach began to churn. She remembered all the days that Jeff had come home filthy. When she asked what happened, the answer was never about Tony. It was always, "I tripped," or "We were just messing around and I fell." Her own son had been the victim of a bully and she'd never known it.

Tony looked at Melanie, then back at his feet. "In high school, I even ripped up a term paper once."

Another memory. The year that Jeff's grade dropped from an A to a C because he turned in his paper late. She knew he'd been working on it and confronted him. "I just forgot to turn it in."

She spent twenty minutes lecturing him about carelessness and how it would hurt his future dreams if he didn't get his act together. If only she had known the truth. She would have comforted him, helped him. Gone to the teacher and explained.

Gotten that punk Tony expelled.

When she looked toward him this time, resentment began to bloom. He was nothing at all like she had imagined him to be. A big fat phony. Just like Jake.

"Then, one morning, a tow truck showed up at school. All the kids were hanging around in the parking lot before classes started, and right in front of everyone he repossesses my truck." He looked around and licked his lips. "It was humiliating.

"That afternoon, I got a call from the tow yard saying I could come get my truck. Somebody had paid off my debt. They wouldn't tell me who did it at first, but I found out it was Jeff.

"I went up to him at school and asked him what he thought he was doing.

" 'I know things are hard for you right now. I saw a way to help you, and I did it,' he says.

" 'But why?' I say.

" 'It's what Jesus would do.'

"That was it for me. I drew back my fist, ready to smash his little do-gooder's face, but my muscles froze in place. I couldn't move my arm. Jeff stood there, looking at me, waiting for the blow to fall. I finally dropped my arm to my side, screamed at him to get out of there, and I took off.

"I couldn't stop thinking about it. Something about that dweeb really bothered me. Then I realized what it was. He had something I didn't. Peace.

"Every day for the next week, I waited for him after school and we talked. Things began to change. Actually, *things* didn't change at all—*I* changed. It took me three months to scrape together the money to pay him back. He didn't want to take it, but I made him." Tony offered a lopsided smile. "With less violence than I'd made him do things in the past.

"My homelife still stinks, my old man's still in prison, and to be honest, I'd just as soon that he stay there. My mom, though, she's real glad that Jeff brought me around. Says she thanks Jesus every day for Jeff." His voice cracked. "So do I."

He rubbed his face against his shoulder and looked up. "That's all I got to say."

He returned to take his seat on the sand. The kids around him pounded his back and whispered encouragement. He never turned to look toward Melanie.

A blond girl stood up. "I was failing geometry freshman year. Jeff spent hours with me. He never asked for anything in return. He was sick a lot that year, and I knew he didn't feel like helping me, but he never complained." She sniffled once. "I'll never forget him."

Melanie had a vague memory of Jeff tutoring a classmate, but sick a lot that year? Jeff hadn't been sick a lot freshman year. What was this girl talking about?

Jeff's friend Dan stood up. "Um, well, Kathy, the *reason* he was sick was because of you. He spent that whole semester trying to work up the nerve to ask you to a movie. Used to throw up after every single tutoring session."

The whole crowd erupted in laughter. Kathy covered her face with her hands—laughing or crying, Melanie couldn't tell.

Dan put his hands in his pockets. "As long as I'm up here, I'll just tell you all that Jeff was one of the greatest guys I've ever known. I miss him every day. He . . ." Dan stared at the ground and shook his head. "He was just great, that's all." He dropped into the sand, his shoulders heaving with emotion.

A blond boy stood and said Jeff sat with him at lunch when he was new to the school. Two girls, leaning on each other for support, talked about how much they looked up to him as a leader in the youth group. One of Sarah's friends talked about how he was the only big brother they didn't mind being around. A slim girl tried to make it through a poem. One after another, they stood, and Melanie listened to them tell their stories of how Jeff had touched them. Sometimes in life-changing ways. Usually just with small kindnesses or a pleasant word. But friend after friend, student after student, boy after girl, they all said the same thing until Melanie swore she heard it echo in her soul.

"I'll never forget him."

When the last student had shared, Jake said a final prayer in memory, and the group began to break up. Melanie knew that she should stay and say a few words of gratitude to the kids who spoke, and to Jake for arranging it all. But, truth was, she couldn't have spoken if her life had depended on it.

She stumbled down the sidewalk and away from the crowd. She passed Stearns Wharf and suddenly couldn't walk any farther. She sat on the stone wall separating sidewalk from beach and stared blindly toward the ocean.

How did any of this fit together in a sensible way? She reached into her purse for a tissue and saw the yellow paper Sarah had given her a few days ago. She picked it up.

How could the same people who would not sponsor this mission trip teach such great love, like she'd heard today? None of it made any sense at all.

———

Andie woke up Saturday morning with a single thought: The Fair had gone on without her yesterday. Early reports indicated it had been a success. She waited until nine o'clock and drove to Christi's house.

Christi looked tired; she'd put in a long week preparing, while Andie had been forced to stay out of sight. "Hey. How did it go?"

"A hit, as usual. In fact, I talked to Carolyn late last night. From preliminary numbers, it appears this has been our most successful year ever."

How could this have happened? Without my help?

Christi's report should have been happy news. The fund-raising effort for Andie's favorite charity had just finished its most successful year. People would be helped, families comforted, advanced treatment given. But Andie had spent the last few years of her life convincing herself that these programs needed her. She was the engine behind the machine, the thing that kept it moving. Now she was faced with the reality. No one needed her at all.

"Andie, you okay? You don't look so well." Christi's forehead wrinkled in concern. The barely noticeable black circles under her eyes hinted at her exhaustion. The Fair took a lot of work.

This was not the time to burden her with Andie's selfish attitude. "I'm fine. I've got some things to do, so I'll be moving along. Just wanted to check in."

"All right. See you tomorrow."

Easter Sunday. Alone. Somehow the thought didn't sound appealing.

As she climbed into her car, Andie realized a week had passed since she'd sat on the beach reenvisioning her life. So far, none of those plans had played out. Her charity thrived without her, her marriage was worse than ever, and she hadn't painted a single thing since realizing how crucial it was to her. Pulling out of Christi's driveway, she decided the only one she could do anything about at the moment was her painting. Sure it was simple, but small steps were important.

Andie drove home and marched into her studio with purpose, ready to start a new painting she could donate. But what? Mattie Plendor's trip to Africa popped to mind, and Andie remembered her own short mission trip to Cape Town years ago. She could see a picture taking form inside her mind. *I'm not sure if a painting would help her cause or not, but I've got to try it.* She closed her eyes and remembered the smells, the textures, the people from her own two-week visit there.

Before she could start, she'd have to drive downtown to the art supply store for a bigger canvas and a few new tubes of paint. A half-hour later, she marveled at her luck when she found a parking spot on Cabrillo, only four blocks from the paint store. A good sign for a good day. She walked up the street, trying to convince herself this was true.

"Andie, how long has it been?" Judy Frist stood behind the counter of the supply store, her waist-length gray hair spilling around her shoulders like a cape.

"Too long. I've made a commitment to get back at it."

"Atta girl. I'll do my part to keep you on track. What do you need?"

"A canvas and I think a tube of ochre and one of cadmium green ought to do it for today."

Judy's face drooped. "You can do better than that. Come check out this new set of brushes we just got it in yesterday. I tell you, the bristles are like a Van Gogh dream."

Andie shook her head. "My brushes are fine. Just a canvas and the paints, please."

"Yeah, yeah." Judy loaded the items into a large plastic bag with handles. "Anything else?"

"No, thanks. Great to see you again." After paying, Andie pushed out the door with her bundle. She rounded the corner onto Cabrillo, and paused for a moment to look at one of Santa Barbara's most famous landmarks—the dolphin fountain at the entrance to Stearns Wharf. It was a favorite photo spot for tourists and locals alike. Andie, Blair, and Chad had taken their Christmas card picture in front of it one year. The memory slammed her.

Chad had been a toddler, and Blair had taken the day off work. They spent the day at the wharf, acting like tourists, asked a passerby to take their picture in front of the fountain, and then bought fresh lobster. Since the lobsterfeast was usually considered a Christmas Eve and anniversary only treat, Blair declared that day's picture would be the next year's Christmas card, and therefore the purchase was perfectly legal.

Her eyes blurred, and she jerked her gaze away from the fountain and its accompanying memories. She watched a group of college students coming down the bike path on Rollerblades, laughing and joking, then looked at the people seated on the concrete wall that separated the bike path from the sidewalk. A movement drew her attention. There, sitting on the wall.

The woman whipped her head back around toward the ocean, but Andie had seen her. She had seen Andie. Once again, with a bag in her hand.

Better get back to the car quickly.

Coward. Don't you have something you need to do about now?

Andie stopped. Could she really bring herself to do this? *God, if this is really what I'm supposed to do, then I want to do it. But it's really hard for me, and I don't want to mess things up even more. Please show me the way.*

The light at the corner turned green, and she crossed the street, feeling she might have a stroke at any minute. She walked behind the woman, who kept her head turned, and sat down beside her. The woman looked over. Her face showed absolutely no emotion.

By now, Andie could actually feel the blood moving from the top to the bottom chamber of her heart. "I . . . I'm sorry."

Melanie Johnston turned back toward the ocean and shrugged.

Andie's instincts told her to stand, to run away. She'd done her part, but she couldn't make herself move. "I had no idea Chad would be driving that night. I would never have allowed it." She leaned her bag against the wall and looked over her shoulder out at the ocean. "I should have hidden the keys . . . something . . . I don't know. Maybe I should have stayed home that night. There are so many things I see now I could have done differently."

A gurgling sound came from Melanie Johnston's throat, but she didn't speak or look at Andie.

Andie grasped the handles on her bag, prepared to take flight. "What I mean to say is, I am sorry that my mistakes cost you your son. There's nothing fair about that. Why couldn't my mistakes have cost me, and left both our boys alone?"

She stood, but wasn't quite finished. "I've wanted to say this to you ever since the accident, but people kept saying I shouldn't. I don't know why doing the right thing has been replaced by doing the thing to protect yourself, but it has. Now I don't think it much matters one way or the other."

Finally Melanie Johnston looked straight at her. She wiped her right hand across her eyes and jumped to her feet. A piece of paper fell from her lap and floated to the ground. She turned and fled.

Andie watched her go but didn't try to stop her. *I guess I blew that one, huh, God?*

She started to walk away, but the flash of yellow drew her attention. She picked up the piece of paper, read it, and then put it in the bag with the canvas.

———

Melanie shoved past tourists, tripped over a broken piece of sidewalk, and stumbled forward without thinking of where she was going. She needed to run, escape, but felt like she wouldn't ever be able to run far enough. Her vision blurred behind a thick wetness that burned a path down her cheeks.

She forced herself forward until she got to Ledbetter Beach, where she dropped into the sand. The cheers and laughter of holiday weekend beach-goers came from all around her, but it seemed a great distance away. Here, where she was, there was nothing.

The look on Andie Phelps' face haunted her. All this time, she'd never thought of her as a grieving mother—only as the guilty party. But there was no mistaking the look on her face. It was cut-to-the-bone, barely-able-to-move grief.

Melanie knew it intimately. She put her head on her knees and cried.

So much loss. So much.

The moment replayed itself over and over in her mind. She saw Andie across the street. Felt her approach. Heard the fear in her voice. *"I'm sorry."*

The words changed absolutely nothing. Jeff was still gone. Right?

The other woman's face was ghostly pale, her eyes wide with fear. She couldn't have expected a warm reception, regardless of what she said. Yet she had said it. Come all the way across the street and said it.

Melanie looked at the ocean, choppy today, churning with insistent, uneven breakers. It was just the way this entire day had felt for her. "Oh, Jeff, it's all so messed up. Everything. I don't understand anything anymore. I just know I miss you."

When she was certain enough time had passed that she could retrace her steps and avoid Andie Phelps and any remaining teenagers from the memorial, Melanie returned to her car. She drove with no clear destination in mind, even as she turned onto South 101.

Suddenly she knew very clearly where she was going. She just wasn't sure what she would do when she got there. Or even if she'd be welcome.

chapter thirty-two

As evening fell, Andie forced her attention to the canvas. She needed to focus on her work. Forget about what happened earlier that day.

She cranked up the volume on her old cassette player. The African chants that she had recorded twenty years ago helped put her in the right frame of mind and brought the scene before her to life. She added more shading to the buckled wall of the tin shack. Yes. That was better. Perhaps a touch more.

She dipped her brush back into the paint on her palette, then slowly pressed it against the canvas. One smooth stroke and she leaned back again. That was enough.

"I'd forgotten how talented you are."

Andie dropped her brush. "Blair. What are you doing here? I thought . . ."

"You thought what? That I had checked myself into the clinic for a two-week stay, so you had seven more days to be home without worry?" The accusation in his voice stung, but it was tempered by something else. When Andie looked at him, she thought perhaps she sensed an air of defeat. Still, there was no point arguing with him. He spoke the truth.

"I'll just go get a few things."

"Andie, please. Stay."

Andie carried her brush over to the sink. She wanted no part of the conflict that lay ahead if she didn't leave right now. She wanted peace and quiet.

Yet she remembered her resolutions.

She washed her hands and tried to find a shred of courage. There had to be a little left, somewhere deep inside her. "I'm sorry for the way I stormed out on you last weekend. I know you have a lot of things to work out, and my support would make that easier for you, but I have things to work out, too."

He leaned against the wall and looked at her. "And I won't make things easier for you, will I?" His voice was soft. Broken almost.

She started to walk out but grasped the doorframe with her hand and held on. Her body willed her forward, but the hand would not let go. "You never do."

She glanced back over her shoulder to see that the dart had landed squarely. Blair had doubled over, hands on his knees. He lifted his face up toward her. "Has it been that bad? All this time?"

"I don't want to do this right now. No, it hasn't been all bad, but it's been bad enough. Maybe the fact that you've been running around with another woman should give you a clue that you weren't so happy, either. Maybe deep inside you wanted to give me a reason to leave you. Ever thought of that?"

Her hand finally relinquished its grasp on the doorframe. She walked from the room, down the hall, and toward the stairs. She heard Blair's footsteps behind her. He grabbed her arm and spun her around to face him. "What do you mean 'running around with another woman'?"

"Having an affair, a paramour, whatever you want to call it." Andie felt the anger flash through her gut again. "And don't grab me that way again!"

Blair took a step back, stunned. "Andie, I have never cheated on you."

"Come on, Blair. Let's at least move past the lies. You've been staying out half the night, and when I called you the other day, I heard her voice in the background."

Blair leaned his head forward and furrowed his brows. "You heard Ruby, the sixty-five-year-old cocktail waitress—never anyone else. I've never been with a woman. I've been alone. Drinking. But alone."

"Then why do you come home smelling like perfume?"

"Smoke, maybe. But perfume? You must have imagined . . . No, wait. Just once, right?"

"Maybe somehow the fact that it was only once makes it seem less a problem to you, but that's not how I see it."

"You don't understand. I let Ruby use my jacket that first night. It was cold, and she was taking out the trash. After a few martinis, I fancied myself quite the gentleman by offering it to her. Of course, when I sobered up the next day, I realized I'd given her an Armani jacket to carry garbage to the Dumpster."

"I think your story is a little too convenient."

Blair released his grip. "I can see why you would. But I swear it's the truth. I've yet to meet the woman who holds a candle to you."

"I'll bet." She turned and started up the stairs.

"Please. Stay. I'll sleep in the guestroom. I'll give you space to work things out, but I don't want to lose you without a fight."

"I'm tired of fighting. I'm tired of grieving. I'm tired of being told what I'm supposed to do by everyone else. I'm tired of trying to be someone other than who I am, trying to make everyone else happy."

"Go back to your painting. I'll go get Chinese and a movie. We won't even have to talk—we'll just get used to being in the room together again. Okay?"

Had he actually told her to get back to her painting? Could he really be serious? He was desperate and would say anything to get his way at this point, and she understood that, yet shouldn't she be willing to at least try? "Chinese sounds good." She forced a smile she did not feel.

Blair whirled around. "Great. I'll be back soon. Now, get back in there and work on your painting." He followed her to the door of her studio. "You really are talented. You've always supported my dreams; I'm sorry I didn't return the favor."

"You say that now, but what about next week? Next month? It'll be my selfish hobby after things calm down."

He shook his head. "Uh-uh. When I saw the painting you did for the Fair, I knew then I'd been wrong not to encourage you more."

She turned to see his face, but he had already disappeared into the garage. She shut the music off and stared at the painting. Only then did she get the best idea of all. She reached for her brush and added exactly what the painting needed.

People.

Two people, rebuilding a shack that had collapsed—whether from rust, disuse, or poor construction, she didn't know. The fact was, they were working together to make something worthwhile from the rubble that remained.

———

The boy who answered the door looked to be twelve, maybe a little younger. His black T-shirt with a surfboard across the front was two sizes too large for his skinny frame. Melanie attempted to smile, but her lips seemed stiff and heavy. "Is your mother home?"

He didn't answer but turned his head. "Mom!" He continued to hold the door close to his side, as if he expected Melanie to suddenly shove her way inside, and only he stood between her and the total decimation of his home.

"Who is it?" the voice called from farther back in the apartment.

"I don't know. Some lady." He turned his head only long enough to answer his mother, then turned back to guard this potential intruder.

Candace walked up behind him, wiping her hands on a dishtowel. "Melanie. What a pleasant surprise. Please come in."

The boy backed away from the door, but seemed reluctant to do so. He took a seat on the faded tweed sofa, folded his arms across his chest, and watched.

Candace made up for his lack of hospitality. "Come into the kitchen with me. I'm chopping some onions for my meat loaf, and I need to get it in the oven."

"We're having meat loaf again? Yuck." The boy's words were spoken quietly. They were intended to be heard, but not so loud that a mother could prove it. Melanie knew the tone well. She winked at the boy as she followed Candace to the kitchen. He scowled in return.

Candace casually resumed her work in the kitchen. If the fact that her co-worker, who lived seventy miles away, just happened to drop in on a Saturday evening, hours before Easter, surprised her, she didn't show it. "So, as you've just heard, we're having yucky meat loaf tonight. There's plenty, if you'd like to stay."

"Thanks, but I've got to get back. But, well, I wanted to talk to you."

"Sure. What about?"

"God. Forgiveness. I don't know. Lots of things."

Candace looked up from her work at the cutting board, studied Melanie's face, and then nodded. "Okay. Why don't you start from the beginning?"

Melanie spent the next hour telling her everything. Tony's story. Jake. Andie Phelps' apology. "I'm just so confused by it all. That forgiveness stuff sounds great, but to tell you the truth, I'm justifiably angry, and I don't want to start handing out free passes to the people who have wronged me the most."

"Okay. In your life, who have you felt anger toward for the longest period of time?"

Melanie didn't even have to think about that one. "My parents. They left me on the doorsteps of the Children's Home when I was two years old. No note. Nothing."

The knife clacked against the cutting board. Candace leaned both hands on the counter, took a breath, and then picked the knife back up. "No child should have to go through that."

"Tell me."

"But does your anger in any way punish them?"

"No. They don't even know about it."

"How about you? Does it hurt you?"

"A little, I guess."

"What about Sarah?"

"Absolutely not. I've made certain that it never would. I've made it a point that she never ever feels abandoned. I'm always there for her." The words sounded different when spoken aloud. "That almost sounds smothering, doesn't it?"

Candace dumped her minced onions into the bowl. "What would Sarah say?"

"She says I smother. Sometimes."

"So maybe your anger has affected her, huh?"

"Yeah. But this thing is different. That family's son killed my Jeff. If ever there was an anger that was deserved, that's the one."

"I'm a mom. You'll get no argument from me." She began to work the onions into the meat. "Hey, God can understand this one—His son was murdered. Thing about that was, He allowed it to happen so that He could offer forgiveness to the killers and people like them. That's incredible."

"Maybe so, but that's God. I'm human, and I'm mad."

"Fair enough. Do you think your anger changes anything for the better?"

"Yes. I'm hoping that I'll raise public awareness. Maybe save the life of another kid like Jeff. At least then Jeff would have some sort of legacy."

Candace began to shape the meat mixture into a loaf. "Why would your anger help raise awareness?"

"By suing those parents I'm sending a message to other parents. You know, that they are responsible for their children."

"Didn't their son die, too?"

"Yes."

"Which do you think sends the stronger message: 'Watch your children or you might lose some money' or 'Watch your children or you might lose them'? Do you think people are more motivated by this lawsuit, or the pictures of two teenage boys who were alive and healthy one day, and gone forever the next? Don't you think most parents would be more moved by the second?"

Nothing made sense anymore. Where was the truth? "I want Jeff to have a legacy. It's important to me."

"Judging from what you told me about the memorial, sounds to me like he's already got one."

———

Blair reached up to his visor, pushed the button, and held his breath. Why had he volunteered to go get food when it would give her another chance to run? What a fool he was. The garage door seemed to take forever as it inched higher, taunting him with his stupidity. Finally, it lifted high enough to reveal her car, parked in its usual spot. *Whew.*

Once inside, he found that Andie had set the table and changed into a shirt without paint smeared on it. He looked at her, the plates she'd set, then tilted his head toward the living room. "Why don't we eat it straight from the boxes? On the couch. In front of the television."

Andie's face lit with surprise. This had been one of her favorite habits early in their marriage. Why had she stopped? Flashes of memory told the reason—him. All those years of "Not on the new sofa" and "You'll ruin the carpet" and "Let's eat like civilized people." When he thought back now, pictured the scenes, he could see the light dulling in her eyes as he said the words. At the time he'd been so convinced he was right, he didn't take time to notice.

"Are you sure?" Her shoulders stiffened as though she sensed a trap being set.

"Yeah. It will be fun."

She nodded. "Sure."

They walked into the living room, and Blair unloaded the boxes onto the coffee table. Andie brought two glasses of Diet Coke and set them on coasters at each end of the sofa. Blair sat, and so did Andie, taking the farthest possible spot from him. Common sense told him it was so she could keep her drink on the end table while she was eating. Inside, his gut screamed at him that his own wife didn't want to be anywhere near him.

He pointed at the DVD he'd rented. "I couldn't find much that looked interesting. I got an old western. *My Darling Clementine*. Have you seen that one?"

"I don't think so. Black and white?"

"Yes."

She nodded. "Those are always best."

Blair inserted the movie, and they ate and watched without speaking as Henry Fonda, playing Wyatt Earp, avenged his brother's death. Strange how silence could suddenly feel awkward with your wife of almost twenty years, yet it did. He wanted to say something ... no, not just something, the *right* thing. Words failed him. He could think of nothing.

Instead, he looked around the living room, wondering what Andie would say if she knew they might lose the house—the tile floors she loved, the primrose border she'd painted around the ceiling, the rooms where they had lived with Chad. She would hate him if he lost all this—if she didn't already.

When the movie ended, Andie picked up the drink glasses and carried them to the sink. Blair tossed the containers into the bag he'd brought them home in, then walked into the kitchen. Andie turned toward him when he entered. "Don't you need to go back to the clinic? I'm afraid my little tirade made you leave before you were ready."

He shook his head. "Kathleen worked it out so that I can come in for counseling sessions on an outpatient basis for the next two weeks. After that, I'll need to attend a meeting every night for the foreseeable future. I needed to get out of there—to make things right with you." *And to save my company.*

"Blair, if we're going to try to work through all this, we can't have secrets between us."

No way could she know anything. Unless . . . had Mike Daniels called here this week? Surely he wouldn't have said anything. Better to play dumb and see what she knew. "Andie, I swear, I have never cheated on you."

"Not that." She paused. "There's something I think I need to tell you." She glanced at him then.

What a relief. It wasn't his secret; it was hers. From the look on her face, she was expecting a bad reaction to what she was about to say. He had to make certain not to give it to her. He dropped the bag in the trash. "Tell me."

"I apologized."

"Apologized?"

"To Melanie Johnston." The words were barely a whisper. She leaned against the kitchen counter.

His resolve to remain calm ripped apart like paper in a shredder. "You did what? What did you need to apologize for?"

"Because I am *sorry.* I wanted to call her or send a card right after the accident, but everyone kept telling me I couldn't because we'd be sued. That happened anyway, now, didn't it?"

Emotional women and common sense. Did the two never meet in the middle? "What are you sorry for? You didn't do anything."

"Chad was my son. I left him at home alone, with a set of car keys in the house. I knew he was upset. I should have stayed home and worked it out."

"Andie." Blair stepped forward, but Andie pressed tighter to the counter. He stopped. "That wasn't your fault—it was mine."

"Right."

"I'm the one who wouldn't let him go on the trip. I'm the one who fought with him, then left the house without trying to work things out. It was *me.* Me. Get it?"

"If I'd been a better mother, I would have found a tutor before he got the bad grade, which would have prevented the whole fight in the first place. You know it, too. I see it in your eyes. You've hardly looked at me since Chad died, and when you do, I see the accusations there."

"You don't see accusations. You see guilt. Think about it, Andie. What did they find at Cachuma? The envelope *I* made for Chad, trying to *encourage* his Ivy League future. Trying to force it down his throat is more like it. I'm the one who always insisted that he strive for perfection. You're the one who always loved him for what he was. That's why he told you that you were the greatest person he'd ever known before he died. What did he say to me? 'I was going to get it back.' Like he wanted to let me know he was going to get his grades back up. What kind of final words are those? Not the ones you'd say to a decent father—I'll tell you that."

"So all these months, I've been hating myself, thinking you did, too, and you've been blaming yourself, thinking I hated you?" She watched him nod, and her expression softened. "Guess that shows we're not the greatest communicators, huh?"

Blair fought the next question, but he needed to know the answer more than he feared what it might be. "What did she say? Melanie Johnston."

"Nothing. She jumped up and ran away." She walked over to the counter and handed him the yellow piece of paper. "She dropped this. Funny, it never occurred to me they would be involved in church and mission trips."

There was a lot they didn't know. Including how much damage Andie had just done. *Keep your mouth shut. Don't lose it now.*

She turned away to load some glasses in the dishwasher. "I know our lawyers are going to have a fit, tell me it was the wrong thing to do. But I've done a lot of thinking and praying, and I'm going to stop listening to people constantly telling me what I should and shouldn't do. I have to follow my heart, and God's leading—a leading I've mostly missed for the last ten years. No more. I'm not going to get talked into committees I have no business on. I'm going to do the things God has called me to do."

"Like what?"

"Like the Fair for the Cure, my work in the soup kitchen. Painting." She looked toward him, waiting for a reaction. He gave none. She lifted her chin a fraction of an inch. "And trying to work things out with you."

Blair reached out and touched the softness of her cheek. "I like that last one."

She moved back just enough to break the touch. He knew better than to push the issue. She would need some time. So would he.

He thought back to early in their marriage. Andie was right. In the beginning they had been so tuned in to God and His will for them, but somehow it had slowly changed into working harder and staying on top. They needed to get back to the beginning, and they could. Together, with God, and maybe a really great counselor.

But there was another issue, one that Andie didn't know about yet. "Andie." He looked into her eyes, knowing that what he was about to say might destroy the thread of trust that held them together. "I have something to tell you, too." He took a step backward. "It's about work. I didn't want to worry you with it. I thought I could take care of it. But I've made a huge mistake, Andie. And it could cost us everything."

chapter thirty-three

Melanie pulled into the mostly empty parking lot behind Les's office. She knew it was a lot to ask, but she was a working woman. It was the weekends or nothing.

Well, okay. She also liked seeing the man dance a little for her. She remembered his response when she'd called last night. "Important meeting? Tomorrow? Melanie, it's Easter. I've got plans for brunch." He'd said it like he was joking, but she knew there was some truth in his irritation.

"Let's meet at seven, then. You'll still have plenty of time."

When she walked in, he was studying something written on a legal pad. She cleared her throat, and he flipped the page.

"Thanks for meeting me."

"I'm your lawyer. That's what we do." He offered his most charming smile, which was when Melanie trusted him the least.

She sat in the seat across from him, wondering how he was going to take her news. Not well, she imagined. "A couple of things have happened. I don't even know where to start."

The calm confidence on his face was absent in his eyes. A before-the-jury practiced smile curved across his mouth. "Why don't you start from the beginning?"

"I ran into Andie Phelps yesterday."

A spark ignited in his eyes. He picked up a pencil, leaned forward. "Did she threaten you, make obscene gestures?"

Melanie looked evenly into his face. "No. Nothing like that."

"What happened, then?" The pencil seesawed in his hand.

"She . . . apologized."

His jaw actually dropped open. It took a full fifteen seconds before he restored an all-business look to his face. "Good for her." His voice came out calm and measured, but he fidgeted in his seat like he wanted to jump up and pump his fists in victory. "Tell me exactly what she said. Everything that you can remember."

Everything we can use against her in court, you mean. "I . . . it made me feel funny."

The pencil stopped moving. "Of course it did. No doubt she did it trying to gain your sympathy. Defendants who know they're backed into the corner will say anything they can to escape. And remember, this is not about punishing them, anyway. It's about making your son's death mean something."

Somehow, these words did not act as the call to battle they had in the past. This time they felt hollow. Empty. "I don't know."

Les leaned back in his chair. "I had a client once, Cedric Tims—the same thing happened to him. It was a business deal gone bad. His partner had cheated him out of a lot of money.

"Just before the trial, his partner came to him on his knees, promised to pay back everything, recalled their friendship since high school, their children's years on the soccer field. My client dropped the suit days before the trial was to begin."

Maybe Les did understand. This wouldn't be so hard after all. "Did things work out for him?"

Les snorted. "Hardly. His newly repentant partner skipped town the day after we withdrew the lawsuit. Moved to some island in the Caribbean with all the money he'd stashed away and never had any intention of returning. My client, on the other hand ..." Les straightened some papers. "He, of course, owed me."

"Owed you?"

"Our contract clearly stated that I would take a percentage of whatever we won. If we won nothing, then I got nothing. When he dropped the case himself—a case we would have won—he was required by law to compensate me at an hourly rate for all the preparation I'd made. Not to mention office expenses, filing charges, etcetera."

Les tapped his pencil against the legal pad. "Yes, it was a sad deal. He came out far worse than he went in. All because he believed an apology meant something." He looked into her eyes, letting the information sink in. "You have to be very careful about these things."

A chill crept up Melanie's spine.

Les bestowed a gracious smile. "You said there were a couple of things. What was the other one?"

"I . . ." She couldn't afford to wreck what remained of Sarah's life. And hers. "I've forgotten."

He nodded. "Not a problem. Feel free to come by again if you think of it, okay?"

"Sure." Melanie walked from the room, her shoulders drooping with added weight.

———

Andie walked up the aisle of the church, Blair at her side, feeling the stares at her back. Everyone, by now, must have heard that they had been separated. Most knew Blair had been in short-term detox until yesterday. Lots of tinder to fuel the gossip in the church foyer this Easter morning. At least the issues with his company were still a secret—for now. She almost regretted the decision to come today, but skipping this service of all seemed deeply wrong. And she still was not sure if she wanted to spend an entire day at home alone with Blair.

"Andie, darling, don't you look divine?" Mattie Plendor rushed across the sanctuary to give a hug. Not an air kiss, but a true hug. She pulled Andie's arm until she had her out of earshot of Blair. "I've been just praying like mad for you. I know things seem so hard, but you hang in there. The same God who helped me through will do the same for you. Never forget that." She patted Andie's arm and moved away, but not before Andie saw the glistening of moisture in her eyes.

"Andie, Blair, so good to see you. What are the two of you doing for lunch? We've got plenty of ham come spend Easter with us." People approached them on all sides. "Andie, do you want to play tennis tomorrow?" None basked in the light of superiority, or even cast looks of judgment. No. They were here to help her. They were praying for her.

How had she come so far from her roots? The people who would love her through the darkest of times were the people who served the God who loved her through the darkest of times. The thought lit a light of hope that she had believed long extinguished. She looked at Blair and smiled. She knew the road would not be easy, but she hoped they could still walk it together.

She found it difficult to stay focused on the sermon—too many thoughts cluttered her mind. After several moments, a single thought separated itself from the rest and would not be ignored. She looked at her husband and willed the service to end.

She forced herself to wait until they were in the privacy of their car before she voiced it. "Blair, something occurred to me this morning during the service. I know I'm right. You misconstrued Chad's last words."

He flinched as he put the car in gear. "How so?"

"Think about it. *'I was going to get it back.'* Remember which direction he was driving? Away from town. He was on his way back to Cachuma to get the envelope."

"Why would he—"

"He'd calmed enough to realize his mistake. Don't you see? He didn't hate you for pushing him, he saw the value and went to get it back."

"Either way, it's a pretty strong indictment against me as a father."

"No. It shows he respected your dreams for him and knew you had his best in mind."

Blair moaned. "I wish I could believe that."

She reached over and squeezed his hand. "I do."

———

Melanie sat in the parking lot, taking deep breaths, searching for her courage. "Okay, God. You've got my attention. Jeff and Sarah's friends, Candace, Jake—they've all got a peace I know I don't have. I know you've got to be the difference.

"But this forgiveness thing. . . . I mean, it kind of made sense when I was talking to Candace, but now . . . I don't know. I want that family to pay for what they did. I want them to suffer as much as I have." *Whoa.* This was starting to sound less about Jeff's legacy and more about personal vengeance. Jeff wouldn't want that.

"Okay, but if I do this, it could ruin us. What would happen to Sarah?"

Although Melanie heard neither an external voice nor one inside her head, a calm peace flowed over her like nothing she'd ever experienced. "Better do this before I lose my nerve."

She climbed from the car, closed the door, and started back up the steps. It had been almost an hour since she'd left Les's office—perhaps he had already left. Deep inside she knew she hoped so. That would give her time to talk herself out of this crazy thing.

She got to the door of his office just as he was coming out. "Melanie, what are you doing back so soon?"

He was using the accommodating voice that Melanie had never been able to stand. The irritation it sparked gave her the courage she lacked. "I need to talk to you."

chapter thirty-four

Andie stared out the window. As soon as they had arrived home from church, Blair announced he needed to run an errand. He disappeared out the door without a backward glance.

She pictured him at some bar, tossing shots of whiskey down his throat. So much for starting over.

Andie paced, as had become too much a habit of late. Nothing had changed.

When his car pulled into the garage, she rushed to meet him. The door opened and she pounced. "Where have you been?" She sniffed the air, alert for the telltale scents of smoke or alcohol. Nothing.

He shrugged. "You were right all along. I decided it was time I apologized, too."

"Apologized. To whom?"

"Jeff Johnston's mother."

"You went to see her?"

"No. I apologized in my own way." He walked inside and started up the stairs. "Why don't we change clothes and take a walk on the beach? We can walk past the spot where we released the lobsters and wish them good luck."

A gleam was present in Blair's eyes that Andie hadn't seen in a long time. It seemed a great burden had suddenly lifted from him. She wondered what exactly he had done, but knew he would tell her in his own time and in his own way.

Several hours later, when they returned from the walk, the phone was ringing. Andie picked it up. "Hello."

"Andie, this is Sam Campbell. Is Blair home?"

Oh no. Couldn't they have one moment of peace? Andie considered lying but thought better of it. "Yes, he's right here." She handed the phone to Blair. "Sam Campbell."

Blair's face stiffened. He took a deep breath before putting the phone to his ear. "Hello, Sam." He walked toward the living room, phone still pressed to his ear. "Yes. When? Okay, thanks." He picked up the remote from the table, pointed it toward the television, and pushed the button.

"Blair, what's going on?"

Blair shook his head. "Sam said to turn on channel three. He said the other side has called a press conference."

"What does that mean?"

The local station switched to a shot of Les Stewart standing on the courthouse steps, his face grim. Beside him, Melanie Johnston's face was so white she looked as though she might pass out. She stepped toward a large podium with microphones attached.

"Today, Easter Sunday, I'd like to announce that I am withdrawing my lawsuit against the Phelps family." She paused, then seemed to falter before straightening and looking toward the camera. "I wish them comfort in their grief." She stepped back.

One of the reporters called out, "Do you no longer feel that the Phelps family carries the blame for your son's death?"

She didn't move forward, so her words were harder to make out. "I . . . I forgive them. That's what Jeff would want."

The reporter asked something else, that the microphone did not pick up. She shook her head and looked toward her lawyer. He stepped forward. "Mrs. Johnston has made her statement. That's all she has to say."

"What about you, Mr. Stewart? What's your feeling about this?"

He did not look happy. "Mrs. Johnston has to do what she thinks is right."

"So you don't agree with her decision?"

"In my opinion, it's a mistake. But it's a mistake she has the right to make." He glanced at her, then back at the camera. "No further comments."

Blair let out a whoop behind her. *Blair, whooping?* That had to be a first. He pulled Andie into his arms and swung her around in circles. "Can you believe it? One major worry gone, just like that."

What just happened? She looked at Blair. "Okay, in exactly what way did you apologize?"

He shook his head. "That wasn't because of something I did. What I did was anonymous. She doesn't even know about it."

"Then why is she doing this?"

"I think it's obvious. You. You did the right thing, the thing we should have done from the very beginning. God honored that, and obviously so did she."

Andie let herself smile, but instantly the phone rang and she knew this one beautiful moment was a dream. The woman had changed her mind; it had all been a mistake. But instead it was Sam calling back with congratulations. And then the Baurs. And all afternoon the phone rang and rang and rang, and she never stopped smiling.

———

Jake sat at the desk in his office, Bible opened on the desk before him but his mind somewhere else. So many things had happened today he found it difficult to concentrate on his reading. He finally gave up, looked toward the ceiling, and said the thing he felt deepest in his heart at the moment: "Thank you, God."

Behind him, the door to the garage rattled. He approached it, wary. Who'd be out on Easter at an hour like this except someone looking for trouble? He peeked through the security hole, then threw the door open.

"Melanie. Come in." He held the door for her, then locked it behind them. "I was just in my office, thinking. Care to sit awhile?"

"Sure." She seemed more ill at ease than he could ever remember.

He thought he could help by breaking the ice. "I saw the news this afternoon. That was an incredible thing you did."

She looked at him, her eyes pleading. "Was it the right thing?"

"What does your heart tell you?"

"Listening to those kids yesterday, Tony in particular, I realized I was doing something in Jeff's name he would never have done himself. His legacy, if that's what you want to call it, was kindness. And forgiveness. That's what would honor him most, by acting in a way that he would have me act."

"Then it sounds like you did the right thing."

She stared at the ceiling. "I . . . I came here to apologize. To you." She dropped her gaze level with Jake's. "I was out of line. I know you did what you thought was best for your kids. Probably was. Who knows? But it's not my place to say. I shouldn't have jumped on you like that." She paused. "Forgive me?"

"Nothing to forgive. Some of what you said was true. I've been doing some checking, seeing if I can track them down."

"Well, I wanted to say I'm sorry. I'd better get back home, I've got to work tomorrow."

"You never stick around here very long, do you?" Jake joked. "Say, you want to deliver a little good news to Sarah when you get there?"

She looked surprised. "Sure. What?"

"The mission trip is back on."

Her face lit up. "You're kidding. How?"

"We got the funding we needed this afternoon."

"Are you telling me that within three hours of my announcement, the money has already come in?"

"No. I'm telling you that one hour before your announcement, it came in." He hesitated, not sure if he should give her all the details. But he felt God's nudge, so he continued. "I got a visit this afternoon from Blair Phelps. He had one of those yellow flyers in his hands. He asked me if your kid was scheduled to go, and said he'd like to pay the remainder needed for the whole group. Any idea where he got that flyer?"

Melanie looked away. "Yeah. I've got an idea." She didn't elaborate.

"Anyway, he wanted it to be strictly anonymous. I'm not sure why I told you just now. I probably shouldn't have, but somehow it seemed important."

"And you're telling me he did this before the news conference?"

"Yes."

She shook her head. "Incredible." She stood to go. "Sarah will be thrilled when she gets home."

Jake didn't want to watch her walk away. He couldn't stand the thought. "Where is she now?"

"At the Pizza Palace with some kids from church."

"Why don't we go tell them? Together. You can ride on the back of my bike."

"Well, I . . ." She squirmed and looked over her shoulder. When she turned back around, her eyes gleamed. "I haven't been on the back of a bike in fifteen years. I'd say it's high time I did it again. Wouldn't you?"

"Absolutely."

chapter thirty-five

Christi pushed through Andie's back door. "Andie? Where are you?"

"Back here, in the studio."

Nice. Things were looking up around here. Christi averted her gaze as she walked through the kitchen. *If I don't see the mess, it won't bother me.* She made it to the studio without stopping. "How are you?"

Andie stood at the back wall, straightening a white cloth over a small canvas. "Relieved."

"I'll bet." Christi looked toward the covered square. Odd. What was Andie hiding? She walked up to the much larger painting on the easel, a squalid village scene. "South Africa?"

"Yeah. I've been looking through some of Mattie's pictures. I thought somehow she might be able to use these."

"I'm sure she'll be thrilled." She glanced again toward the white cloth. "So things look a little brighter today, huh?"

Andie nodded. "I honestly do not know how to act. Things had been going downhill so long."

"Sounds like Melanie Johnston still has a little further to drop. Scott told me that her lawyer is going to bill her for his time. Rumor is he bankrupted another client for doing the.very same thing a few years ago."

Andie leaned forward, hands on her knees. "You're kidding me. She's got to pay for absolving us?" She shook her head. "That's not right." A softie to the end. Andie never would understand real life.

"That's the way it works."

"Not if I can help it." Andie paced to the wall and back, biting her bottom lip. "What about that reporter friend of yours?"

"Who?"

"Oh, come on, Christi. You planted those stories, and I know it. What if we plant one about Les Stewart? Remember how *Los Angeles* magazine ran that glowing article about him? Practically made him a saint."

Christi dropped onto a stool, leaned back, and crossed her arms. She grinned from pure delight. "There's a pit bull buried somewhere beneath your poodle exterior." She thought about Andie's idea. *Ingenious.* "Maybe just the threat would be enough. Let me make a call." She flipped open her cell phone, and as she stepped from the room, Andie heard her say, "Mr. Burridge, Christi Baur here. I'd like to offer you a little assignment." A minute later she was back, a sly grin on her face. "Les Stewart is about to get an anonymous phone call. The caller will tell him that the *Los Angeles Times* is about to run its own profile, 'Lawyer With a Black Heart.' That ought to make him think twice."

"Christi, you are brilliant. Evil through and through, but brilliant nonetheless."

Christi nodded. "Thank you very much. Now, what else were you working on?" She looked pointedly at the back wall.

Andie shrugged and averted her eyes. "Nothing much."

With an answer like that, Christi *had* to look. She walked across the room and lifted the cloth.

Words failed her.

She looked back at Andie, who sat staring at her hands. "I couldn't get that face out of my mind. I thought if I painted it, maybe it would stop haunting me."

"It's incredible. What are you planning to do with it?"

"Nothing. It's just something I needed to paint."

"You should give it to her."

"No. I . . . couldn't face her again."

"Well, I could." Christi picked up the canvas and nodded toward Andie. "Talk to you later."

Melanie barely managed to punch the button before the phone slipped from her hands. She slid down the wall and landed on the floor.

Sarah rushed across the kitchen and knelt before her. "Mom, what's wrong?"

"That was Les Stewart."

Sarah scrunched up her face, her eyes flashing. "What did the demon in Armani want this time?"

"He said he . . . has reconsidered."

"Reconsidered what? How many millions you owe him?"

"Owing him, period. He's not going to back charge me after all."

Sarah dropped to the floor. "What happened?"

The doorbell chimed and Sarah scrambled to her feet. "I'll get it."

Melanie didn't move. What *did* happen?

"Is your mother here?"

Something about the voice at the door was vaguely familiar . . . and vaguely unpleasant—though she couldn't quite put her finger on the reason for either reaction. Melanie pushed to her feet. When she rounded the corner, she understood. There, standing at the door, was the woman who had yelled at her across State Street that day. She had something in her hand. Melanie moved forward, prepared for whatever battle lay ahead. "Can I help you?"

The woman looked her in the eye, full of confidence. "Mrs. Johnston, I'm a friend of Andie Phelps."

"Yes, I recognize you."

She didn't flinch. "I've just come from her house. Andie is . . . well, she painted something. I believe you should have it."

What was the catch here? "You believe, or she believes?"

The woman's expression never changed; her eyes didn't even blink. "Both. It's just that she's a bit of a coward. I, however, am not." She lifted her hand and presented a small painting of Jeff.

The sunlight reflected on his face, and his eyes glowed from what seemed an internal source. It was the image that had been in all the papers. Melanie had selected it because it was exactly the way Jeff had always looked.

As Melanie took the offered painting, she felt her throat close. She would not lose control in front of this woman. "It's amazing." She didn't trust her voice to say more.

"There are a lot of amazing things about Andie. This is only one."

"Please send her my thanks."

The woman nodded, turned to leave, and then stopped. "What you did, dropping the lawsuit . . . I know that took a lot of guts." She glanced over Melanie's shoulder. "I think your daughter is one lucky young lady." She floated down the driveway, hopped in a little red car, and sped away.

Melanie sat staring at the same headstone she'd looked at so many times before, but this time it felt different. "Well, Jeff, you're never going to believe all that's happened."

She looked toward the sky. The dark blue of the day was laced with thin trails of white. Did Jeff see her from somewhere beyond those clouds? She no longer doubted that he could. "I think you would be proud of the legacy you've left behind. I'm looking forward to the day I see you again, in heaven, and we can talk about it." She nodded her head. "That's right, you heard me. In heaven."

She looked back toward the tombstone, and this time the lump in her throat made it difficult to continue to speak. "But I guess you see our problem. I understand now that you really don't need me coming down here as often as I do. I know you're in a better place, not just lying here waiting for the next visit from your mom."

The scene before her blurred. "So I'm thinking I'll be just coming every now and then." She looked to the sky. "I hope that's okay with you."

She wiped her eyes. "I know it is. But why is it so hard for me to let go?"

She stood, walked to the headstone, and kissed the granite. The stone felt cold against her lips. "Good-bye, Jeff. I'll always love you." She ran down the hill to her car.

When she drove away, a sudden sense of peace replaced the guilt. It was almost as if she could feel Jeff smiling at her.

———

"Three months. It's been three months." Andie squeezed Blair's arm. "You're doing great."

They both knew this was not completely true. Even though he'd been sober for three months, even though the Vitasoft buyout had come through and saved Blair's company, they still had lost a child, still slogged through each day hoping the next might be a little easier. Many days weren't. In fact, they fought more than ever—though Christi tried to assure her that was a good thing because Andie never stood up for herself before. Today, though, was a very good day.

They sat in the sand at East Beach, enjoying a few moments after breakfast at a little café. In front of them at the beach courts, a summer volleyball clinic carried on in full swing. Scores of kids clustered around the nets, listening to the advice of their high-school and college-age coaches. Squeals of excitement, laughter, and constant chatter blew around the beach like the wind. Sounds Andie only recently could bear without disappearing into grief.

Andie looked at Blair. "Don't you need to get back to work?"

He shrugged. "I told Neil I'd be in after lunch. There's nothing that won't wait a little while."

"Great," she said and stared at her husband. He *had* changed. She did not know if he could change everything, and he was not perfect, but she saw him trying. He was working to save their marriage. And so today was better and maybe tomorrow would be, too.

She smiled to herself and turned her attention to a group of smaller kids, just trying to get the gist of keeping the ball in the air.

Their coach, a beautiful blonde about Chad's age, demonstrated the proper technique for passing and setting to the tykes. She looked up, saw Andie and Blair, and stopped moving. She stared for a few seconds, then turned to her little group. "Okay, everyone practice with a partner. I'll be right back." She walked over and dropped into the sand in front of Andie. "You're Mr. and Mrs. Phelps, huh?"

Andie looked at the girl, trying to place her. Chad's classmate? No. Youth group? Maybe—that group was large enough and fluid enough she had never been able to keep up with all of them.

"Yes, we're the Phelps." Thankfully Blair had the presence of mind to answer.

The girl nodded. "I'm Sarah Johnston." She paused, looked at the sand, let the words soak in. She finally looked up at them. "How are you?"

Andie fought for an answer. It lodged in her throat, but she forced it out. "I'm . . . we're . . . hanging in there."

Sarah nodded, stared out toward the ocean. "Good." She ran her fingers through the sand. "Us, too."

Andie finally found some semblance of her mind. "How is . . . your mother?"

"It's hard. I mean, I don't have to tell you that. You know how it is." She took a deep breath. "But she's making it." Sarah once again looked at Andie. "She really likes that painting—she hung it in Jeff's room. She told me that you went to the store manager at Alfords and asked to have her transferred back to Santa Barbara. She appreciated that."

Andie's face burned with what felt like shame. "I wish I had stopped my friends from the boycott. I *should* have." Facing this sixteen-year-old who had paid the price for her cowardice hurt.

Sarah shrugged. "She's made a terrific friend in Thousand Oaks. It's been good for her."

Andie nodded but could not speak for the life of her.

Sarah drew her knees up to her chin. "Alfords is planning a new store on the north end of Goleta next year. Mom's first in line to transfer back. So she won't have to worry about the commute for too much longer."

"I'm glad." Andie shifted, searching for something to talk about. Then it hit her. "Aren't you about to go on a mission trip?"

Sarah's eyes lit with surprise. "Yes. We go to Mexico next week. Mom's even coming as a chaperone." She buried her hand in the sand. "She was never a Christian. Before . . . all this. Jeff was always so worried about her."

Blair cleared his throat, reached out, and touched Sarah's free hand. "He would have been happy to see this, then." His voice sounded thick.

Sarah Johnston looked at Blair, then Andie, her eyes misty. "He would have died for it."

She blinked fast, pushed herself up, and jogged back to her students. "Who wants to learn how to serve?"

acknowledgments

There are so many people to thank, I hardly know where to start. But I'll give it a go....

First and foremost, thank you, God, for blessing me with the dream of my heart.

Lee—for the support, the love, and the laughs. You really are the man of my dreams!

Melanie—for putting up with such a nerd of a mother.

Caroline—for all the hugs and smooches and general joy of life.

Dad—I know I still owe you several million sheets of printer paper and several gallons of ink. I'll put them in the mail ... soon.

Carl, Alisa, Katy, Lisa, and Leah—your enthusiasm inspires me.

Gary and Katie Horwald—for being willing pre-readers, and terrific neighbors, too!

Lori Baur—you've lent me laptops, encouraged the dream, and pounded the pavement on my behalf. "Thanks" is not a strong enough word.

James Scott Bell—for the teaching, coaching, and cheering. I want to be like you when I grow up.

Michael Berrier and Shawn Grady—you always encourage me to dig deeper.

Everyone who helped critique—Kathleen Rouser, Susan Falck, Kris Jensen, Bonnie Engstrom. Lois Carlson, Tom Macy, Diana Campbell—for encouraging the dream (and keeping it secret) for so long. Also, to Scott Campbell—for answering tons of legal questions with patience and grace.

Terry Foil, Christine Charlton, and Joy Van Wickle—for the prayers and the support. Special thanks to Rick Van Wickle—for answering my questions about the inner runnings of a grocery store.

Austin Boyd—for your enthusiasm and encouragement.

Les Stobbe—for guiding me through the process.

Extra special thanks to my extra cool editor, Dave Long—thanks for believing in this story.

Dave and the BHP editorial team—for making it so much better.

Steve and the entire marketing team at BHP—your enthusiasm overwhelms me. Special thanks to Brett, Debra, and Tim, who made me feel so welcome.

All the folks at Bethany House—I still can't believe I get the privilege to work with you.

questions for conversation

1. Which mother did you have the most empathy for at the beginning of the book? Did it change by the end and why?

2. Have you ever found yourself protecting your own interests rather than doing what you knew was right? Why is it so hard to do the right thing? What were the repercussions?

3. How did you feel about Christi Baur's "help" in sticking up for Andie? Was she being a good friend or an interfering one?

4. Grief can often devastate a marriage. Do you think Andie and Blair are on the right path? What do you think is most important for a marriage to survive a tragedy?

5. What do you think would have been the outcome if Melanie's case had gone to court? Should parents be held responsible for their child's negligence? Do you think that lawsuits do more good or harm in our country today?

6. What role does class play in our culture today? Have you ever seen an individual or family treated preferentially because of their status or encountered prejudice against a poorer individual?

7. What kind of comfort can you offer a person facing deep grief? Is it possible to offer the hope of eternal life, especially to a person who isn't sure what she believes?

8. What role did Andie's painting play in her recovery? What is your "outlet" in times of distress?

9. Ultimately, what would you have done had you been the mother of Jeff? How about Chad?